TH
PERFECT
GARDEN

GUY SHEPPARD

SOCCIONES

© Guy Sheppard 2023
All rights reserved.
Guy Sheppard has asserted his right under the Copyright, Designs and Patents Act 1988 to be identified as the author of this book.
This is a work of fiction. Names, characters, businesses, places, events and incidents are either the products of the author's imagination or used in a fictitious manner. Any resemblance to actual persons, living or dead, or actual events is purely coincidental. No part of this publication may be reproduced, distributed, or transmitted in any form or by any means, without the prior written permission of the author, except in the case of brief quotations embodied in critical reviews and certain other non-commercial uses permitted by copyright law. For permission requests, contact the author.

ISBN: 9798377375463

Cover design & typesetting by Socciones Editoria Digitale
www.socciones.co.uk

Other mystery crime novels set in Gloucestershire by Guy Sheppard

Countess Lucy And the Curse of Coberley Hall
Sabrina & The Secret of The Severn Sea
The Silent Forest
The Unwanted Bride
The Raven & The Crow
House of Cristabel

In the 1690s a grief-stricken William Lawrence set about creating the perfect garden in memory of his dead wife and son in the village of Shurdington (England). He called it 'the whole secret of my sorrows'. He died in 1697 before it could be completed.

1

Friday November 26th
Crickley Hill
Nr Cheltenham
Gloucestershire UK

Alison Ellis hated driving this late at night. A police conference in Bristol was all very well, but the party afterwards had been a protracted affair. The food had been awful and she had hardly eaten a thing to her liking. Also chit-chat was not her strong point. Worse still, she hadn't been able to drink and drive. If she had just taken a wrong turning in the dark it was because she felt drained after smiling at too many self-important men for so long.

White fog swirled everywhere as she looked for a safe place on the wintry road to turn her car around.

She turned up the blower on the car's heater, but no amount of hot air could dispel the chill that gripped her now.

Headlamps failed to penetrate the murky miasma that blocked her progress.

'Damn it, I just want to get home and go to bed.'

The floating brume from fields and woods glued itself to doors and windows until she felt uncharacteristically gloomy, in her heart.

The seemingly living cloud was set to mislead and muddle her.

She had to press her face right up to the windscreen to see anything at all…

Night and mist combined in close embrace…

She dropped her speed to ten m.p.h.

…when a shadow shot her way.

She gripped her steering wheel tighter.

Might be a wild deer.

'What the hell!'

She hit the brakes.

Heard a bang.

The shock jarred every bone in her body. Seconds later she was working both hands to unbuckle her seat belt.

It was a miracle the car's airbag hadn't ballooned in her face. She seized a torch from the glovebox, then half fell from her door in a panic.

At first she could see nothing in the ocean of grey.

Didn't think it was a deer.

Alison ran round the car and feared the worst. Surely her victim had just passed under or over it?

The result was more uncertainty. Somebody was groaning and crawling about in the middle of the road…

It was a young man.

A torn, knee-length white cotton nightshirt hung off his skimpy shoulders like a rag. There were no shoes on his feet. He averted his face in the light from her torch, but not before she saw his mostly pale, mostly starved demeanour through his mane of black hair. His cheeks were more bones than flesh and she guessed he was in his mid-twenties. He went to rise, then fell flat on his chin as he used his hands to pull his leg behind him.

'For Christ's sake!' said Alison. 'Didn't you see me? You came out of nowhere.'

He uttered more moans only.

Alison rushed to cover him with her leather jacket. 'I was certain I must have killed you.'

The casualty's dreamy eyes rolled up into their sockets. He had the appearance of a sleepwalker who had wandered out into the night. His expanded pupils indicated he might be high on some drug or other, yet his voice came across as clear as crystal. 'You can't kill me because I'm dead already.'

'Wait while I call an ambulance.'

'Are you mad? I'm dead, I tell you.'

'If you're dead, how is it you're talking to me?'

'Perhaps you're dead too?'

'Are you quite sure you're not seriously injured?'

'You can't die twice.'

She went to help him up, but he shrank from her… shook her off. No wound stained his shroud-like shirt. 'What are you doing out here anyway? It's gone midnight.'

'I wanted to prove to myself I'm not of this world.'

'Sorry, you're not making any sense.'

'What do you care? No one will understand the reason for this.'

'My phone's in the car. I'll go fetch it. You may think you're all right, but you should be checked over by a doctor.'

'I have no heart. I have no blood. I'm rotten inside.'

'Stay still while I make my call.'

'I don't want to go to hospital. I want to go to a morgue where I can be with other dead people.'

'You can't stay here or you'll freeze to death.'

'I can't die when I'm dead already.'

'Do you live close by? Where do you come from?'

'I come from the garden.'

***

Once she had rung for an ambulance she would call the police Incident Room at Bamfurlong Lane, Alison decided. She felt duty bound to log time, place and details of the incident, but first she needed a name. 'Can you at least tell me who you are?'

But there was no sign of him anywhere.

Only her black jacket lay discarded on the frozen road.

'Damn it,' said Alison and groped about in the fog.

The icy vapour wove itself to her face like a damp veil.

Suddenly a scream rent the cold night air.

'Hey?' cried Alison. 'Come back here. I won't harm you.' The somnambulist, if that's what he was, could have chosen any one of four ways from the crossroads.

That voice she heard a second ago was only an echo in the void.

Each exit led to eerie silence.

Back in her car Alison shuddered at the awful expression in her victim's hollow eyes. She recoiled from the colour of his pinched cheeks that were so deathly pale. She could have met a ghost, except no wraith had pressed their cold clay lips to her cheek – no spectral arms had sought to hold her in their embrace.

She peered at the fog one last time, but he was gone she knew not where.

Or someone had reached out and taken him.

2

No garden on the planet will happily endure being totally neglected, it must be cared for by somebody, at least a little. The garden at Green Way House, not happy, lay at the foot of a hill up which ancient tribes once carried their dead to their burial barrows. Fierce Iron Age warriors climbed this path to their hilltop fort five thousand years ago. Romans used the same track to reach their hillside villas, while medieval drovers once drove their flocks of sheep through here on their way to market. Now only dogwalkers, horse riders and eager lovers frequented its shadows.

While the "green way" lent its title to house and garden, the latter had guarded its privacy for hundreds of years. Its trees cracked and fell, flowers withered and bloomed as its tall gates rusted shut. Those who tried to peer over its ivy-clad walls never saw a single soul. Nor were they much tempted to pursue the mystery, instinctively fearing the consequences.

Secrets were safe at Green Way House, since whoever tended its grounds by day and by night had a name but no being in their own Eden.

***

Sixty-year-old Lady Ann Frost had once enjoyed a well-respected career in psychiatry. She had devoted nearly forty years of her life to the causes, preventions, diagnoses and treatments of mental health conditions in very sick people. So intent had she been on curing one young man that she had treated him on a private basis for nearly two years. Her commitment to him was the most intense she had ever felt for anybody other than her own son, but then she frightened herself and decided to end their illicit affair. She failed to anticipate the result. The patient – who had been doing so well – threw himself off a bridge in a fit of despair. He had to be rushed to hospital where he nearly died. She was found to have been in abuse of her professional position, not only because of the sex involved but because she had sent her ex-lover threatening letters, should he squeal. She had also promised to 'finish' his wife, children and friends. She forgot her exact words but they had gone something like, "If I get into trouble for this then I will never forgive you. I will make you pay".

Naturally she had been ruled unfit to be a medical doctor anymore, although this was not the first time she had courted controversy. Already she had set out to find a wife for her son to provide her with heirs. She had advertised for six months in the wanted columns of The Daily Telegraph and The Times. Her list of requirements for the perfect 'breeder' had stated that she should be taller than 5ft 4in – ideally 6ft or 6ft 1in – aged between twenty and thirty, possess a gun licence and be 'house trained'.

Tragedy struck before anyone suitable replied. Her son was killed. Since then she had made local headlines when the police raided her home. She was charged with breaching her shotgun certificate by leaving a weapon unsecured. She pleaded not guilty, only explaining vaguely that she used her guns to shoot foxes and squirrels from her bedroom window. She had been fined £1000 and required to attend an anger management course.

Her refusal to accept that her son was gone forever rendered her increasingly cantankerous. Regret fuelled resilience. She was undaunted, audacious, stout-hearted: she decided to re-invent Green Way House's twelve acres of garden as a memorial to her dead boy. It was a plan born from history. Three hundred and twenty-five years ago the owner of Green Way House had set out to create a garden in honour of his deceased wife and child. By some fateful coincidence they too had been called Anne and Will.

Lady Ann did not consider the idea too outlandish. The Romans had filled their houses with the statues of their ancestors and who didn't hang pictures on the walls of their deceased parents, grandparents et al? The garden at Green Way House already contained more than a few emblems of grief and mortality left behind from the 1690s. It was up to her to revive its true purpose and pluck it from terminal decline. This was to be no morbid obsession but an act of constant remembrance – she would eternalise the memory of her darling son in something that would grow forever. The garden might be twelve acres but several of those would remain trees and fields.

She had acquired her money and title from her deceased husband, while she herself was the illegitimate offspring of a famous stage actress whom she preferred not to mention. But this was not about having sufficient money per se, it was about faith and purity of heart. That didn't mean she was prepared to pay people over the odds to achieve her dream. Ideally she needed enthusiastic volunteers, as in an old-fashioned kibbutz or commune. She favoured amusing ones though. Good right-wing, hunting, shooting, fishing types, but not anybody from Eton or Harrow. She didn't have a swimming pool or a tennis court and she didn't want anyone living in the house (despite eleven disused rooms) because it contained two million pounds' worth of antiques. They could expect to live like aristocracy minus the trimmings.

Fewer than fifty candidates applied to her appeals in newspapers and magazines and on social media. People simply didn't value opportunity over hard cash these days, they couldn't see what an honour it was to help someone so privileged. Her first attempt at saving the garden had gone horribly wrong. As a result she chose to scale back her expectations drastically this time.

A series of interviews via Zoom saw her reject anyone whose roaming eyes settled too long and hard on her valuables. She also showed a virtual door to the simply curious, the obviously insane and anyone else who dared to think for themselves. Her garden project was not to be hijacked by some horticultural know-all whose modish ideas were better suited to the Chelsea Flower Show. She was, she supposed, looking less for garden expertise than a certain optimism of soul. She desired a sympathetic ear into which to pour her memorialising ambitions.

Lady Ann Frost was left with seven hopefuls. When push came to shove only five gardeners agreed to join her at the end of November, the other two would-be workers having newly learnt about the house's gun-toting owner or otherwise listened too closely to idle gossip. One candidate who accepted the job drowned immediately while surfing off the Cornish coast. Another was struck down by an unexpected illness, which rendered his whole right side paralysed. The remaining three set off for Green Way House as planned but pretty much in total ignorance of what they might expect to find.

3

Laura Bloom was by her own reckoning an old-fashioned, bookish person who had just been sent down from university for stabbing a fellow student in the groin ten times with a pair of scissors. Thanks to him she had been forced to pause her course in Classics (Literae Humaniores). The person she hated most right now, apart from the young man who had attacked her, was herself: her rigorous self-defence had seen her banished to a tiny village eleven miles north of Lincoln. This was largely due to the boy's rich parents who had painted her as some kind of intoxicated harpy – she might have a human head but was all wings and claws? She could not remember exactly what had happened but she had woken up at 6 a.m. in her college bed to find her lover had crawled on top of her. He was having unprotected, penetrative sex with her while she still slept. He wouldn't withdraw when she ordered him to, so she had lashed out with the scissors from her bedside table.

Last time she saw him he walked with a limp.

Now Laura lived in fear of his enraged mother, whose emasculated son had brought dishonour on her illustrious family.

To add insult to injury she, not him, had been 'sent down' for a year to let tempers cool.

She had been banished to the one place she hated most, her own home. Lonely brown fields with few trees or hills stretched for miles. It was like living in agricultural hell.

Most of all she loathed her schoolteacher mother who wouldn't stop going on about how she had just ruined both their lives. This, while trying desperately to hush the whole thing up. The village consisted of no more than two hundred people, but every day Mrs Bloom came face to face with far too many of them – even her five-year-old pupils knew her daughter was somehow in disgrace. That wasn't all. Every time the stable lads walked by with the farm owner's prized racehorses they stared in at Laura's gate. The horses too, she fancied, turned their heads her way. She might as well have painted a big red cross on her front door, since notoriety here was as good as the plague. Only Lola, the family dog, was totally accepting. As for her father…

'I might as well be dead,' she told herself despairingly, when she picked up a copy of her mother's gardening magazine and read:

Wanted: volunteers to create a "hortus conclusus". No lefties or Marxists need apply. Successful candidates can bring as much wine as they like, as long as it's high quality and I'm allowed to drink it. Apply Lady Ann Frost c/o Green Way House, Shurdington, Nr. Cheltenham, Gloucestershire.

Laura knew what "hortus conclusus" meant in Latin. It was derived from the Vulgate Bible's Song of Songs: "A garden enclosed is my sister, my spouse, a garden enclosed; a fountain sealed up". The only thing she had truly loved about her short spell at her ancient university had been her college's secluded grounds. They had been a haven from the city's noise, traffic and smells. Already she could envisage a place of supreme delights, a retreat from all cares, as in the Palazzetto del Giardino di San Marco in Venice whose picture she had seen in a book of medieval poetry. Or it would be like the 2011 "hortus conclusus" at the Serpentine Gallery Pavilion in London. This was her chance to escape ugly, vindictive and unjust people by way of a secure space, a world within a world, a garden room in which to sit, stroll and observe the flowers. No vengeful lover would hunt her down. No more nasty solicitors' letters would threaten to destroy her life's prospects… "Needs must when the devil drives… She who hesitates is lost". In short, Laura resolved to go on the run.

***

Ray Knight, not always the name he gave to the police, was in serious trouble. He had purchased a brand new Honda Fireblade 1000cc motorcycle by dint of paying the first month's instalment up front. Short, blond and affable, he had easily charmed the eager salesman into giving him extended credit on the condition that his employer stood guarantor for the remaining £18000. Ray had trained as a fireman on one of Her Majesty's aircraft carriers where he had spent most days doing very little for rather good pay – Royal Navy ships didn't suffer many serious fires.

Highlights of his life so far had been getting exceptionally drunk with his fellow crew when visiting foreign brothels, of which there was a surprising number worldwide. He had particularly fond memories of the Lady Boys in Thailand and girls in the Philippines, but at forty-one years old the fleshpots of the world had begun to pall. Casual girlfriends had come and gone, as had his career on the high seas, but a hankering after his spendthrift youthful ways lingered on – hence the very smart Fireblade with a top speed of 186 m.p.h.

British roads are not made for exceptionally fast motorcycles. The A435 from Cheltenham to Cirencester is well known for its deceptively severe hairpin bends and it was here that Ray skidded two weeks after he had taken possession of his new toy. He had survived but his machine had not. It turned out there was a treacherous patch of oil on the tarmac, but there was no denying his excessive speed. All might have been well had he been insured. He was not. When his employer and guarantor Max Bolger – a kindly old man who had once served in the Navy himself and now ran a builder's merchants in Bristol – learnt he owed nearly £18000 to the motorcycle dealership for the outstanding loan, he collapsed on the spot. The involvement of the police was inevitable. Riding a motorcycle without insurance was a serious crime, but Mr Bolger's two burly brothers were not pleased either. Ray had been put up against the nearest wall and given a month to raise the money or else. He had made a start by selling his solid gold chains and rings as well as three stolen motorcycles that he was 'minding' for a friend in a rundown former stable in a backstreet near Bristol's docks. He was now out of options. So he answered the advertisement that he found in a free magazine while eating fish and chips in a café overlooking the Floating Harbour and set out for Green Way House a.s.a.p. He bobbed along on his 'borrowed' second-hand 50cc moped with a wonky rear light at a steady speed of 35 m.p.h.

***

Barry Barnes was a convicted murderer. He had been imprisoned for the killing of a drug dealer late one night in the City of Gloucester. A jury had found him guilty in the absence of any real evidence against him. He had confidently told police that DNA tests would clear his name. Instead a witness picked him out of a video identity parade – she told the court that she was more than 100 per cent sure she had seen him stab the dealer to death, even though he did not match her original description of the attacker at all.

For sixteen years Barry – once head gardener to a local castle – had feared he would never see freedom again. Now he had been let out for good behaviour. If he had accepted his 'guilt' and gone through the usual rehab programmes, he could have been released ten years earlier. Yet the more he protested his innocence the longer he had been forced to remain behind bars in a bizarre quirk of the British legal system.

At 9.10 a.m. on a wet Wednesday, Barry walked through the gate of HM Prison Leyhill (Category D) in South Gloucestershire. Only his terminally ill, seventy-three-old mother was there to meet him. 'I never thought I'd live to see the day,' she said. 'I thought I'd be dead in my grave by the time it happened.'

'It's all over now,' said Barry, although until he cleared his name he would have to live under a shadow.

The evidence he craved for so long had – cruelly – come on the day his release was agreed. Now the Criminal Cases Review Commission had decided his case should go to the Court of Appeal. Twice it had turned him down, but this time it looked set to rule in his favour. It would also reopen the murder case years ago. Barry had been silenced once but he would not be silenced again. All his protests of innocence while he was in prison had not gone unnoticed. He knew things. *Other people knew he knew these things.* If they had bribed a witness years ago they could get to him now to stop the truth emerging.

Already a note had been pushed through his door showing a face with its lips sewn shut as a warning.

When his mother pointed out the advertisement for a job at Green Way House he applied the same day. He had been 36 when he was arrested and he was now 53. He had watched real murderers, rapists and paedophiles do their rehab courses and be released when their tariffs expired. He'd even seen people escape (three in one month) when he had chosen to stay behind. That had been very hard to stomach.

While ensconced behind bars Barry had dreamt of feeling the sun and rain on his face. He longed to hear the wind in the trees. He wanted to smell every kind of flower from lilac to roses. Tread grass under his feet. He had vowed he would one day tend somebody's garden again, but never did he think he would have to hide in one.

4

Police Headquarters
Prism House
Gloucester

DI Prickett was having one of his rants. His theatrical march up and down the office in his new jacket and tie was undercut by his habit of wearing dirty brown shoes. 'These new gun rules will never work. It'll be the south-west all over again. The killer uses a legally held shotgun to murder five people including a toddler, before blowing his own head off…'

'Uh-huh,' said Alison, without looking up from her desk.

'There won't be any *legal* onus on doctors to place firearms markers on the medical notes of certificate holders.'

'Sorry, what?'

'If a firearms licence-holder develops an obsession the police will not necessarily be notified. I'm talking about that shooting in Plymouth last year.'

'Right oh.'

'The killer was heavily influenced by "incel" culture.'

'Beyond a doubt.'

'It turns out there's this misogynistic online movement of men who blame women for their own sexual failings.'

'Uh-huh.'

'Already some doctors have refused to take part in firearms applications. Some are citing conscientious objections while others say they're not experts in mental health. The placement of a marker on the medical notes of a gun owner should be obligatory, don't you agree?'

'I suppose.'

'That includes an assessment of their mental health. It will make explicit that firearms applicants must be subject to social media checks.'

'I guess.'

'Are you even listening to me, sergeant?'

'I really am.'

'You're really not.'

Alison popped a mint in her mouth. 'I can't stop thinking about that man I ran over last night.'

'Fine. Yes. Whatever. Where did he go?'

'One minute he was lying all winded and bruised in the road. Next minute he was gone in the fog and dark. I'm worried sick about him, to be honest.'

Prickett stopped pacing the floor. 'Or maybe the fact that he didn't hang around says it all. He didn't need your help.'

'But I could so easily have killed him.'

'Except according to him he was already dead.'

'He did say that, yes.'

'You said you were driving very carefully and slowly. It was hardly your fault.'

'I've rung every local hospital. No one remotely like him has been admitted for traffic accident injuries. Where did he come from? Where did he go? There's not much habitation on those hilly roads. The only thing he mentioned was someone's garden.'

'Do you good to forget all about it.'

'I'm seriously wondering if I imagined the whole thing.'

'What you saw was someone's idea of a bit of fun.'

'I really can't say.'

'I'm thinking stag night. His mates dumped him in the middle of nowhere and he had to get home with no money, or even his clothes.'

'No, it's more than that.'

'You quite sure he didn't give a name?'

'None,' said Alison, scratching a mole on the side of her nose, 'but I think I should try to find out, don't you? I should do it today.'

'Don't even think about it.'

'What if he's in serious trouble?'

'And you don't get paid to investigate ghosts.'

5

'Absolutely not!' said Mrs Bloom. 'What about your studies?'

'What studies?' said Laura. 'My university tutors don't want to know me. I've been sent down in disgrace.'

'And whose fault is that?'

'It's certainly not mine.'

'You went to bed with a drunken lad. Then you stabbed him in… in the…'

'Balls.'

Mrs Bloom resumed polishing the already gleaming floor. 'This is you running away Laura. This is you failing to face up to what you did.'

'You mean what he did to me.'

'You could at least find a decent job that pays. I really don't know what you are thinking. This will be a whole year out of your life.'

'Consider it gardening leave.'

Mr Bloom wandered into the kitchen wearing his dirty brown overalls. A short man with big hands, he liked to cultivate everything from beans to potatoes on his large allotment. 'What's going on? Why is everyone shouting?'

'Your daughter wants to work for a pittance in a stranger's garden.'

'It's not a pittance,' said Laura. 'I get somewhere free to stay and all my food is provided.' She exchanged looks with her father. There had always been an unspoken bond between them, forged by their mutual love of growing things – they spent whole days together cultivating lettuces, cabbages, turnips and strawberries. She tended orchids in the heated glasshouse. Whereas her mother abhorred all germs, Laura was happiest with dirt under her fingernails. When she was not reading books about ancient Rome she wanted to see things blossom and fruit which always fascinated her.

'What work are we talking about exactly?' asked Mr Bloom. He began removing a wellington boot on sheets of newspaper. He hopped from page to page like stepping stones across the shiny floor.

'All I know is that it involves creating a garden in the memory of the owner's lost son. Lady Ann Frost…'

'Lady? You're not going to work on someone's estate?'

'That remains to be seen.'

'Laura should stay here with us,' said Mrs Bloom, butting in. 'She can perfectly well help me with the housework. It seems to me I have to do a bit too much round here…'

Laura reddened. 'I don't want to upset you, I really don't.'

More sighs followed as her mother sought to cajole, undermine and generally criticise her. If she was a big disappointment to her, so was life. Mrs Bloom fretted at having married a local lorry driver – even if he did love her dearly – but most of all she chafed at her own *lack of recognition* in this world. Unfortunately her reputation had been forged in her childhood – she would never live down her older brothers' dubious behaviour. Both had been renowned for stealing apples and pears from neighbours' gardens and they had once 'liberated' a whole set of solid silver cutlery from the farm owner's kitchen. Worst of all, one brother had twice exposed himself to the bus driver as she drove by on the top road. Being an excellent schoolmarm made not one jot of difference in the villagers' minds. She would always be 'that person' from 'that family'. Her daughter's acceptance by a famous college was meant to fix all that. Thanks to Laura the Blooms would be top dogs in the village at last. Now it was all messed up and she felt so embarrassed.

'If you leave you're on your own. Don't expect any help from me,' said

Mrs Bloom. 'You've already made such a hash of things…'

'Naturally I won't go if you don't want me to, mother.'

'Good, because I won't be praying for you when it all goes wrong.'

***

It was six a.m. next morning when Laura walked out the door with her suitcase in her hand. She had some cash, her phone and credit card and a promise from her father to delay all knowledge of her departure for at least an hour.

In reality she was safe enough since her mother had always steadfastly refused to learn to drive. Mrs Bloom couldn't jump in the family car and come storming after her.

She was going not to spite her mother especially, but going nevertheless. I'll walk up to the top road and hitch a lift into Lincoln and continue from there, thought Laura. "Nothing ventured, nothing gained… Hope for the best and prepare for the worst… She who hesitates is lost".

Lady Ann Frost had sent her directions which were both straightforward and a little mysterious: "Leave the M5 Motorway at Junction 11A and take the A417 for Cirencester. This road will take you to a roundabout at the top of Crickley Hill. A road on your left goes to Cheltenham. Proceed along this route for less than a mile until you come to a small crossroads at Ullenwood. Turn left into Greenway Lane. Descend the rough track (not all of which can be traversed by a car) for two and a half miles and you will come to Green Way House. My butler John Mortimer will open a side gate for you in the garden wall. Do NOT attempt to approach the house any other way. Local villagers are too apt to show an interest in my affairs, which is why you'll find the main gate to the driveway is kept permanently chained. No one goes in or out without my say-so. I am very grateful for your offer of assistance in my little project and look forward to meeting you very soon."

The old Roman road called the Fosse Way runs straight as a die from

Lincolnshire to Gloucestershire. England is not a large country but even so her journey totalled about 150 miles. Laura was all set to follow in the footsteps of many a footsore centurion. Unhappily, people are less likely to give rides to strangers standing at the roadside these days, so it was a relief when a lorry finally stopped and its burly driver offered to take her as far as the City of Leicester.

He offered to go the rest of the way in return for a blow job.

She found another driver, but what should have taken most of the morning took until 2 p.m. That's because her courier, a friendly Polish woman, stopped to deliver carpets in Worcester, Tewkesbury and Gloucester. When Laura stepped out of the van at the top of Crickley Hill she badly needed a drink. Also, her driver had played rap music very loudly for hours on end and her head ached.

City lights pinpricked the distant valley. Otherwise she was standing in a bleak place that had once been home to forts and ancient graves. The only nearby building was a Cotswold stone inn called The Air Balloon.

I won't be long, she thought and braved the traffic to reach the pub's lit doorway.

'I'll have a cheese burger please,' said Laura to the beady-eyed girl serving behind the wooden bar. It felt good to get warm again. 'And a coffee.'

'What sort of coffee?'

'Any sort.'

'Vienna, Demi-crème, Frappe…?'

'Expresso.'

Even for a dull, weekday afternoon her welcome hostelry was exceptionally empty. The only other customer was an old man wearing a faded blue cap, who leaned on the bar while reading a copy of "Amazing Spider-Man". His dirty wax jacket smelt musty. Mud caked his boots. She took him to be a farmer.

'Never heard of a pub called The Air Balloon before,' said Laura loudly. 'It's usually something much more boring like The George or The Bell.'

The old man glanced up from his comic. Coarse grey stubble covered his chin. 'It was built in 1777 when it was called The New Inn. It changed its name after Edward Jenner launched an unmanned hydrogen balloon in 1784. The balloon flew from Berkeley Castle and landed near here. That's all there is to it.'

'I'm sure it must have been quite a sensation at the time. It must have been one of the first ever flights in Britain.'

The farmer resumed reading adventures of his own. His calloused hands grated each page he turned.

Laura had to move stools to regain his attention. 'You look as if you live locally. Do you know a place called Green Way House? I'm on my way there now, only these winter days are so short that I'm afraid I won't find it in the dark.'

He raised his head. The bartender did the same. 'Don't tell me Lady Ann is expecting you?'

'I'm going to help her with an exciting new project.'

Grin turned to grimace as the farmer raised an eyebrow. 'Sounds to me as if her ladyship is up to her old tricks again.'

'What tricks?' asked Laura.

He shot the bartender a look. 'There will come a time when someone will tell all.'

'Tell what exactly?'

'No one in their right mind goes near Green Way House any more, not after what happened.'

'I'm only going there to do some gardening.'

'That's a bad idea.'

'I'm quite sure nothing bad is going to occur.'

'Let's hope not.'

The bartender shot her a look of her own. Said nothing.

'Do either of you know Lady Ann at all? Have you ever met her?' asked Laura cheerfully.

'I know that the last people who went to work for her didn't last long,' said the farmer. 'One of them was a young woman about your age.'

'Oh really? When was that?'

'Must be several months ago now.'

'Do you remember her name?'

'I know it was Lauri or Lillie. No it wasn't. It was something else... I met her at the old army camp at the top of Greenway Lane. I graze sheep there and I had a sick ewe to tend to. There's a whole collection of huts left behind from World War II. It's a real warren and you can get lost in its ruinous maze. She asked me if I'd seen a man dressed in a white nightshirt. I joked she'd seen our local ghost.'

'What ghost?'

'Never you mind.'

'Did you see hear from her again?'

'I *heard* she and her fellow gardeners left Green Way House in a great hurry.'

'Why?'

He hid behind his comic. 'Something's not right about that place.'

'That's your honest opinion, is it?'

'Just accept it.'

'Are you saying that Lady Ann has tried to create her garden once already?'

'People say she is another Miss Havisham. You know, as in...'

'Charles Dickens's novel "Great Expectations".'

The bartender, wiping a glass, took up the story. 'Lady Ann's husband was a computer software builder. He was one of the first to start a company providing internet access to 230,000 subscribers. When he sold out to Scottish Telecom in the 1990s he made sixty million pounds. He died some years ago in mysterious circumstances. The general opinion was that he had somehow poisoned himself with a plant *from his own garden.* As a result Lady Ann inherited his fortune. Ever since then there have been dire rumours.'

'Rumours? What rumours?'

'There are those who say she did away with him. She tried to marry again almost immediately, but it turned out the new groom only wanted her inheritance. As a result she jilted him at the altar. She has been a recluse ever since.'

Laura smiled. 'Sounds like a very sensible person to me.'

'People can be needlessly cruel. They like to make trouble. Some suggest her son died in suspicious circumstances too.'

'They do?'

'Okay, that's enough for now.'

'Or you know more than you're telling?'

'And I'm no blabbermouth.'

'If her ladyship is so shy, why is she so keen to hire people to remake her garden?' asked Laura.

The farmer buried his face in "Amazing Spider-Man". 'Someone has to give her hope she'll find redemption one day.'

6

Ullenwood
Near Greenway Lane

'You can't possibly be serious detective?' A look of disbelief filled Olivia Bennett's face. Normally unflappable, she went pale. 'We are a further education college for people with physical disabilities, acquired brain injuries and associated learning difficulties. No one is allowed to wander off. I doubt they'd even want to.'

DS Alison Ellis shared her discomfort. 'I know it sounds strange, but are you quite sure you haven't lost anyone in the last forty-eight hours?'

Olivia had total confidence in her own competency as she tapped her gold pen on her desk. 'As residential manager at Ullenwood College I can assure you everyone here takes their responsibilities very seriously.'

'Yes, but I have to check.'

'Can't we do this another day? I'm very busy.'

'It can't wait, I'm afraid.'

Their eyes met. 'Oh very well, say what you have to.'

'Two nights ago I was on my way home from a conference in Bristol when I ran into a distressed young man in his twenties. I hit him with my car at the crossroads not a quarter of a mile from your front gate. It was extremely late and very foggy. Fortunately I was driving very slowly. If we rule out some stag-do prank he can't have come far. You see what I'm getting at?'

'Of course I do, but I don't like it.'

'I'm not here to get anyone into any trouble.'

'Forgive me if it doesn't look like it to me.'

'The young man I met said some pretty peculiar things. That's not all. He was dressed only in a flimsy nightshirt. Some people here are residential, are they not?'

Olivia adjusted her large brown spectacles on her nose. 'We have seventy single rooms and nine shared rooms and our night nurse is on site at all times to assist anyone in need.'

'So you haven't lost anybody recently?'

'Really detective, you ought to know better. Our residents are quite happy here. They have a kitchenette and TV in their rooms… That's only part of what we do. Much of our time is spent providing day care, independent living training and physiotherapy for those who come and go on a full or part-time basis…'

'Nevertheless someone could wander off if they chose to?'

'Bear in mind most people here use wheelchairs.'

'What about staff?'

'I don't know of any trouble among the staff. They're a dedicated bunch. One in ten has a declared disability of their own. What's more, they have all achieved Disability Confident employer status.'

Alison found it hard to hide her disappointment. She had very much hoped that this centre for disabled youth would quickly solve her mystery for her. 'I'm sorry to have wasted your time. I'll see myself out.'

Olivia, relaxing a little, shot her a smile. 'Fact is detective, you're not the first person to meet somebody at that crossroads.'

'How's that?'

'I once saw someone there myself.'

'What? When?'

'It must have been a year ago, almost to the day. I'd been working late and was very tired. I was all set to turn right in my car to descend the hill into Cheltenham. The night was cold and dank and the windscreen kept misting over. I was trying to clear its glass with a cloth before proceeding when I looked up. My lights were on full beam and lit Greenway Lane directly opposite me. Coming straight at me was a naked man – he was about to rush headlong across the crossroads. I don't know if I'd dazzled him, but I really thought he was going to run into the traffic. I dimmed the lights and he was gone!'

'Would you recognise him again? Can you describe him?'

'Long black hair hid his face.'

Alison took out her notebook. 'What happened then? Did you manage to go after him?'

'I didn't know what to do. It sounds stupid now, but there was something about him that gave me the shivers. It wasn't like seeing an apparition exactly, yet I felt I was looking at someone that didn't belong in this world. He could have come straight from the grave.'

'Sounds about right.'

'At that moment my phone rang and distracted me. Forgive me, I probably did wrong to mention it.'

'No actually you didn't,' said Alison and handed the manager her card.

As she walked out the door a voice cried after her.

'Who do you think it is detective?'

'I don't know, but I don't believe in ghosts and neither should you.'

***

Alison drove as far as the crossroads. Stopped her car. She had meant what she said: she didn't believe in ghosts, but it could do no harm to study the scene of her accident again by day.

Black wrought-iron railings fenced the entrance to Greenway Lane, while a hedge and a stone wall enclosed grassy fields on either side. A sign warned her that the way ahead was impassable for motorised vehicles.

Trees shed leaves on a freshly killed deer that lay bloody and broken at the kerbside.

She checked the map on her phone. She was looking for a place that might have a garden. Greenway Lane was the quickest way up the escarpment from the valley below as the crows flies. Her screen showed a farm as well as another dwelling called Green Way House at the bottom of the climb.

The house clearly had substantial grounds. To reach it she would have to descend the hill on foot via the lane for some considerable distance.

A map could only ever measure a journey in kilometres or miles, not pain.

It was a pity to ruin a new pair of shoes…

Next minute her phone rang. It was Detective Inspector Prickett.

'Something's come up. Get yourself to Coombe Hill Nature Reserve. Looks like we have a major incident on our hands…'

Any thought of exploring the track ahead was suddenly out of the question. Alison switched on her car's flashing blue lights. Sounded her siren. She would have to call on Green Way House some other day – she would stop by it unawares a different way.

7

The dying sun in no way dampened Laura's spirits. That farmer in The Air Balloon really was something else, she thought happily. Her only real gripe was her suitcase. It bounced and bumped along the verge as she regretted bringing something quite so heavy. She really hadn't thought this through. Oh well, she laughed. "The Road to Hell is paved with good intentions… What does not kill me makes me stronger".

Her trek from the pub to the start of Greenway Lane turned out to be cold and lonely. At the crossroads the moon already looked down on her in silent motion.

The lane's entrance resembled a dark cave. Its red and white T-sign told her she was heading for a dead-end.

A high hedge and fence stretched either side of her, should she be tempted to stray from its one true path.

Next minute she nearly jumped out of her skin. Something shrieked at her from the trees' black branches. It went ke-wick, ke-wick, ke-wick. There followed almost immediately a soft hooo, hooo, hoo-oo-oo-oo-oo-oo, the final hoot with a quivering waver.

Laura walked faster. The sound was echoey and eerie, as much like a poor, lost soul as a bird.

Almost human.

It hurt her ears.

'Who's there?' she shouted to the empty lane. Only tawny owls screeched like that she told herself firmly, though she hated the silence that followed even more. It was telling her don't go, don't go, don't go-oo-oo-oo…

She soon descended a stony path more fit for horses. From here on, Greenway Lane was dirt and rock, not a real road at all.

In total she walked another mile and threequarters, when she looked up and saw the sun glint red on broken glass that fortified the top of a high brick wall.

She remembered what she had been told: a gate led from the lane into Green Way House's private grounds.

The gate was locked but there was no buzzer or bell. Laura peered through its rusty iron bars as the last of the afternoon sunlight lit the dirty glazing of derelict cold frames. Beside the ruins of a kitchen garden stood a white, metal garden seat complete with two long handles and a front wheel which had to date from Edwardian or Victorian times – you could push it anywhere like a wheelbarrow. A cracked and weatherworn terracotta pot stood as tall as a person, while several impressive stone statues of scantily clad men and summer maidens adorned weed-filled flowerbeds.

She was all set to shout more loudly when someone appeared at the gate, scolding and scowling. 'Be quiet. Do you want to disturb the whole house?'

'I'm Laura Bloom. Please let me in. Lady Ann Frost is expecting me.'

He looked her up and down and said rather haughtily: 'It's your own fault. You should have been here hours ago.'

'But it's not yet four p.m.'

'Her ladyship takes tea at four.'

'I stopped at the pub on the hill for something to eat and drink.'

'What pub?' said the crooked gatekeeper and rattled his keys in her face.

'There's only one. It's called The Air Balloon.'

'Last I heard it has been demolished.'

'Excuse me?'

'You didn't speak to anyone, did you?'

29

'What kind of question is that?'

The gatekeeper brought his head back to the bars. Squinted at her with his totally white eye. 'That pub has been under a cloud for years. It sits on a road that joins the M4 and M5 motorways. It's a notorious accident blackspot. There have been hundreds of casualties. The new, replacement road can only be routed through the middle of the inn – to go anywhere else will destroy nearby Barrow Wake which is a site of Special Scientific Interest.'

'The farmer I chatted to didn't mention anything about a new road…'

'It's all gone, I tell you. Months ago. Only the dead drink there now.'

'Sorry, but you're mistaken.'

'Like to think not.'

He turned the key in the gate at last. 'Come in and come quietly. There's no disturbing Green Way House after dark.'

Laura giggled. Perhaps a modern-day Miss Havisham really does live here, she thought. 'I quite understand. Lady Ann Frost likes her routines.'

'What? Oh yes. That too.'

'Are you John Mortimer the butler?'

'Who else would I be? Except I'm less of a butler than an all-purpose maintenance man these days. My wife Betty and I take care of her ladyship.'

'She must be lonely.'

'Lonely? Why do you say that?'

'Forgive me, but Lady Ann must crave company after the death of her husband and only son?'

John carefully twisted the key shut in the gate again. He left her to carry her suitcase herself. 'If you'd come any later I would have given up on you. No one *lives* in the house anymore except her ladyship. Not me, not you, not anyone. She won't allow it. Betty and I have a place in the village and we go home every evening.'

Laura refused to let his resentful evasiveness get her down. 'So where will I be staying, if not with her ladyship?'

'In one of the caravans of course.'

'Caravans?'

'Where else?'

'Naturally I assumed…'

'Like the others.'

'What others?'

'Two more people are due to arrive first thing tomorrow morning. You don't think you can landscape a whole garden by yourself, do you?'

'I'm sorry, it's just that…'

Mr Mortimer sniffed loudly. 'You didn't suppose you would be living in luxury in some country mansion? You'll soon see. Otherwise you'll wish you hadn't come after all.'

***

Laura hurried to keep up with the butler across the grounds. A red mini-digger stood rusting beside a large hole into which this autumn's dead leaves had blown. The slit in the earth was no bigger than a grave. Whoever had stopped work here so abruptly had forgotten to remove the key from the excavator's ignition. Someone had also left behind their pretty blue cashmere pointelle scarf draped across its seat. Lacy scarves like that didn't come cheap.

She had in mind a mansion of magnificent rooms with lavish wainscots and decorated plasterwork. She hoped for something delightfully Gothic with hideous gargoyles and heraldic lions, at least some of which might yet prove true. "Forewarned is forearmed… Fools rush in where angels fear to tread". Except her initial impression was rather different. Pointed finials should have adorned the stone slate roofs of all three gables, but one finial was missing in the incomplete skyline. An octagonal turret crowned the house with its globe of glass, some of whose storm-tossed panes were missing or broken. A tall chimney had been shortened, with the result that the other imposing pairs of ashlar stacks failed to look symmetrical. Similarly the newer, three-light bay windows on the ground floor no longer resembled the older and squarer, more Jacobean windows elsewhere. This was an ancient, misshapen place whose scars mirrored those of its many previous owners.

'Wait here while I fetch you a torch from the kitchen,' Mr Mortimer barked at her. 'Whatever you do, don't wander off. Never go in the garden after dark without a light.'

'But I...'

No sooner had he vanished down the side of the house than she heard him whistle a cheery tune.

She assumed it was him.

Whoever it was, the jolly song lost nothing of its boldness despite its sadness.

'Hallo?' she cried, but the singer was lost in a sudden swirl of snow in the air. Mr Mortimer had done what she should never do and left her to fend for herself in the dark.

The song's words dissolved like the crystals on the palm of her hand:

In my garden grew plenty of Thyme,
It would flourish by night and by day;
O'er the wall came a lad, he took all that I had,
And stole my thyme away.

She really couldn't get the solemn voice out of her head. Or it was Green Way House itself that so unnerved her? Its want of contentment was less architectural than emotional. There was something almost wounded about it. Fresh doubt gripped her. The house was warped, distorted, twisted. *Leave here Laura while you still can...*

8

Coombe Hill Nature Reserve

'I'm James Wickes but you can call me "Rusty Boltz".' With one front tooth missing and a bulbous beer belly the short, stocky man greeted her with an excited smile at the edge of the canal.

'My name is Detective Sergeant Alison Ellis from the Gloucestershire Constabulary.' She really needed to talk to the First Responders about what they had discovered, only "Rusty Boltz" was not about to give her that chance. Also the light was as good as gone – the dying sun left behind a deep grey sky. Even that faded fast.

'This way detective. We'll have to walk along the towpath. It's about a quarter of a mile from the terminal wharf, isn't it Jane?'

A beaming blonde teenager in a big yellow waterproof coat nodded hard. She chewed gum even harder.

'And this is?' asked Alison switching on her torch.

'She's my sixteen-year-old daughter.'

'Pleased to meet you detective. I'm "Magnet Maid".'

Alison set off meekly along the grassy path that bordered the canal. 'What were you doing when you made your discovery?'

"Rusty Boltz" gestured at the nearby water. Wreaths of white mist steamed on its icy surface like a boiling cauldron. 'Jane and I go magnet fishing all over the country.'

'Last summer I fished a gun out of the Regent's Canal,' said "Magnet Maid" proudly. 'And you found a Second World War bayonet in Birmingham, didn't you Dad?'

'Not to mention a 1980s cigarette machine in Liverpool.'

'I'm still envious!'

'That's what we thought we had here because it was so heavy.'

'It's lucky Dad uses the "Evolution".'

'I can't pretend to know what that is,' said Alison, beginning to feel very cold in the damp, mizzling afternoon.

'The "Evolution" gives you 1600kg's worth of pulling power. Dad won't let me try it yet. He says I'm not ready. I'm still on the "Beast" which is 1000kg.'

'Why don't we start at the beginning,' said Alison calmly. 'You came here today to fish for junk because…?'

'It's our hobby.' "Rusty Boltz" tugged on his cap and grinned from ear to ear. 'You should see our footage on YouTube.'

'We mostly pull out bicycles and shopping trolleys.'

'Don't forget that ladies' sex toy we bagged last week in Gloucester.'

"Magnet Maid" giggled. 'Dad didn't know what it was. I had to tell him it was a Rampant Rabbit.'

'To be honest detective, we didn't expect to get much at all today. It's not as if we're in the centre of a big city or anything. If the Wildlife Trust hadn't bought it as a haven for birds everything would have vanished from the face of the earth years ago. This canal hasn't carried coal from the Forest of Dean via the River Severn since the 1870s.'

'Dad's right. We thought it would be an absolute dead loss. We were about to call it a day and go home, but now we'll be right up there with that man who found a woman's severed leg in a bin bag in London. The magnet only picked *her* up because she had a chain round her ankle to weigh her down. We'll be famous on the internet.'

'Absolutely we will,' said "Rusty Boltz". 'This has to be on a par with "Bondi Treasure Hunter". You know, the Australian guy who hauled two safes out of a canal in Amsterdam.'

'I do hope so. He got 1.4 million views for the cash and jewellery he found inside.'

'Of course we called the police as soon as we realised what we'd found.'

'We've recorded it all on film.'

'That's what bothers me,' said Alison.

'Meaning what?' asked "Magnet Maid".

'Just to be clear, this is now a crime scene. None of this can go to the press or social media.'

'It sure beats hairgrips and rusty nails.'

'Which is why the answer is still no,' said Alison grimly and watched the hellish mist creep closer to her on the water's surface. There was something other-worldly about this place, yet the scene looked peaceful enough apart from the stripy DO NOT CROSS police cordons across the path. Each strip was turning white with the glittery frost. Moorhens scooted on the cold water, while noisy ducks climbed the bank hoping to be fed.

'But this is BIG detective. As big as those magnet fishers who pulled a man out of the River Itchen in Southampton in 2019. The magnets stuck to his handcuffs. It made national TV…'

'When you put it like that.'

'We deserve to be stars.'

'Not a chance.'

'All I have to do is press SEND.'

'Not yet.'

The canal rapidly degenerated into a series of lagoons divided by large clumps of broken, brown bulrushes. "Rusty Boltz" was right, thought Alison. All pretence of a navigable waterway was long gone – no one would ever again haul a sixty-ton barge full of coal three miles from the river to the foot of Coombe Hill. She stopped by a pollarded willow. In summer these canal banks would be a riot of purple-loosestrife and the air would buzz with dragonflies, but right now everything was dark and still.

She had once come here to watch birds from the wooden hut called Grundon Hide that gave commanding views of water-filled scrapes, marsh and swampy lowland. Back then she hadn't always been able to tell the difference between a teal and a wigeon. She still couldn't, although the great gathering of birds making so much noise right now – as they chose their roosting places for the night – was most definitely a flock of lapwings. A stately grey heron stood in a tree overlooking the crime scene. It mounted guard as silent witness.

A muddy refrigerator stood on the side of the canal, attended by a police officer. He and Alison exchanged brief greetings.

'We thought it was just a "UMO" at first,' said "Magnet Maid".

'A what?'

'A "UMO".'

'Just say it.'

'Unidentified Metal Object.'

Black skeletal trees reflected in the reedy water as Alison pulled on her latex gloves. She approached the refrigerator from the front.

'As you can see detective, we opened the door and tried to shut it again pretty quick,' said "Rusty Boltz".

'Only his arm wouldn't…'

Alison covered her nose with one hand and shone her torch straight ahead. Inside the white metal box sat a naked man. His legs were at the top of the refrigerator and his head at the bottom. The condition of his face was slightly green. Some skin and hair had parted company from his cranium, mostly because of the weight of his body pressing down on his skull. She had no way of telling whether he had been alive or dead when he had been sealed in his aquatic tomb, but a forensic investigation looked viable. The sick, sweetly smell was overpowering. She turned away before she felt compelled to throw up.

'Are you quite sure neither of you has touched the remains?'

'Absolutely not,' said "Rusty Boltz".

'All the better. Decomposing bodies can be nasty things. I'll need formal statements from you back at my car.'

'I bet it's a gangland killing,' said "Magnet Maid". 'I do hope I'm right. Everyone loves a good murder on YouTube. What do you say detective? Do you think someone has done for him?'

'That's what I need to find out.'

9

'Yours is the yellow one,' said Mr Mortimer and opened the door to a decrepit caravan that stood in the shadow of the high garden wall. 'You'll be dry and comfy now I've fixed the leak in the roof.'

Laura's heart skipped a beat. 'I'm really staying *here*?'

'No one told you?'

'No.'

'That's so her ladyship.'

'It's awfully small.'

'You're looking at a Thomson '52 Almond.'

'As in the year *nineteen* fifty-two?'

'Stately and handsome, your '52 Almond was built for the mountains or on the plains. There was a time when you could find vans like this in the snows of the north or the heat of the African veldt. You're looking at the worthy successor to all the famous Thomson caravans, travellers of the world's highways.'

'What about the blue one over there? Can't I have that?'

'The Classic Sprite with the seized wheel bearings and flat tyres?'

'It looks bigger.'

'Please believe me, it isn't.'

'What about that caravan with the green door? That looks newer.'

'The 1966 Sprite Musketeer has a window that won't shut properly.'

Laura surveyed the travellers' graveyard. 'It's funny the three of them should end up here. It's sad they'll never go anywhere again.'

'Can't be helped.'

'I've never lived in a caravan before. I trust it has a shower and a loo?'
'You'll have to visit the house for those.'
'Well, I'm not sure I approve.'
'Did not Lady Ann promise you board and lodging?'
'True, but it's what she *didn't* say.'
'I don't make the decisions round here. My duties are strictly domestic. I don't interfere where I'm not wanted.'
'Clearly not,' said Laura tartly.
'Mrs Mortimer and I generally stick to Green Way House.'
'Okay.'
'So it won't be us you see in the grounds.'
'That's quite all right.'
'We don't even go for walks in the garden if we can help it.'
'I understand.'
'You definitely won't ever find us picking up fallen apples or shovelling dead leaves into wheelbarrows.'
'Should I not report to you if I see…?'
'You shouldn't *see* anyone. Nobody *should* be in the garden. No one has the *right* to be here whose job it isn't.'
'I meant if I see something that needs fixing,' said Laura, sticking to her guns.
'Above all, you can have absolutely no visitors. That means no boyfriends,' he added darkly and handed her the key to her van.
Laura couldn't help smirking. It was almost worth bringing home a lover just to spite him: watch out John, *there's someone in the garden,* upon which she gave a little shudder.

***

Laura flicked a switch in her new abode and the caravan lit up with a small twelve-volt bulb. Her suitcase filled the gangway and she already felt thoroughly cramped beneath the sloping roof. She was mildly claustrophobic at the best of times. "She who pays the piper calls the tune… Hope for the best and prepare for the worst" she told herself while she wondered if she should clear out while the going was still good. She was already missing her dog Lola. Do they really expect me to live in this box for a whole year? Where will I wash my clothes? "Failing to plan is planning to fail". But she couldn't go home now, she couldn't admit to her mother that she had made a terrible mistake.

She wasn't about to lose face that soon.

It's definitely no worse than my student room at Uni, thought Laura rallying, because it had been designed for compactness and efficiency. The forward half of the van contained a double-bed-settee with locker space beneath. She spun right round and the other, rear apartment revealed two single beds with a removeable table in-between. There was a handy oak-faced cupboard whose top served as another mounting for the table. She opened the door to discover a ventilated locker stacked high with provisions. There was enough food here to keep her fed for a month and more. 'Somebody has gone to a lot of trouble. They've assumed I'll be staying that long.'

She was looking at tins of baked beans, tomatoes, lentils and sardines. There were a jar of coffee and a tea caddy as well as packets of cereal and crisps. Judging by the expiry dates, some of the things had been here a while. Whoever had stocked the caravan had done it for someone before her.

There were four fresh eggs in the refrigerator, as well as half a dozen cartons of Long Life Milk in a box on the floor. She found a kettle and cooking utensils inside a built-in cabinet beneath the gas cooker. There was further space in the gas cylinder storage locker. Opposite the cooker and next to the door there was a ventilated wardrobe to hang coats and larger items of clothing. "Nothing ventured nothing gained" thought Laura gratefully and placed her suitcase on the full-width bed-settee.

Two bed lockers with more roof lockers overhead would take everything else. 'I just have to put everything in its proper place and then I'll be able to move around without tripping myself up in such confined quarters.'

No one had told her exactly what to bring with her, but since she was meant to be working in the open air she had jettisoned dresses in favour of jeans. She had left behind a pair of high-heeled shoes in favour of trainers. A last minute decision to pack some wellington boots had seemed sensible. She had her waterproof coat and a thick pair of trousers, as well as a dark blue beanie and gloves. Her world had suddenly changed to Green Way House and its ruined garden. She baulked at her brief feeling of unease but not the thrill.

If her surroundings had shrunk, her heart had already swelled?

'Tomorrow the rest of the workforce arrives,' she told herself cheerfully. 'Together we'll make our presence felt. We'll make a good team, I bet.'

***

Meanwhile that bath or shower had to be her priority, thought Laura and peered through one of the caravan's windows at the path to the house. Her hot breath misted the cold glass, but not before she registered how the garden had undergone an extraordinary transformation in the time it had taken her to unpack her things. Spectral paths, hedges and a frozen stone fountain shone white in the moonlight beneath a sky of bright stars. What she had thought was snow was hoarfrost. Its cold silence coated everything, even as it flashed and cracked like diamonds on fire.

Suddenly there came a succession of loud taps on her window. Flying and fluttering shook the pane most violently. It quivered ready to shatter, leaving her exposed. But it was only dozens of winter moths hitting their side of the glass. Hers was the first light they had seen in the caravan for a while and they were in a frenzy…

With the wings came someone's strident humming. It drifted her way in all the commotion. Their voice appealed directly to her heart. Someone moved close to her door as their tune tried to wheedle its way in.

She grabbed the flashlight that the butler had given her and shone it out of her window. Had he not stressed that she should not expect to find anyone in the garden, least of all himself?

'Mr Mortimer? Is that you?'

He had come back to check up on her?

The fountain glittered and the stars burned brighter.

The image in her head was confused, its details unlikely, imagined, possibly non-existent.

Except she had good reason to dread every shadow.

Dread was the stuff of nightmares she had endured since college.

Dread was threatening calls day and night.

Dread was being followed.

Most of all, it was not knowing when and where her stalker would strike next, but this was the last place she expected to meet him.

Now there were two shadows, one for the garden and one for a figure walking through it. His proximity set icicles jingling on the bramble bushes. The rimy air powdered his head and shoulders with icy crystals, lending him a frostbitten look on top and sides. That's not to say he was entirely frigid, since there was also something sparkling and electric about him. He leaned heavily on his cane as he paused to sniff a pretty rose that bled red at his fingertips.

Next minute he started towards her, as though ready to embrace her in mid-gait.

'*The garden is mine*,' he declared loudly, before hurrying off to another part of the grounds.

***

Cold air set fire to Laura's lungs. She could opt to go after her unsolicited visitor, but it might be dangerous to track him down in the dark? She shone her torch all round. Saw nothing. That's because proximity in space was not the same as time.

Whoever had just sung her his song was gone where light met shade.

***

Back in her caravan, Laura took care to lock its door securely and leave its bulb switched on. Any inclination to go to the house deserted her. She sat on the full-width bed-settee and clenched her fists. Safety was as much about feelings as physical presence. She might not be back at university but fear travelled with her – it could be triggered anywhere at any time for no reason. She would not be forced to relive the moment! No one should be able to hunt you inside your own head. No one had the right to taunt you with your own worries. Someday she would walk down the street without looking over her shoulder.

A truly bad experience rotted a vital part of you. Something shrivelled and died as anxiety ate at the memory.

Like a maggot in the brain.

She wanted to expose and face the ugly thing for what it was.

He's not real, he's not real.

I'm real.

She had just taken someone else for her pursuer – mixed man with monster – but that didn't mean his song didn't ring in her head with its empty hopes and refrains:

> My garden with heartsease was bright,
> The pansy so pied and so gay;
> One slipped through the gate, and alas! Cruel fate,
> My heartsease took away.

10

Green Way House

'Quite the place you have here,' said Ray Knight, sitting astride his spluttering moped. He had left Bristol at 8 a.m. to be sure to arrive on time.

Mr Mortimer eyed the newcomer's tatty motorcycle leathers. Sniffed loudly. 'You'll be residing in the green Sprite Musketeer caravan over there.'

'That old thing?'

'Her ladyship won't tolerate noise in her own home.'

'Bit of a shy bird, is she?'

'If you'd just like to park your... *ahem*... machine.'

Ray gave the moped's throttle a quick twist. Then he wriggled it and himself through the gate. He rode straight down the path to where the caravan stood in the shadow of the garden wall.

'As I say, her ladyship values her privacy,' said Mr Mortimer, struggling to catch up.

The pathetic roar of the moped's tinny exhaust died, hot and smelly, after its forty-three mile stint on the open road. Ray unclipped the strap on his crash helmet. 'Nobody is good enough for her, is that it?'

'You can't blame her for tiring of people's hurtful comments.'

'So I'm to keep to the confines of the garden, am I?'

'I think it's for the best.'

'And if I say no?'

'You won't.'

'I'd better make myself at home then,' said Ray, accepting the key to the shabby van.

'If you wish, you may put your moped in the stables.'

'Which stables?'

'Is this the sum total of your baggage?'

Ray unhooked two bungee cords that secured a blue plastic milk crate that he had strapped to the back of the moped's seat. He didn't own a suitcase and his kitbag from his navy days had fallen to pieces. 'All you see is all there is.'

'Please come to the house in an hour. Her ladyship is expecting you. A word of warning. She abhors lateness.'

'Bit of a harridan, is she?'

Their eyes met but nothing more was said. Instead Mr Mortimer stalked off. Ray unloaded his crate of belongings on to the floor of the caravan. He took out a photograph of himself standing on the sunny deck of an aircraft carrier and propped it on a shelf by a bed. Otherwise he left the rest to be dealt with later. 'It's a bit like being back on board ship,' he thought, surveying the cramped but orderly interior. 'Quite like old times.'

Meanwhile the stables sounded an excellent idea. The butler hadn't told him where to find them so he would do it himself. His recently 'acquired' moped was best kept hidden from curious eyes. He remounted his machine with a devil-may-care glint in his eye. Then he let go of its clutch and took off down the nearest path through the overgrown garden – he reckoned there was enough time to embark on a quick lap of his new abode first.

Ray started at an upper court, rode by Green Way House's front door, then went via a knot garden and orchard before entering more of the grounds...

'Yeehaw!' he cried at the top of his voice. In his imagination he was once more racing along on his £18000 Honda Fireblade 1000 motorcycle. He skidded and scrambled as he roared down an avenue of cherry trees.

He came to an iron gate that barred his way. 'Everything's so blooming quiet in this place,' Ray thought. It was easy to feel stifled, smothered, drowned. The very stillness was a stimulus – he needed to remind himself he was alive and well in a garden that was as cold as the grave. Its quietude was not just the noiseless sleep of winter, it was a stubborn reservation, a taciturnity, as of something written but never pronounced.

Like the non-betrayal of a secret?

There was a brief delay while he lifted the gate's rusty latch in order to enter a broad rose walk. Soon he was leaning sideways out of his saddle. He twice tore round the statue of an old bearded man who was dressed in a long robe and stood at the intersection of four weed-strewn paths. He waved his arm at him as his moped's rear tyre spun into plants overwintering in the hard, frosted soil that was like concrete.

He laughed and aimed his moped at the weary, slightly stooped statue – he gave the tip of its stone scythe a quick kick as he swept by at five m.p.h. 'What's up old man? Don't be sad. I'm Ray Knight. I'm here to have some fun.'

***

'Oh God. Is that the time?' Laura rubbed her eyes. Grabbed her phone. 'My first day at work and I'm about to be late!'

Whoever revved their motor cycle so loudly had just done her a favour.

She dressed and left her caravan in a hurry to brave the frozen garden in her chilly wellingtons. Had not Mr Mortimer told her where to find the bathroom? Green Way House looked different this morning. Not many places were more unsettling by day than night, as if the garden was doing its utmost to bury the whole residence alive. A mass of deciduous and evergreen vines scaled its tall wings to the very tops of its gables. The tangled, parasitic tendrils percolated through fissures in the pebble-dashed limestone walls – they lived in and on their host as if drawing nutriment directly from it. She could see them feeding off dangerous cracks in the mortar.

'The rooms must be very dark inside,' thought Laura curiously, as long twisted boughs covered most of the windows. Deprive a place of light and it had to be like living in a perpetual winter. Perhaps she was better off in her caravan after all?

She entered the porch to find its big front door slightly ajar. She was struck how oddly detached, indifferent and drab the house appeared within. Nothing had been painted for years. No new furniture had been bought and a bulky brass chandelier was strung with dirty cobwebs.

'That's okay,' laughed Laura. 'I'm not here to dust the house. I'm here to resurrect its garden.'

A centuries old fireplace had once heated the entrance hall. A vase of wilting red roses stood on its mantelshelf above pretty stone panels decorated with fruit and scallop shells. One triangular pediment carved with leaves and grapes was broken, which was possibly why no fire had been lit in its grate for years.

She ducked through a round-headed archway with fluted pilasters and started up a staircase with turned balusters and ball finials. Another vase of shrivelled roses stood in a shell-headed alcove on the quarter landing. She was in a maze of dusty, deserted passageways where it was hard to imagine anyone ever lingered long. That warning voice in her head sounded louder: 'Go Laura. Go far from here. *Go now.*'

***

'Who the devil are you?' The sudden reprimand broke the silence with its hurried whisper, as though talking loudly in Green Way House was expressly forbidden.

Laura spun round. A woman dressed all in black stood before her. 'And you are?'

'I'm her ladyship's housekeeper. I'm Betty Mortimer. What are you doing up here?'

'I'm Laura Bloom. I arrived yesterday. Mr Mortimer kindly let me in.'

The woman's face hardened. 'Where do you think you're going?'

'I'm looking for the bathroom.'

'Well you won't find it up here. You shouldn't be walking about as if you own the whole place.' Betty was a short woman with a strong physical presence. The distinct twinkle in her eye could not mask her sternness.

'Did Mr Mortimer decide to stay late last night? Did something happen?'

'What business is that of yours?'

'I heard someone singing in the garden.'

'You come with me,' said Betty, looking horrified. 'It's nearly 10 a.m. You're needed in the drawing room.'

'Her ladyship told me I was to make myself at home.'

'But not like this.'

Laura found herself shooed, driven, almost pushed along. She came again to the quarter landing and found herself eye to eye with a half-length oil painting of a man at the turn in the stairs.

She loved old portraits. Older the better. The flowing black curls of his wig hung down each side of his embroidered coat and his long, distinguished face was very striking. He wore a white lacy shirt and dark stockings covered his knees. How she had passed him on her way up without noticing him she didn't know. His close-lipped stare was rather serious. Some discontent lay behind the concentration. With his mouth so neutral it was his eyes and eyebrows that created the strongest facial expression – together they conveyed an aloofness that could have been quiet menace. He was sitting in the doorway to a beautiful garden while his hand rested on something on a little table beside him. His prized possession was pointed at one end and indented at the other. Anyone else might have said it was fan or bell-shaped, like some vital human organ.

It appeared to be broken in two pieces. Meanwhile an inscription could be seen on the table's edge that read "et genus et pectus" in elaborately sculpted letters. Their exact significance eluded her for the moment.

'Who is this splendid gentleman?' asked Laura. 'He's very fine.'

'That's William Lawrence. He created the garden here. He did so in honour of his dead wife Anne and his son Will, who died within a few months of each other in 1691. That's why you see him holding his broken heart. The garden was meant to be one of mourning and remembrance, only he died in 1697 aged sixty-one before he could fully realise his dream. He called it "my little Canaan, my Promised Land".'

'How sad to lose wife and son so quickly.'

'Anne died of dropsy and Will succumbed to a fever. She was forty-one and he was twenty-three. Mr Lawrence stayed on here as a recluse. Grief-stricken, he was. That's when he hit upon a plan to erect a tomb for them both on a hill at the edge of the grounds. He intended to remove their bones from Badgeworth Church and rebury them here at Green Way House, so they would have a view of the whole vale and be seen from a distance of many miles.'

'Their bones are in the garden?'

'Not theirs.'

'What then?'

'His second wife Dulcibella inherited Green Way House when she was only thirty-nine. Mr Lawrence's will specifically instructed her to build the garden tomb to rehouse the family bones, only she never did.'

'Why not?'

'I really can't say.'

'Perhaps she lost interest?'

'Unlikely,' said Betty darkly.

Portrait painters could be unsparing or flattering, but the three-quarter view of William Lawrence's face struck Laura as extremely realistic. Strikingly lifelike. Human faces were asymmetrical at the best of times and the artist had depicted his with many subtle left-right lines and shadows.

'If William Lawrence set about creating a garden here over three hundred years ago, then I hope I can do the same. We should seek to invoke his inventive spirit. That might not be such a bad thing?'

'That's a very bad thing.'

'His painting gives us a glimpse of his garden as it was in his day. That could be useful. It could give us good ideas.'

'Lady Ann makes all decisions about the garden, not you.'

Betty could not have made matters clearer with her no-nonsense tone. Nobody had any business doing things they shouldn't! Most probably that went for other things too, thought Laura, so she didn't say any more about hearing any singer in the grounds.

The housekeeper threw open a door downstairs and said bluntly: 'There you are. *This* is the bathroom you can use and no other. Don't make me tell you again.'

Fifteen minutes later Laura greeted the other, newly arrived gardeners. She gave them her best smile, even if it was a bit of an anti-climax. Had she not just met the house's *real* incumbent, whose only task now was to spend long, lonely hours hung on his wall?

11

Police Headquarters
Prism House
Gloucester

'Just my luck,' said DI Prickett. 'Who wants to investigate a dead body with Christmas so near?' He was being largely serious but with a wry smile.

Alison cracked a mint in her mouth. 'No man willingly shuts himself in a refrigerator.'

'Oddly enough.'

'Someone wanted to dispose of his body without chopping him up.'

'So you keep saying.'

She pointed to the report on her desk. 'Preliminary investigations by Forensics have yet to come up with a definitive cause of death.'

'I'd hate to think he was still alive when he sank.'

'It gets worse. It says here his nails and teeth have begun to fall out.'

'Which means he's been dead for some weeks?'

'The airtight container slowed the whole sorry process, but the lack of air didn't prevent gases exploding. As soon as his body stopped breathing and its blood ceased to circulate, it had no way of getting oxygen or removing wastes. Excess carbon dioxide creates an acidic environment, causing membranes in cells to rupture. His abdomen split wide open. Basically he blew himself inside out.'

Prickett sighed. 'Poor bastard.'

'He did his best to double in size due to the bloating. That's why our magnet hunters couldn't shut the refrigerator's door after they broke open his prison.'

'He was put in there before rigor mortis set in, that's for sure. But why Coombe Hill?'

'The canal is a remote place only frequented by a few dog walkers, bird watchers and horse riders,' said Alison. 'No one goes there after dark.'

'Makes you wonder why they didn't tip him straight into the basin.'

'Mothers and young children stand at the edge of the terminal wharf to feed the ducks on the shallow water. Much better to ditch a big white object in a place full of mud and bulrushes. It would be relatively easy to wheel the refrigerator along the towpath on a sack truck or trolley, which is also most likely now in the canal.'

Prickett sighed again. 'The coroner won't be happy. He won't like it if he has to record the name of the deceased as unknown.'

'I'm not done yet. I've spoken to the pathologist. It turns out our victim has a metal repair in his left leg. He must have undergone a relatively recent operation because the titanium plate has not yet fully fused with the bone. He was most probably walking about with a limp when he died.'

'Do we care?'

Alison shot him a hard look. 'The plate's serial number will tie it to a manufacturer. They should be able to tell us the name of the hospital to which it was delivered. After that we can trace the patient's name via their health records.'

'I do hope you're right.'

'In the meantime I've asked the Face-lab experts to produce an image of what our victim looked like before his face slid off his skull.'

'That's good. That's progress.'

'If we have to, we'll issue the image to the press and hope some relative or friend recognises him.'

'Anything else sergeant?'

'DNA has been taken from his bone. It remains to be seen if any match shows up in British Missing Persons or police databases. He could have ties with known criminals?'

'Do we even know how old he is?'

'Our dental expert says his teeth are healthy and well looked after. Reckons they belong to someone about twenty years old. There is one other thing we know.'

'What's that?'

'Several of the corpse's fingernails are broken and clogged with clay. My bet is our man worked outdoors. It may be that he's a builder or a gardener.'

'Among others.'

'So why has no one reported him missing?' asked Alison.

'That bothers me too.'

'It suggests he isn't local but may have just moved here? For work reasons? Conversely, whoever dumped him in the canal knows the area well. That nature reserve is invisible from every road. You could live within a few hundred yards of it and not know it exists. I suggest our killer could be a lover of birds.'

Prickett scratched his stubbly chin. 'Let's not get ahead of ourselves.'

'I've visited that reserve. Twitchers keep a log of which birds they see from Grunden Hide. They put the time, date and their own name in a book that they keep on the hut's shelf. The main route to the hide is along the canal. I should compile a list of regular visitors. Maybe one of them saw someone acting suspiciously on the towpath in recent months. Perhaps they noted an unusual vehicle parked in the carpark beside the wharf.'

'I keep forgetting you're interested in birds.'

'My father took me and my brother to see rare migrants all over the country when we were kids.'

His face altered. 'No news I suppose?'

'News?'

'Admit it. You feared our dead man might be your Paul? You thought he might be your lost brother?'

Alison buried her face in her computer. 'How can you tell?'

'You've got that look in your eye.'

'I'd rather not talk about it.'

'You are all right, aren't you?'

'Of course.'

'I remember how close you came to finding him last year.'

'At least I can say Paul was still alive then. That has to be cause for hope.'

'You can say that again.'

'Except I'm a police officer and I can't find my own brother! What does that say about me?'

'I'm sorry too, sergeant.'

'It'll soon be eleven years.'

This time it was Prickett who frowned. 'I'm mortified to think you're wasting your life because of him.'

'Now our father is dead all I have is Paul.'

'You have your partner Ravi.'

'You know what I mean.'

'It might be time to move on.'

'That doesn't mean I should,' said Alison flatly. Not having her brother by her side was like a waking grief. He could fall ill or be killed at any time and she might never get to hear about it. He had left home soon after their mother had died, but not before he quarrelled with their father – he had got into drugs and gone rogue. Last year she had discovered that he had been living for a while at an eco-warrior's camp deep in the woods near a village called Cranham. Now he was off again she knew not where.

She wanted him back. 'I swear to God I still love you Paul,' she thought, 'but what good is that if I'm not in your life?' She wanted to sow the seeds of love for him like some exotic flower. She wanted to grow it like any gardener would nourish their most prized bloom in their very own garden.

Alison clawed at the freckles on the back of her hand. Scratched blood. It wasn't only her interfering boss she found so irritating today, she was annoyed at herself. With all this business of a dead body she hadn't yet had time to visit Green Way House.

12

What a lovely sunny person, thought Laura the minute she walked into the drawing room. The blue-eyed Lady Ann Frost appeared to be neither young nor old. Her long grey hair would have added grace to her brittle elegance even if she had not been clad in such striking clothes. Her circular, calf-length dress gave her all the lightness and spring of a ballerina – its crisp glazed cotton was a riot of green, pink, mauve and blue flowers. The dainty straw hat on her head dangled strings of red cherries, while her small feet were encased in powder blue suede court shoes decorated with small bows. The two other people in the room were quite spellbound by their host too. One of them, a large, strong and serious-faced man, perched on the edge of a cream sofa. Meanwhile his short blond companion smiled at Laura and patted a chair close beside him.

Laura smiled back and chose a chair of her own.

'Welcome to Green Way House,' said Lady Ann. 'You must be Ms Bloom. Gosh. You're a funny, old-fashioned thing, aren't you?'

'My father drives lorries for a large farm in Lincolnshire.'

'I don't doubt it. Let me introduce you to Barry Barnes. Barry, please say hello to Laura.'

'Pleased to meet you I'm sure.'

'Barry has experience as a head gardener. He hasn't worked for a while, but I hope he will prove invaluable to us with his skills.' She then pointed to the younger, blond man seated on the other chair. 'And this is Ray Knight. He was once a fireman aboard a Royal Navy aircraft carrier and should be familiar with discipline and teamwork.'

'How do you do,' said Laura. She had rather hoped her co-workers might be more her own age. At the same time she was thoroughly disillusioned with the preppy young men she had encountered at university – far too many of them had been educated at Eton or wherever. They had all dressed and spoken alike, like clones. They had the same chubby cheeks and floppy hair. Her attacker was one of those. He had no boundaries. No respect. Frankly she had no idea how this was going to pan out, but she had no intention of flunking it in front of her new friends. She'd nearly given up on people once already and mustn't do so again – this time she had to be more open-minded. "Needs must when the devil drives".

Ray gave her a wink. His mop of fair hair was thinning on top but it still hid his hazel-coloured eyes. Even from where he was sitting he smelt strongly of cigarettes and alcohol. She had nothing against people having a few beers when she was disinclined to drink much herself. She had certainly never taken up smoking. She had tried it once and found it wanting. It was sometimes difficult to have fun with those whose only purpose in life was to have a great time. She might have to watch out for Ray Knight. She would certainly keep her caravan door locked tonight. He might be like that lover who had spiked her drink at college. He might turn out to be another reason why she had yet to regain faith in so much.

Lady Ann clapped her hands. Called for their attention. 'Three perfect strangers, will friendship blossom or will it wither and die on the vine? Will you love or hate each other? Don't worry, I'm sure you'll get to know one another in time.'

'You make it sound as though we're here to take part in some sort of bizarre social experiment,' said Barry and scratched the scar he had acquired in prison.

'Just because I'm a psychiatrist doesn't make this any less of a risk. Human nature needs nourishment,' added Lady Ann mischievously. 'We all have it, but that doesn't mean it won't grow into something twisted and stunted if we don't take good care of it.'

No sooner had she spoken than flames flared in the drawing room's crackling fire. Hot yellow tongues licked the fireplace's round-headed alcoves, arches and Ionic capitals – they singed the carnation-like flowers carved on each column. The fiery eruption was brief but left Laura wondering. She hadn't noticed them until now but the chimney piece was alive with amazingly hideous figures. She found herself admiring grotesque human heads, lions and slippery serpents. The fire might have died down but the semi-human menagerie went on watching, snarling, grinning.

Their host's ice-cold eyes suddenly forgot where she was.

Her face froze for a moment…

She blenched as somebody passed by outside the window.

…with fearful hope.

'You'll be wondering exactly what I want you to do for me. For the garden,' said Lady Ann, hastily correcting herself.

Seconds later Betty entered the room carrying a tray of tea and biscuits.

'Any chance of a beer?' asked Ray.

Betty glowered at him. 'I don't run errands for people. I'll never agreed to that. If I thought I had to be a skivvy round here I'd leave at once like all the rest.'

'That's quite enough Betty,' said Lady Ann sternly. 'Mr Knight has only just arrived. He doesn't yet appreciate our little ways.'

'All I want is a can of beer.'

Betty stroked her close-cropped hair. Patted her black dress. This was not someone who felt it necessary to indulge in any self-depreciating humour. 'The nearest pub is up the road, but don't expect me to lock and unlock the gate for you at night because I go home by nine p.m., as does Mr Mortimer. Her ladyship won't take kindly to being woken up with the sound of you singing drunken songs. She retires early to bed. It's only right. You shouldn't go crashing about in the garden by yourself, not ever. No one should.'

'Thank you Betty,' snapped Lady Ann. 'I'm sure Mr Knight won't be raising the roof any time soon.'

'Sorry ma'am, but you know how people like to take advantage.'

'I've put all that behind me.'

'All the same, they will say such awful things.'

Lady Ann looked flustered. Glanced again at the window. 'First let me tell you about the garden. I call it a garden when really it is a whole collections of courts, walks and orchards laid out largely in the Dutch style. You'll also find fields and a wood gone wild. Once upon a time the walled grounds formed part of an estate of seven hundred acres, most of which has been sold off to local farmers. That leaves us with twelve acres that go with the house.'

'Is it true that someone called William Lawrence created it to honour his dead family in the 1690s?' asked Laura eagerly. 'Is it true he never finished it before he died? Is that why his spirit can never rest?'

'Who told you that rubbish?'

Laura saw Betty glower at her. The look she gave her was pure hatred, so much so that she instantly regretted her conjecture. 'I think I must have read it in a book somewhere,' she added hastily.

'I can assure you it is all nonsense.'

'To appeal to his spirit is to capture the essence of the garden, surely?'

'I really can't say. Talking about spirits is a very bad idea.'

'That's funny,' muttered Laura, 'because Betty said the same thing.'

'What's that?' snapped Lady Ann.

'Well, I...'

'More to the point, what's the soil like here?' enquired Barry in his rough voice. 'We can't plant anything until we know what we're up against.'

Lady Ann was most eager to talk practicalities. 'The top soil at Green

Way House is mostly clay. Below that you'll find gravel and sand.'

'Sounds to me like heavy work,' said Ray. 'I once dug my stepdad's allotment and that was clay. Back-breaking it was. That stuff sticks to your spade like putty.'

'Clay's good for the roses,' declared Barry.

'Just saying…'

'We can grow Black-Eyed Susans and asters.'

'You need wooden boards to walk on clay otherwise it gets too compacted.'

'We can try bearded irises, daylilies and hostas. I saw some lilac on my way through the garden. Weigela might be good. That's a pretty shrub that blooms in spring. Its tubular flowers are white, pink and deep red colours…'

'I've already drawn up some preliminary plans,' said Lady Ann and directed everyone to a nearby table. 'You will see at a glance what goes where.'

'These sketches point to a very formal style of garden,' declared Barry with surprise. 'Did you mean to draw something quite so rigid and old-fashioned?'

'How so?' said Lady Ann. She gave him the same guarded look she had given Laura a moment ago.

'You've denoted an upper court, knot garden, a rose walk, old orchard, new orchard, wild wood, lake et cetera. From what little I've seen of the grounds so far, I'd say you want us to go back to the garden's original design?'

'It sort of came to me. Once I drew a line it was there. I didn't touch it. It became my theme. Then I worked round it, trying it out in different sizes and different places, until I exhausted all other possibilities.'

'How about I design something much more modern?'

'Oh no! The garden won't allow it! That's to say… *I* can't allow it.'

Barry gave a start. 'Naturally I won't do anything you don't want me to.'

'Thank you,' said Lady Ann, looking relieved. 'I wouldn't insist if it wasn't important. Now where was I? Oh yes. You will find tools and other equipment in the stables. Please don't hesitate to request anything else you need. There should be sufficient gloves, boots and overalls for you all. One word of warning: everything you do will be closely observed if not by me then by... That's to say, nothing must be left to chance. Everything has to go right this time.'

'This time?' queried Laura, recalling the red mini-digger she had seen rusting in the grounds. 'So it's true? Other gardeners have been before us...?'

'They used weed killers and a rotavator to clear things they shouldn't. I had to put a stop to them before they destroyed perfectly good plants that had survived in the grass.'

'Who were these people?'

'Does it matter?'

'Is it true they weren't here long?'

'Not long.'

'Why did they leave?'

'There was an accident involving a tree.'

'By the sound of it the garden isn't very safe?'

'Of course I know that now.'

Laura smiled. 'In my Zoom interview with you, you said you wanted to create a memorial for your dead son William.'

'You told me that too,' said Ray. 'I didn't know what that meant exactly. I still don't.'

'It's quite simple,' said Lady Ann. 'My mission is to create a private garden within existing walls. Think of it as a "hortus conclusus" or refuge from all the cares of this world. It is to be a contemplative room to heal someone's broken heart and grieving soul.'

13

'So what's this "hortus" thingy again?' asked Ray on their march to the stables. 'I still don't get it.'

'A "hortus conclusus" is a garden with walls, like the one we're in now,' said Barry. 'You see them in medieval paintings and manuscript illustrations. There was a "hortus conclusus" at the castle where I once worked. High walls separate the garden from the rest of the world, creating a division that renders its private and sacred. Mother Nature guards the gate while a naked Venus, the goddess of love, resides inside. Carefully laid out beds grow flowers and medicinal herbs in the shelter and shade of tall trees. Roses are trained to grow up the walls. That's because roses were sacred to Venus in ancient times but later became symbols of Christianity. The Virgin Mary was called a "rose without thorns", recalling the legend that before the Fall roses had no thorns.'

Laura skipped for joy. The winter day was bright and breezy. Having spent a year cooped up in gloomy university libraries, lecture halls and having to eat with the other students at dinner (crowds and noise made her doubly nervous), she was looking forward to *doing* instead of *thinking*. 'In the Vulgate Bible's Canticle of Canticles 4.12 it says " Hortus conclusus soror mea, sponsa, hortus conclusus, fons signatus". That's Latin for "A garden enclosed is my sister, my spouse, a garden enclosed, a fountain sealed up".'

'Aren't you the clever one?' said Ray, wrinkling his nose.

Barry nodded. 'Laura's right about "The Song of Songs". As I was saying, such gardens now represent the Virgin Mary and Immaculate

Conception. The Virgin is often shown in paintings accompanied by a unicorn. The walls close off the garden – the womb – which remains untouched and protected from sin in a place of perfection.'

'Sounds like a lot of hooey to me.'

'Such gardens often have a central grove of trees with box-bordered, gravelled paths. You'll find benches and fountains, raised beds, blossoming trees, trellises and bowers to create physical, visual and sensual harmony. In the herb garden you'll find everything from mint, sage and basil to thyme, rosemary and rue.' He broke off to wave. 'Here we are. These must be the stables Lady Ann mentioned.'

'I could have told you that,' said Ray and pushed open a large wooden door to a series of grill-topped stalls, one of which now housed his stolen moped.

Lady Ann had not exaggerated: the former horse stalls contained every sort of thing they would need for the garden. Here they had their pick of tin buckets, wheelbarrows, rakes, forks, spades, trowels, hoes, pick axes, lawn rollers and lawn mowers as well as a great many other things, all of which were very well-made but also very old. There were saws, hammers, nails…

'I'm still confused,' said Ray, unhooking a pair of brown overalls from a peg on the wall. 'How can a garden heal someone's soul? It makes no sense.'

Laura chose a pair of thick canvas gloves. She held up a trowel and the initials WL had been burnt into its polished wooden handle. 'I don't think we should dismiss her ladyship as some sort of crank. If the person you loved most in the world had died very young, how far would you go to mend your broken heart?'

'She didn't actually say the garden is for her,' said Barry, finding his overalls a little too tight for his broad shoulders.

'Barry's right,' said Ray. 'She simply said there is *someone's* soul she wants to heal.'

Laura leaned in. 'She means her dead son.'

'She didn't name him.'

'Who else can it be?' asked Barry. 'Who else gets the perfect garden all to themselves?'

'Hope it's not our prowler,' laughed Laura, finding her overalls didn't fit very well either. Her breath blew white in the winter air. The minute she said it she regretted it.

Her companions' faces turned quizzical. 'Prowler? What prowler?' they said in unison.

'I heard someone singing in the garden last night.'

Ray burst out laughing. He was delighted, Barry less so.

'You honestly think someone is creeping around Green Way House after dark?'

'The grounds anyway.'

'We should put this person to work,' said Ray. 'We could do with the extra help.'

'Of course I can't say it was an intruder as such. I don't know who it was,' declared Laura, blushing. 'The window in the caravan was all misted up and I couldn't see him very clearly in the darkness, but somebody walked by me after Mr Mortimer went back inside the house. He sang me a pretty song.'

'We're supposed to be worried because someone sings songs?'

'Now you're here perhaps you'll hear him too.'

'He really sang to you?'

'Not to me especially, more to his garden.'

'Is there a difference?'

'Damn right there is,' said Laura, vowing not to mention the matter again. No one wanted to believe anything she said! They always dismissed her as an over-imaginative, truth-embroidering hysterical *girl*.

'Better get on,' said Barry hastily. His opinion of her had just gone down a peg or two.

She should never have used the word 'prowler' – it made her sound too 'dramatic'.

Ray smirked. 'I'll say one thing for our Lady A. The grieving mother looks good on her. I reckon she's only hired us because she's lonely. Perhaps she likes to seduce her gardeners like that film I saw. What was it? It's on the tip of my tongue.'

'"Lady Chatterley's Lover,"' suggested Laura.

'The lovers run about naked in the garden.'

'It's really a book written by DH Lawrence.'

'Who cares?'

'I do,' said Barry brusquely. 'Remember what her ladyship told us. I propose we start by doing a methodical tour of the grounds. All interesting, salvageable plants can be marked with these bamboo canes. That way we'll avoid destroying anything of value when we begin our big clear up.'

'Don't see why he has to be leader,' said Ray, after he and Laura departed. 'Don't see why *he* gets to tell *us* what to do.'

'Barry's not so bad. We should give him a chance.'

'Damn this. Here, have my sticks. I'm going to see if I can get that mini-digger started...'

'I can drive it if need be.'

'Yeah right you can.'

'I've driven JCBs on the farm. My dad taught me.'

His face clouded. 'I should at least find out it if still starts.'

'Good idea.' He had hoped to impress her, thought Laura with his man-knowledge. He wanted her approval because approval led to other, more exciting things. Except she was beyond being impressed by other people – she didn't intend to be taken in like that again any time soon. Her abuser at college had liked to sing old west country songs and ballads. He had been clever and talented enough to harmonise and arrange them for the pianoforte and put them on YouTube. If she had learnt one thing, it was that monsters came in all shades of betrayal.

***

Laura took a path which led to an iron gate. This in turn led to a former herb or scent garden. Beds were bare or covered in grass but that didn't mean perfectly good plants weren't lost among the weeds as Lady Ann said. It was not going to be easy to determine what was alive and what was dead.

A second gate yielded to her touch, until she found herself strolling among dozens of dwarf trees of various fruits. Come spring this place would most likely be a mass of pretty cherry, plum and apple blossom. She walked to the end of the orchard where she came face to face with another gateway. 'This garden is a puzzle but not a muddle. There's method in its madness. This is the careful product of someone's wonderfully obsessive brain.'

The gate opened into the rose walk. Laura strolled enjoyably as far as a statue of a very old, heavily bearded man who was dressed in a long robe. She loved old statues as much as she loved old paintings. A stone wolf lay at his feet beside a cunning-looking serpent. The edge of his plinth was inscribed with the words "Perfectio vera in coelestibus" which she translated as "true perfection is to be found only in heavenly things".

That's when she studied the rather ominous scythe he carried. 'Damn it,' she said aloud and her dismay bordered on outrage. The blade's tip was lying on the ground and the damage was obviously recent. She trod narrow tyre tracks all around. 'Who did this to you? Let me guess! I think I know who.'

She shuddered at the thought of Ray Knight being so reckless on his moped. It felt like a crime. Like sacrilege…

Laura didn't linger. Instead she entered a sizeable grove, again by a rusty gate. Two large letter "0s" adorned its ironwork. She had noticed such letters on the other gates, but only now did she stop to consider what they might mean.

She must have walked in a complete circle because suddenly she found herself back at the stables. How she had returned to where she had begun quite so soon, she didn't know. She still had in her hands some of the bamboo canes to mark plants worth saving. In reality it must have taken her an hour to walk the grounds' inner limits, but that was not how it felt. It was like looking through the wrong end of a telescope. A whole new world was compressed into a very small space with her inside it.

Before her stood the unusual, white metal seat with handles that she had seen on her arrival yesterday.

Somebody had wheeled it to a new place in the garden.

They had followed the sun.

She sat on the bench and her head swam, not unpleasantly. She had somehow just trodden an interior place that was different from the physical. She could sit, walk and admire the trees and flowers in a whole new state of mind… To sit here was to envisage how her "hortus conclusus" was going to be an emblem of serenity and privacy. "Hortus conclusus soror mea, sponsa, hortus conclusus, fons signatus", she repeated: a garden enclosed is my sister, my spouse, a garden enclosed, a fountain sealed up. She was here to help create somewhere that was to remain untouched and protected from all evil, but first she had to free her own mind?

Seconds later the brief, blissful sensation faded. She was at the base of a brick wall too high to scale. Laura panicked. Then she laughed. For a moment she supposed she might be walled in forever. Apart from the distant view to the escarpment there was no reason to believe that Green Way House existed anywhere other than in its own oasis at the foot of the hill. It was a secluded place that time forgot.

A familiar voice reached her ear.

The sound travelled from tree to tree and from bush to bush, shifting invisibly, as might a bird…

The unseen singer couldn't rest for as long as his garden needed tending?

His voice grew louder, as did her anxiety and sense of anticipation. She was soon in a flutter. 'Who's there? Is that you Mr Mortimer? I'm over here.'

Laura made a move towards him, but what right did she have to interrupt him? She stopped in her tracks. Ray and Barry would have to believe her now, only they were nowhere within reach. Instead he shared his ballad as he departed:

>My garden grew self-heal and balm,
>And speedwell that's blue for an hour,
>Then blossoms again, O grievous my pain!
>I'm plundered of each flower.

14

There were never enough hours in the day, thought Alison. It was less about the long spells spent in the office than the late evenings brooding about cases at home. December was here and she still hadn't collected a Christmas wreath for her father's grave or bought presents for her partner Ravi. Police colleagues had only just forgiven her for forgetting their festive cards last year. And now this! As if she didn't have enough to be getting on with. Solving the case of a body in a refrigerator would always be a team effort, but the near-naked man she had hit with her car was her responsibility alone. Her fellow officers had made it quite clear with winks and smiles that they weren't about to help her in any way at all.

So why couldn't she stop thinking about him?

It had been such a shock to drive straight through someone at Ullenwood's foggy crossroads. Every night she relived the moment in her dreams.

She couldn't help but suffer nightmares and flashbacks. Surely when the young man had said "I'm dead" it was because she had just run him down?

'I didn't kill him. I didn't kill him. I didn't kill him,' she repeated out loud as she stepped out of her car. It was four p.m. and the day was almost done. Remaining patches of deep blue sky turned pale, almost white before her eyes. Clouds grew bloody before they went grey in the lost light. I really should not have come unannounced, thought Alison. As it was, Green Way House, set well back in its own grounds, mocked all callers with its stern aloofness.

She stopped at two tall pillars topped with stone urns. This had once been the mansion's front gate from the main road, she realised. From here she could see the house itself. Pretty much. Great vines of ivy scaled its walls with woody stems as thick as trees. The building was trapped in one big bower which would eventually crush it? Creeper crawled from the garden as if greedy for something – it had demands it considered its dues? The vines overtook the highest windows in every gable and sent branches sprawling across the stone slate roof. Such exuberant abundance buried the front porch, whose heavy oak door might well have come from some ruined priory or abbey.

Two large double gates, sealed with a heavy chain and padlock, barred her way to the abandoned driveway.

Green Way House turned its back on all cars and pedestrians that passed by on the nearest road.

Scarcely a living soul inhabited it, apparently.

She took out her mobile phone and tried again to ring the owner, but there was no reply.

Alison returned to Greenway Lane where she had parked her car. A second, single iron gate guarded this side of the walled grounds.

She put her face to its rusty black bars and shouted. 'Hallo? Anyone in there?'

The sound of a voice reached her from a distant block of stables. Someone laughed... Whoever had been digging in the extensive garden had just finished work for the day. She went to call once more, but her words were drowned by the all-embracing darkness.

She glanced at her watch. Have I really been here this long, she wondered, questioning where the time had flown, if indeed time inside and outside the garden were the same. I have come too late, she sensed – Green Way House is not open to nocturnal callers. Not in the cold grip of winter. No one can hear me, no matter how loud I holler. She had the uneasy notion that no one would let her in because she was judged to be too covetous, jealous, evil? They said KEEP OUT KEEP OUT KEEP OUT.

***

From here the track continued uphill to the crossroads. This had to be the route down which the young man had fled on the night of their collision, or this was where he had been taken? Alison was shut out of the garden he had mentioned? She had no option but to follow its high brick wall along the lane.

She shone her torch at track and trees until she came to a place called Cherry Tree Farm on the opposite side of the road.

A man in blue overalls stood mending a tractor by the light of a barn. His collie dog scratched its ear and eyed her carefully as she advanced.

'Sorry to bother you sir. My name is Alison Ellis.'

'I don't do charity or church.'

'That'll be Detective Sergeant Ellis from Gloucestershire Constabulary.'

'You mean to say you've decided to visit me at last? How long has it been? Two months? I'm Frank Smith. I'm the one whose tractor got damaged. Whoever stole the Sat Nav from its cab is well-organised. Part of a gang. This is the second time this year.'

'I'm very sorry to hear it,' said Alison, 'but I'm not part of the Rural Crime Team. I'm not here about any Sat Nav.'

'So where are they? Where is the RCT?'

'I'm sure they'll pay you a visit very soon.'

'They caught sod all last time.'

'The Rural Crime Team don't have a lot of officers in Gloucestershire, but they do their best. Only the other day they arrested five armed hare coursers in a field near Coberley. Confiscated their dogs along with their vehicles...'

'Next time anybody comes snooping round my yard they'll find themselves on the wrong end of my shotgun.'

'That bothers me too.'

'This lane is a dark and lonely place at night, believe me.'

'At the first sign of trouble you should call 999.'

'I feel better already.'

'I mean it.' It was hard to define Mr Smith. This was clearly not a person known for his wit and humour. That's not to say he couldn't shock her with his mean and snarling ways. 'Fact is, a road accident occurred recently near here at Ullenwood. I'm talking about the night of Friday 26th of November. The person involved ran off into the fog. I need to find out if he was badly hurt. Did anyone call at your farm that day? Have you come across anybody lying injured anywhere? Has anyone spoken to you about a collision at the crossroads at the top of this lane?'

'Better check the old army huts up there.'

'You think?'

'They're totally derelict. Otherwise it's all fields hereabouts.'

'What of the people living in Green Way House? I tried to visit it just now. I thought I heard voices, but I couldn't make myself known.'

Frank Smith laughed. 'That doesn't surprise me. Lady Ann Frost keeps herself to herself. Trying to make contact with that place day or night is like trying to raise the dead.'

'Does any young man live there by any chance?'

'Her ladyship did have a child called Will or William, but that's all in the past now.'

'What about him?'

'You don't want to know.'

'What do you mean?'

'William died, is all. It made the front page of the local newspaper.'

'When was that?'

'Five years ago.'

'How did he die?'

'He was hit by a truck at the top of this lane.'

'At the crossroads?'

'As I say, the press made a big fuss about it at the time.'

'Okey-doke. Thanks for your help.'

Frank Smith wiped oil off his hands. Shot her a curious look. 'If your man ran away he can't have been critically hurt. Why all the interest detective?'

'I'm the one who ran him down.'

'What do you say he looks like again?'

'He's in his twenties with long black hair. The oddest part was that he was nearly naked. All he had on was a pale nightshirt. It might have been a hospital gown, I suppose.'

Frank knit his brow. 'Are you sure it was a living person you hit?'

'Who else?'

'Sounds more like your casualty was something different.'

'Not to me.'

'Don't be so certain detective. Rumour has it Greenway Lane is haunted on account of Lady Ann's lost son.'

Alison frowned heavily. 'That's not what I said.'

'Don't underestimate yourself. You met the dead William.'

'Seriously? You telling me I ran into a…?'

'You're not the first to meet a white figure at those crossroads. There's… *evidence*.'

'You literally want me to believe some spectral figure walks Greenway Lane?'

Frank sniffed loudly. Took a spanner to his tractor. 'It's all circumstantial of course.'

'I didn't hit anything the least bit supernatural. I saw a young man. He spoke to me.'

'I know it's a lot to ask.'

'Too right it is.'

'Don't be so sure. Some places harbour sorrow and pain. Bad things repeat themselves there. One tragedy invites another? I read that it was Lady Ann who found her son dead in a ditch. Some people say they still hear her scream, though others will tell you it's just a tawny owl. Her son had long black hair too. Doted on him, she did. In her eyes William could do no wrong, although I heard his biggest wish was to escape both her and home. That's the perversity of parenthood. You lie to yourself long enough and you end up believing the lies must be love.'

'Just to be clear. You definitely don't think any such young man resides at Green Way House right now?'

'Doesn't sound likely.'

'Here's my card. I'd like to get to the bottom of this so-called 'wraith' if I can.'

'Got a taste for it, have you?'

Alison walked away, only to pause at the gate to the lane. 'I remember that hit-and-run accident five years ago. The perpetrator was never caught.'

'All I know is William was the apple of his mother's eye. Sweet Liam, she liked to call him after her favourite pinks in the garden.'

'That'll be sweet williams?'

'Everyone loves their red, pink and white flowers.'

'Not me.'

'If you can't love flowers you can't love life, detective.'

'Whoever killed her ladyship's son is still out there,' said Alison, ignoring him. 'It must prey on her mind.'

'If you ask me, she buried him in the garden to keep him close.'

'What makes you say that?'

'I never went to any funeral. No one did.'

'That's perfectly legal. Of course she would need to register his demise in the official way, once a doctor signed off the cause of death. The only other rule is that you can't bury someone next to a water source, for obvious reasons.'

'Do the dead rest easy in unhallowed ground? I doubt it.'

'Now you're just being silly.'

15

'Which one of you put that seat over there?' asked Laura. She gestured towards the single line of cypress trees that bordered the edge of the rose walk.

Barry shrugged. 'Which seat is that?'

'That lovely long, white metal one with a spoked wheel and handles. You can push it around like a wheelbarrow. When I last saw it, it was near the stables.'

'That boneshaker? It wasn't me.'

'Me neither,' said Ray.

They had made the decision to start work today on the rose walk because it had the prettiest views.

Whoever had moved the garden seat thought the same apparently.

'Damn it,' said Ray as he pulled old bricks, wire and a piece of rusty metal from a thick patch of rough grass. 'We'd do better with dynamite. As for these weeds we should poison the lot.'

Barry shook his head. 'Weedkillers don't work well in the winter. The weeds are too dormant. Poison does its job best when plants are growing.'

'How else are we going to clear them?'

'Use your sickle to cut them down.'

'This relic? It's covered in rust.'

Laura stopped shovelling soil for a moment. She was wearing the blue cashmere pointelle scarf that she had retrieved from the cab of the mini-digger. She coiled it round her neck to keep out the bitterly cold air as she helped to investigate interesting undulations in the ground. Like so much else around her, the rise and fall in the soil could be hiding a lost flowerbed or path. It might even suggest an overgrown rock garden or former pool. 'Barry's right. Lady Ann wants us to tread lightly. That means treating everything with some respect.'

'My point exactly,' said Barry.

Ray lit a cigarette. 'You would say that, wouldn't you?'

'But it's true,' said Laura.

'Not that you would know.'

'Also Lady Ann doesn't want us to use poison. Period.'

'Not even on the brambles?'

'She says she doesn't want to hurt the garden.'

'Good luck working out what that means.'

'Listen to Laura,' said Barry. 'Weedkiller will harm the roots of the trees and shrubs we want to retain.'

'I didn't sign up for this.'

'As ever a bit of imagination would help.'

Ray reversed his cap on his head. 'My back's killing me. We should at least hire a heavy-duty rotary grass-cutter. What do you think Laura?'

But Laura had stopped to listen to the breeze in the trees. It gusted counter-clockwise outside the grounds in an increasingly violent spiral of air. The disturbance pinwheeled up Greenway Lane and sucked at the side gate to the garden. Then it did it all over again. It was uncanny. Yet the dust devil, unable to enter, only huffed and puffed at the walls as she stood in the calm centre within. Trees and clouds were in constant motion, but she felt as though she were standing in a vacuum. The air pressure dropped all round her, until she stepped out of the world's normal rhythm.

That's when she saw him…

Mistook him for another old statue.

…before he stood up to leave.

'Who's that?' cried Laura.

'Where?' asked Ray.

Laura gestured towards the white seat in front of the cypresses.

'Didn't see a soul,' said Barry.

'Me neither,' added Ray.

'What do you mean, you didn't see him?' said Laura. 'He was looking straight at us.'

'There's no one there now.'

'You literally didn't see him get up and go?'

'No, definitely not.'

Laura downed tools. If she hadn't got a proper look at him it was because he was cloaked with inky shade.

'Hey, where are you going?' cried Barry. 'We have work to do. It could snow later.'

'Sorry, but this is important.'

The stranger tapped his cane in the shade of the cypress trees, as if physically attached to their cold gloom.

Won't you wait for me, thought Laura?

Then he was gone.

The next time she caught sight of him he was in the orchard. He had somehow passed through its gate and was now walking at some speed along the remains of what had once been a gravelled path down the middle of the cherry trees – he was going via his own secret way.

'Hey!' shouted Laura. 'Come back! Do I know you?'

The faster she went the less ground she seemed to cover.

A lifetime might have passed before she reached the place where she saw him vanish. There, a very large, old yew tree blocked her progress.

At the foot of the tree lay a stone slab. It was a peculiar feeling. To go beyond it was to go beyond the bounds of life. "Fools rush in where angels fear to tread... The road to Hell is paved with good intentions."

She used her boot to kick aside drifts of dead yew needles to reveal an inscription:

>
> IN LOVING MEMORY
> OF
> WILLIAM FROST
> 1996-2017
> GONE BUT
> NOT FORGOTTEN

Laura stared at the name then hastily covered it again with dirt and leaves. She couldn't decide whether or not she had been meant to find it.

It was her nightmare come back to life…

She did not like it.

… of being followed.

No fear was more formless than one with no face.

It could be her darkest thought.

It could be her monster from college.

On the ground lay fresh footprints.

***

'Well?' said Barry, as Laura breathlessly re-entered the rose walk. 'Who did you find?'

'No one,' she lied. 'I went on a wild goose chase.'

'It wasn't your mysterious prowler then?'

'Sorry if I'm so jumpy.'

'You shot off like a mad thing. Whatever possessed you?'

'It's those cypresses over there.'

'What about them?'

'They cast odd shadows. Don't you find them rather incongruous, not to say disturbing?'

'The Greeks and Romans called them "mournful trees",' said Barry. 'They used their wood in funeral pyres. That's why you find them in graveyards throughout the world.'

'So what are they doing so close to the rose walk?'

'If I'm right then the garden we're working on is a substitute for something else more meaningful.'

'I don't follow you.'

'Consider this garden a poor copy of one created years ago.'

'All I see is a big mess,' said Ray.

Barry waved his hand about. 'Take our statue of Saturn or Time with his scythe, for instance.'

'This old codger? I wondered who he was.'

'Old Man Time is forever pointing at the cypresses for a reason.'

'I agree with Laura,' said Ray. 'Those cypresses aren't at all like the other trees.'

'Their roots point down to the dead in the underworld while their spiky tops point up to heaven.'

Laura was still baffled by what had just happened. 'Are you really suggesting a whole other garden is waiting to be revealed right under our feet, if we know where to look?'

'That's to say *how* to look?' said Barry. 'See here. These overgrown rose beds are in a bad way today, but once they were a riot of colour. Whoever designed this part of the garden intended it to represent the joys of *this* life whereas that orchard over there, with all its apples, plums and cherries, signifies the fruits of the *next* life. No bit of the garden stands alone, to tell a story. Those cypresses that you so dislike link the rose walk to the orchard – earth with heaven – in a line so straight and thin because it can, like all human existence, be so easily broken.'

Laura thought of the rusty, wrought iron letters she had seen attached to the gates. She recalled the "0s" and wondered if they could signify the futility of material things? 'You might be right.'

'Come on, let's do some serious pruning. These roses are particularly straggly. We need to cut back the branches and start again, even though it means missing next season's blooms.'

Laura glanced again at the white metal seat. It remained empty. If anyone had intended to sit and watch them working then they weren't doing so now. Meanwhile she used her saw to slice through a thick, prickly stem. Each bush was like a small tree.

It was such a relief to engage in a new and worthwhile project. Suddenly everything she did filled her with increased optimism. Enthused her. She was about to put her recent troubles behind her. The *humiliation*. She was no longer somewhere whose staff prioritised the reputation of the college above her safety and wellbeing. No stuffy university chaplain was about to ask her if she was aware of the effect she had on men, as if she should be wary of the impact of her claims on her "alleged" attacker. It was the chaplain who had implied that her drinking might have been a problem when it was obvious she had been given the date drug Rohypnol…

'Are you all right Laura?' asked Barry. 'You look as if you're having dark thoughts again.'

'Me? Oh no.' She was really thinking about her mysterious observer she had just attempted to follow. The more she replayed it in her mind, the more she concluded that he had been an actual person rather than a three-dimensional shadow.

It left her with a big lump in her throat. Ray and Barry were adamant that they hadn't seen anybody at all, which was why she had been careful not to divulge what else she had found.

To reveal the grave's existence was to deny that she alone was worthy of its secret?

She considered it very odd that Lady Ann had not referred to her son's last resting place. The idea of accidentally digging up or damaging the gravestone gave her the goosebumps. If I were you, thought Laura, I would have mentioned it straight away – I would have taken great care to point it out on my plans for the garden.

16

That night Laura woke in her caravan with an awful start.

Whatever she'd just heard was a loud boom.

Like a gunshot?

The deafening aftermath split the air with a cleft, fissure, chasm. Her whole caravan rocked, or she did inside it…

'What the…!' she cried and rolled off her bed. She wrapped herself in a blanket and rushed to the door in her llama slippers.

Frozen dew glittered like jewels on the ground, bushes and trees. It chilled the garden and turned it silver. Everywhere was trembling as if from the severe noise.

'Did you hear that?' said Barry. He had raced to throw open his caravan's door too.

Ray followed suit. 'That was someone's shotgun, I'm sure if it.'

Next minute another bang rent the air.

It sounded too close to Green Way House for comfort.

'We should investigate,' said Laura. 'Someone could be getting killed.'

Barry nodded. 'Yes, but it's none of our business.'

'Why would you say that?' she snapped and set off alone.

'Wait,' said Ray, dressed only in leather jacket and boxer shorts. 'I'll go with you.'

They had not ventured far when they met Lady Ann coming towards them by way of the knot garden.

'Thank God. Are you all right?' asked Laura. 'We heard shots.'

Lady Ann paused to pick smoking cartridges from the twin breeches of her gun. She tossed the empty black shells at her feet on the ground. Next she reached for two new cartridges from the pocket of her pink nylon housecoat printed with large blue-and-red cabbage roses. 'Oh it's only you. I thought you might be someone else,' she said, barely able to conceal her frustration.

'What are you doing out here so late at night?' asked Barry.

'I'm sorry I disturbed you.'

'Are you sure everything is okay?'

'You didn't notice anyone prowling about the garden just now, did you?' The look in her ladyship's brazen face was less than remorseful, thought Laura. Instead there was an absolute resolution to inflict pain… be cruel. At the same time her gaze was far off in place and time – she continued to peer right past them at a point some distance away.

'No, but Laura thought she might have seen a man earlier today, didn't you Laura?' declared Ray.

'Is that true Laura?'

Laura bit her lip. 'Well, I…'

'Who was it? When?'

'This afternoon. I followed him as far as the big yew tree where he disappeared.'

'We assume it was Mr Mortimer,' added Barry quickly.

'Absolutely,' said Laura, glad to save face.

Lady Ann looked less panicky suddenly. 'Yes, I'm sure you're right. Who else could it be?'

The fact that Mr and Mrs Mortimer rarely chose to venture into the grounds conveniently slipped her memory. Laura did not remind her.

'No worries,' said Lady Ann. 'I'm out here scaring off foxes. Every night they like to test the chicken wire under the cover of darkness.'

'That's where our fresh eggs have been coming from!' said Ray with delight.

'There's a coop near the range at the back of the brewhouse. I also have twenty bee hives and make my own honey. It always pays to be self-sufficient.'

'We'll leave you to it then,' said Barry, as he and Ray turned to walk back to their caravans. 'Happy hunting your ladyship.'

Laura watched her host resume her armed tour of the garden. Now was the time to go after her and quiz her about the grave she had found.

She had to know why a beloved child's last resting place went unvisited?

I should do it now thought Laura. If she chose to delay it was because Lady Ann had been so persistent. It was unlikely that she pursued only wild animals quite so rigorously. The sheer strength of her desire to track something in the garden struck a chord – *her ladyship was prepared to brave hostile shadows too?* Something about the intense way she reloaded her gun, ready to fire, struck her as nothing short of admirable and necessary.

She gave no quarter.

17

The Round House
Mercombe Wood

'Unbelievable,' said Alison and drove fast along the last few yards of the stony track to her home. Ever since moving into the old toll-keeper's house this high on the hills she had grown accustomed to the winter's inky darkness. That's because her little round house, built of tufa stone in 1830, had no mains electricity.

So it was a shock to see "The Round House" all lit up now. Christmas fairy lights dripped like icicles from its gutter with three, six and nine-foot LED drops. An acrylic reindeer and sleigh balanced precariously on the low roof of the outhouse and woodshed. She was suddenly at a magical place whose blue and white bulbs all winked, blinked and twinkled in the night-time.

Ravi was carefully arranging a plastic dachshund with a red and white hat and bell on its head by the front door. He still wore his hospital ID photo on its cord round his neck from his day at work, she noted. He gave her a big wave.

Alison parked her car on a patch of muddy grass. To go any further required a tractor or a quad bike. Even they weren't much use since a tree had come down in the recent gales and blocked the footpath to the nearest village beyond the hill.

'Who said you could wreck my house?'

'And ruin the surprise?'

'Honestly I don't know what to say, it's so OTT. How on earth…?'

Ravi stood back to admire his handiwork. The lights were the only ones visible in every direction in the black wood. 'An inverter changes the 12-volt DC power of a car battery to AC to power the bulbs.'

'I hope you used a relay.'

'Think of it as Santa's grotto.'

'No Santa ever visits me.'

'Well, how would you put it?'

'Don't be surprised if it all gets stolen. Thieves have already gone off with a seven-foot high goblin in Cheltenham.'

'Unless it ran away.'

'I wish it were that simple.'

'Who wants a seven-foot goblin anyway?'

'Search me. But someone had to climb up on to the roof of the Hanover Inn to acquire it. They cut through several heavy-duty cable ties and wires attached to the battery pack. They'll be after the illuminated reindeer on the Snow Queen Trail next.'

'You did say the police are having trouble with poachers.'

'Very funny.'

'Consider it part of my plan to persuade you to enjoy Christmas this year.'

'Won't be easy.'

'Any progress on your naked man in the fridge?' asked Ravi, following her into the round house. He opened the door of the stove and fed a fresh log to its fire.

'We're still trying to trace the number on the surgical plate in his leg.'

'No one is nobody.'

Alison poured herself a glass of wine. 'That's easy for you to say. Interpol can't find his DNA on any of their fucking databases.'

'I don't expect you to come home full of fun....'

'You're the one who's always telling me that you prefer your nice comfy flat in Gloucester.'

'...not in your job.'

'So it's my fault?' she said with a smile. 'Sorry, I'm being narky.' They both knew she suffered from Seasonal Affective Disorder. Lack of sunlight was its chief cause since the short December days could be so gloomy. SAD stalked her like a malicious shadow.

After a twelve-hour shift on the wards he could do with a bit more cheer. 'So tell me, what's really going on?'

'What do you mean?' asked Alison innocently.

'I don't know. Something's not right. You want to tell me what it is?'

She opened her book on her lap. 'Okay I admit it. I'm reading up on Gloucestershire ghosts.'

'What on earth for?'

'Frank Smith of Cherry Tree Farm believes I met Lady Ann Frost's dead son who haunts Greenway Lane. The residential manager of Ullenwood Manor says the same. Either that or they're winding me up, which I seriously suspect is the case.'

'No one believes in all that ghost stuff.'

'You've heard of white-cloaked figures seen on lonely roads…'

'You're telling me this because?'

'My favourite story so far is this one set on Dover's Hill. A lady-in-white appears there every first night after a full moon…'

'I doubt that.'

'Her name is Beatrice and her story begins in the 1640s. It goes like this.'

'Please don't.'

'Her brothers fight for Cromwell in the English Civil War. When the war ends the victors do very well, but a Royalist neighbour they know called Sir Roger is left bankrupt – he becomes so poor he resorts to highway robbery. One day he ambushes a coach in which Beatrice is travelling on the Bristol Road. She and Sir Roger recognise each other and fall hopelessly in love…'

'Talking to myself here.'

'The lovers arrange to meet secretly by the gate on Dover's Hill. As a precaution Beatrice signals to Sir Roger by waving her white cloak high in the air. They plan to elope, except her treacherous brothers have been spying on her from the very beginning. They lie in wait and wave a cloak of their own. That way they lure the highwayman to his death.'

'Don't tell me, Beatrice goes mad with grief and dies.'

'She has haunted the gate on the hill ever since.'

Ravi shrugged. 'Who knows, the story may once have had a kernel of truth to it. There might even have been a murdered lover, but more likely it's all made up and can never be proved.'

'Then what do you make of sightings like this?'

'What's *this*?'

'Proof that some ghosts might exist. Sort of.'

'What possible proof could that be?'

'One night on the 19th September 1936 the well-known photographer Indra Shira and his assistant Captain Provand are photographing a country house for Country Life Magazine. All is quiet when Shira suddenly shouts to Provand to press the trigger on the camera. He has no time to explain that a ghostly figure is coming down the oak stairs towards them. Sure enough, the misty shape of a dead woman appears in the photograph when it is published three months later…'

'Cameras do odd things.'

'Shira especially recalled the awful expression in her glazed, hollow eyes and the parchment-colour of her pinched cheeks. He said her dishevelled hair and ashen face grinned in a malicious and diabolical manner as she held aloft a flickering lamp in one hand.'

'I'm sorry, I still don't get it.'

'The country house that features in the magazine story is a lot like Green Way House.'

'What ghost doesn't like to haunt an old mansion?'

'More to the point, it's the only place within miles of my accident that has a proper garden.'

'Wait, are you trying to tell me that your spectral young man fled back to Green Way House, after you ran him down at those crossroads near Ullenwood?'

'Everywhere else is farmland. I've even searched some nearby huts left over from World War II, but there's no trace of him there. No broken body!'

'It's easy to imagine that an ancient country pile harbours a spectre from years old, but a modern one?'

'If a house can have one ghost it can have another.'

'I guess.'

Alison refused to back down. 'If Greenway Lane really is haunted, it can be no coincidence that it leads to a house of the same name.'

'You'll be telling me next it harbours some awful secret.'

'Ghosts manifest themselves at gates and crossroads at times of trouble.'

'Not that it changes a thing,' said Ravi with a frown. 'Even if ghosts could exist – which they can't – I'm quite certain they can get along very well without you and me.'

'It says here such apparitions can be a warning of death.'

'You sound very convinced.'

'You think I'm being irrational?'

'No, not irrational. Just upset. You still think you might have maimed someone with your car. You even think you might have fatally injured them. You heard what your doctor said: the situation remains unresolved, which is doing something to your brain. It means you have begun to haunt yourself.'

Alison winced. 'There speaks the orthopaedic nurse. If it doesn't have bones and muscles *it ain't real*.'

'Say what you like, he's not your problem. Never was.'

'No, you're wrong. Whoever he is, he needs my help.'

18

Green Way House

She had decided to take Lady Ann at her word. What surprised her most was the relief she felt, thought Laura. A rabbit lay bleeding to death in the flowerbed. She had shot plenty of wild rabbits on the farm back home, so she picked up the bundle of fur by its warm, bloody ear and threw it into her wheelbarrow. It expired on impact. She laughed. The rabbit had to be proof of Lady Ann's recent kills? Forget any needless alarm or suspicion. She ought to do the same for her own worst fears before she terrorised herself with any more dire imaginings. There was no hostile prowler. *He's not real, he's not real, I'm real*, she told herself firmly as she scraped thick, green clay off her boots before pruning more bushes in the rose walk.

Work on the garden was going well. Barry had shown her how to remove all dead white wood and cut back the main branches, in some cases to just above the ground. After much mulching and feeding the new and strong shoots should grow from low down. Even so she had to make sure she cut above old grafting points, she had to identify the telltale knobs at the base of each stem. Otherwise she would encourage fresh suckers from the rootstock. Each bulge marked a season to keep a remarkable record of the garden written in wood.

'Why not plant new roses?' said Laura. 'That way we'll save ourselves a lot of trouble and see them bloom much sooner…'

She broke off with a loud 'ow'.

A thorn just pierced her glove and pricked her thumb.

The stab felt spiteful, painful, cruel.

'Never add new roses to old,' said Barry, forking weeds into his wheelbarrow. 'The soil will poison them all.'

'That can't always be true, can it?'

'Believe me it is.'

'Why would the old want to kill the new?'

'See here, this bush with the shiny label has been planted in the last twelve months, but already it has sickened and died. The soil must be totally replaced before you can even think about doing something like that. That's why we're going to dig new beds nearer the house.'

Laura sucked blood off her thumb. The wound was worse than she thought. 'So we can plant new roses if we leave the old alone?'

'Why should that bother you?'

'It's as if the garden has its own set of rules.'

'Doesn't every garden?'

'That's not what I mean.'

'What then?'

'I can't help wondering why the previous gardeners lost heart so soon.'

'Isn't it obvious? They left because they weren't up to the task.'

'Or something stopped them?' said Laura.

'You make it sound very ominous.'

'Lady Ann mentioned a falling tree.'

'No doubt they scared themselves silly with their own incompetence.'

'Or they broke the rules.'

'Lady Ann hired the wrong people, that's a fact.'

'Or they saw sense and decided the garden was beyond resurrecting? Look around you.'

'What about it?'

'You have to admit it has been neglected for an awfully long time.'

'"Neglected" is not the word I would use,' said Barry. '"Neglected" suggests someone has wilfully failed to give the garden proper care and attention. In truth those blackberry and bryony bushes over there have been going strong for years. Take a good look at that clematis? It's busy flowering, as will that Bergenia in a few weeks' time. While the borders have succumbed to grass, the more substantial herbaceous plants such as those euphorbias and heucheras are still flourishing. The same is true of the elderberry. All those perennials have grown from seeds dropped by birds. You could say the garden knows how to look after itself without our interference. Despite everything it goes on quietly recreating itself in its old form.'

'I thought you were going to say someone secretly tends it.'

'I won't. You might.'

'Not me. I'm done with other people's nasty snooping and sneaking.'

'Why, what happened to you?'

'It's complicated. I don't want to talk about it.'

'Better go wash that thumb.'

'Don't worry, I'll be fine.'

The heftily built ex-prisoner looked glum, not to be trifled with. 'Do as you're told. Go to the house and ask Betty for some antiseptic. Go now.'

'It hurts like hell I must admit.'

'Rose thorns can soon turn nasty.'

'Okay, I won't be long. "Better safe than sorry". You and Ray will have to go on working for the garden in my absence.'

If she said 'for' rather than 'in' the garden it was because, in the last few days, she had begun to think of it as something not entirely inanimate… not entirely without feelings. We are not like the self-seeding shrubs and flowers, she told herself. We don't belong here. Not yet anyway. Perhaps we never will.

***

'Mrs Mortimer? Hallo? Is anyone about?' cried Laura, the minute she entered Green Way House's tranquil hall.

She expected to see Christmas tinsel draped over its silent clocks or hung from its banisters, but there was no sign of any festive spirit. Green Way House was as dim, bare and draughty as it had been in the 17th century. Her call was lost in its labyrinthine collection of unresponsive corridors, shut doors and dying flowers.

Surely this house has not celebrated anything for hundreds of years, she decided? A chill hung in the air which went beyond the mere lack of heating.

Laura walked through the stone archway into the kitchen. A glassy-eyed rabbit lay on a wooden table where somebody had begun to peel bloody flesh from bone. Clearly this had been one of Lady Ann's better shots: this lucky rabbit had died instantly. She grinned. Her ladyship liked to eat her kills, or she had them cooked for someone else.

Laura turned on a large brass tap in the lead-lined sink. Ran icy water on her thumb. There was a green bar of soap to cleanse her wound, but no antiseptic was to be seen anywhere.

It was necessary to mount the stairs to the next floor where the loneliness of long, empty corridors struck her deeply.

That was not to say all rooms were completely unfurnished, only that there was no sign of any inhabitant… This had been a person's home for generations, yet now it seemed no one's at all.

Except the feeling of vacancy was so strong it almost constituted a presence.

Someone still walks in these unloved spaces, thought Laura. *Someone* still breathes the freezing cold air besides me? Tapestries and paintings decorated the walls in a full-sized billiards room, while in a library a great many leather-bound books gathered dust on its shelves.

Something other than the wind through the window caused the door to creak behind her.

'Mrs Mortimer? Betty?'

A rat with a pink spotty tail pattered across bare boards strewn with broken glass and fallen plaster.

Other than that, no living creature stirred visibly anywhere.

Laura came to another, short flight of stairs and started up them to a door. It wasn't locked and she went in.

She was immediately impressed by an enormous oak desk that stood in the middle of the room. Here was evidence of some visitor's recent visit. Pen and ink lay on the desk's green leather veneer. Papers sat piled beside books on medicine. Someone spent many hours here poring over the human brain and body.

Their search had all the hallmarks of something frantic.

Someone worked hard in this retreat which, unlike the rest of the house, was not so dismally dark by day. When Laura lifted her eyes she saw why. An imposing octagonal cupula, with glazed sides all round it, took the place of a ceiling. The tall lantern was mounted high atop the mansion's roof where nothing could impede the sky that shone through its panes. That still didn't entirely account for the exceptional luminosity. Rather, the windows themselves magnified the sunlight through the clarity and refractive quality of their thick flint glass. She might have been standing inside a lighthouse's fiery lens or prism. It reminded her of some ancient Pharos.

One of the chamber's eight windows had some words carved over it, she noted: "hinc itur ad astra", which translated as "from here the way leads to the stars". A second window read "ex umbra in solem" which meant "from the shadow into the light". A door led out on to a small balcony that was enclosed by an iron rail.

Laura emerged into the cold winter air to see Barry at work in the rose walk directly below her. From giddy heights she saw what she couldn't see so well on the ground. She was simultaneously dazed and delighted. 'This house is like its garden,' she decided. 'The outside world looks very different from within.' Where the four intersecting paths quartered the rose walk it was possible to chart how each part was drawn with some specific design in mind. Previous gardeners had laid bare numerous lines of brick edging with oblique notches, whose shapes represented patterns from heraldry? She could make out one complete escutcheon whose bars were formed from black brick set against pale stone.

She had noted the same impressive device on a stone coat of arms mounted over the front door to the mansion.

'Barry is right. Nothing here is by chance,' thought Laura. 'Everything has a purpose which is to remember.'

She turned back to the study and closed the door carefully behind her. More words were carved in the waist-high dado rail that ran right round the room "ad perpetuam memoriam of Will. Decessit vita patris". "To the perpetual memory of Will. Died in the lifetime of the father".

She was all set to open a drawer in the desk when she heard a cry. It was a drawn-out, ugly squeal from downstairs.

'That's no rat,' thought Laura and rushed to descend very quickly.

She saw Betty emerge from a doorway partway along the corridor – the housekeeper carried a tray in her hands on which lay a plate of half-eaten food, along with a glass of water and a packet of pills.

'Why are you up here?' asked Betty, nearly dropping everything. 'Did I not tell you never to wander about this house by yourself?'

'I was looking for you,' said Laura. 'See here, I've pricked my thumb on a rose thorn. I'm in urgent need of some antiseptic.'

'What do you want me to do about it? This isn't a five star hotel. We're not Claridge's!'

'I was admiring the unusually shaped room upstairs. It must be so warm and sunny in summer.'

'You shouldn't go up there. Not even I go up to the lantern. It's not safe. Only Lady Ann dares to.'

'But it must be the nicest room in the house?'

Betty eyed her intensely for a moment. 'That's because hundreds of years ago William Lawrence designed it as a study for his son Will who – God help us – did not live to see it finished. Now come downstairs with me. That wound looks nasty. I may have something for you if you're lucky.'

'Thank you.'

'You should be more careful. Hasn't anyone told you? The garden can be a dangerous place.'

***

That night Laura stood alone in the doorway of her caravan. Its stuffy atmosphere saw her in dire need of some fresh air. Barry and Ray were playing cards in Ray's van but she had declined to join them. When people, even strangers, socialised they were bound to ask questions. She felt no great inclination to explain why she was here and not still at university. Not yet. Not ever?

Two men twice her age were hardly going to understand how the female master of her college had refused to meet her face to face and had not replied to her emails for weeks. It was not as if dozens of students hadn't signed an open letter and held a protest rally in her support – they'd turned their backs whenever the master or chaplain had tried to address them publicly. Not being believed was like having no roots suddenly. She had felt small, dry, withered. Mostly she was angry that the master referred to her as the "alleged" victim only. This woman (a Dame no less) wanted to discredit her testimony and all because the chaplain had informed her that he was aware of some *factual inaccuracies* in her account of her experience.

Laura looked skywards to admire the stars, only to see a light burn in the study high on top of the house. Someone was holding a torch to its octagonal windows. The glass globe flashed more than ever like a lighthouse in the dark sky, as its occupant walked about inside. Its reflective panes backlit their head and shoulders when they emerged through its door and on to its railed balcony. It was Lady Ann.

Her ladyship was restless, agitated, inconsolable as she shone her flashlight left and right at the garden below.

'Why are you up there at this late hour?' Laura wondered.

Something must be making you do it, she decided.

The chatelaine wasn't stargazing.

'Did you lie to us the other evening after all?' queried Laura. '*Did* you expect to see someone in the grounds? Do you now?'

Laura quickly shut and locked her caravan's door against the lantern's keeper. Had not Betty said that only her mistress ever dared go up there?

***

Laura couldn't sleep. She threw off her blankets and looked out of her caravan. No light shone anymore from Green Way House's rooftop cupola. Its observer had abandoned her solitary watch for another night?

Instead her ladyship's silhouette could be seen pacing a room on a lower floor where she had not yet drawn the curtains. Back and forth she went like someone possessed. She traversed the space between bed and window. She held both hands on her head as she changed direction most violently.

She argued with herself and not only for a short while.

Laura was about to return to bed when a song sounded in the garden…

Her first thought was her stalker.

…with more words designed to taunt her?

Had her abuser really tracked her down to resume his horrible game? He had tried it before and now he was doing it again. Laura waited to hear the tap of his stick as he came nearer. Like Lady Ann, she braced herself for the expected occurrence which had yet to happen. She was disgusted with herself. It did no good to anticipate someone who might never come. Anxiety was like a gate, it let things in. *He's not real. He's not real. He's not real.*

I'm real.

The ugliest shadow deserved no credence! She was here to banish the man but also the memory. Except this singer was bashful and timid... about to weep. He maintained his lament, albeit with a less serene and more hurried tune than before.

As if her hurt could be his and his hers.

Suddenly he nerved himself to sing much louder. His brittle voice rose in a show of strength, despite Lady Ann's hostile surveillance.

He did so as one gardener to another.

It reminded her of what Barry had told her about the rose walk. The old was apt to destroy the new:

>There grows in my garden the rue,
>And Love-lies-a-bleeding droops there,
>The hyssop and myrrh, the teazle and burr;
>In place of blossoms fair.

'It seems I alone am not afraid to listen to you,' said Laura as Lady Ann blundered about insensibly, her hands still clamped on both her ears. 'Or there are none so deaf as those that won't hear.'

19

River Severn

The call had come on her way to work. Alison was feeling distinctly sleepy, having sat up too late at night reading more outlandish ghost stories. It got her nowhere. Ravi was right, it was time to forget about Green Way House and any spectral crossroads.

She drove down the steep hill to The Red Lion Inn near Wainlode Cliff. She and her brother had once cycled here with their fishing rods when they should have been at school.

She kept going down the narrow lane with the great, curving expanse of water on her left until she crossed one small redbrick bridge, then came to another. Suddenly a police officer waved her off the road. He directed her by way of a gate whose crudely drawn black and white sign said **PRIVATE. NO ELVERING**.

The rough dirt track took her across two fields to the river again where DI Prickett stood waiting for her with his arms folded.

Beside him stood a gaunt, red-haired man with the eyes of the devil.

'Damn it, what is the Environment Agency doing here?' hissed Alison as she stepped from her car under the wide open sky.

'Be nice,' said Prickett. 'I know you can.'

'The Agency do a great job protecting the river, but I prefer it if they stay out of my way.'

'Just because they made a total balls-up of everything last time…'

'I swear to God they won't have any balls at all if they mess me about again today.' They both knew to what she was referring. That **NO ELVERING** sign she had just driven past was there for a reason. Netting endangered baby eels was big business when they sold for £175 per kg, but three years ago an international crime syndicate had been reselling them for twice that price in the Far East where they sold like caviar. All she had needed was final proof. The Environment Agency were experts at detaining illegal fishermen by way of their night patrols on land and water, but sometimes it didn't pay to be a stickler for the rules. Thanks to this particular agent she had been prevented from releasing two local poachers as bait to catch their bosses later. Somebody had to see the bigger picture. Much better to net a big fish instead of a minnow, she reminded herself as she adopted a brave face. 'James! Good to see you. It's been a while.'

The red-haired agent eyed her with a mixture of sternness and sympathy. 'Good morning Detective Sergeant Ellis. A lot of water has passed under the bridge since we last met.'

'Can't disagree with you there.'

'Have you forgiven me?'

'It's about time, isn't it.'

'No hard feelings?'

'Can we just get on with it?'

'What makes you think I haven't?'

'I won't know until you tell me.'

'Yesterday afternoon we began inspecting the old canal lock in this side of the riverbank. Gates and sluices are long gone and it has been silted up ever since it closed one hundred and forty years ago. After the recent floods we were concerned that its brick walls might collapse and be a hazard to boats. We came back this morning to take another look and that's when we saw it. It doesn't look good, so we called you.'

'I have to see for myself.'

To those who didn't know her well her refusal to be fazed could be a little intimidating.

'The bonnet is facing down into the riverbed,' said James, 'and the back is standing up at a precarious angle. We think the partial collapse of the dock caused the vehicle to shift in a gyre of water.'

Alison took a deep breath then advanced past the fire engine, ambulance and police cars. A white lorry the size of a horsebox stood at the side of the river. A short ladder led to a door in the rear of the command centre organising the whole operation. These were specialist divers from Gloucestershire's Underwater Search Team. They at least ought to know what they were doing. Meanwhile she watched a crane manoeuvre its telescopic boom out over the river. The Police Diver Attendant monitored the lifeline to the diver whose head appeared above the Severn's rippling surface, ensuring contact by way of a cable at all times – he made sure he knew where the frogman was without restricting his movements. He signalled to check his condition as he reported back to the Diving Supervisor.

Alison called him over. 'How long, in your opinion?'

'It's pretty treacherous down there,' replied the Attendant. As he spoke the diver unclipped a hammer from the D-ring on his dry suit. Then he disappeared underwater with a flap of his large, open-heel fins. Bubbles burst to the surface from his closed circuit rebreather. 'There's so much silt suspended in the river after the recent rain. You can't see a thing.'

'Can't he use some sort of torch?'

'He has a flashlight but the particles stirred up by the currents are rendering it pretty pointless. He's diving in a black fog and the beam can't penetrate it. He says he literally can't see his hand in front of his mask.'

'I wish we didn't have to ask him to do it.'

'Makes a change from shopping trolleys and traffic cones that we usually find on a dive.'

Alison heard the frogman's two-way radio crackle. He confirmed that he had successfully smashed the glass in the two rear doors of the submerged wreck. He was now passing a heavy duty recovery strap from one hole to the other, he said. She saw the boom of the crane swing ninety degrees over the site as the diver reappeared to attach the sling to the hook.

'Won't be long now,' said the Dive Attendant. 'We need to get our man ashore and then we'll be safe to go.'

'What about traffic up and down the river?' asked Alison. She was wary of the Severn's wide, deep and powerful body of water which could wreak havoc on whole towns when it flooded from the Welsh Hills.

'I have two men in dinghies observing the scene from a safe distance,' said James, 'should any boat, barge or tanker come along to disrupt the lift.'

'God forbid, but what if something does go horribly wrong?'

'We have a tugboat on standby from Bristol.'

Minutes later Alison saw the diver stagger up the muddy cliff to the shore. Other divers, always on hand should there be any mishap, helped him discard his shoulder, waist and crotch strap assembly to free the twin tanks of air on his back. He tore off his regulator and face mask and gave his head a good shake. 'Christ! It really is as black as pitch down there. Absolutely diabolical!'

Next minute the recovery sling pulled taut as the mobile crane driver began to ease the wreck from the water. Bit by bit a filthy metal object began to surface. It was so covered in mud Alison couldn't tell whether it was grey or green – it slowly slid from dark currents oozing silt, weeds and debris. Somewhere amid the sludge was a sizeable car. At a guess she would say it had to be a Volvo Estate.

She waited for the salvaged vehicle to swing through the air. She saw it settle on the grassy bank with a heavy bump as grimy water sloshed through its broken windows. It took a few minutes to release the hook from the sling.

'After you,' said James.

'Thanks a lot.'

'Don't mention it.'

Alison stopped to gag and gasp as she approached the driver's door. James and the diver had hinted at what to expect but it still took her breath away. The stench was foul, putrescent, *evil*...

20

Green Way House

'No joy?' asked Laura cheerfully as she cast her eye over the defunct mini-digger. She had yet to tell anyone about Lady Ann's nocturnal vigil – she was loath to admit it as more evidence of a prowler. The best she could do right now was to get on with her work. Defer the thought. Defy the logic.

Ray shook his head. 'There was a sparking sound when I went to turn the engine over, then all the lights went out on the panel. Now I'm having trouble getting it to start at all.'

'Try cracking open one of the injectors to see if any diesel is getting through.'

'I've done that. It squirted fuel like it should.'

'Have you bled the whole system so there's no air present?'

'Still won't start.'

'You checked all lines for holes and splits?'

'You bet.'

Laura rummaged happily through his box of tools. 'My guess is the primer ball pump.'

'What makes you think that?'

'The farm digger I've driven has a pump like this – it has a one-way valve that gets bunged up with gunk.'

Ray reluctantly watched Laura wield her spanner. 'I was thinking we should have a Christmas party.'

'I'm not into that Santa stuff. You won't catch me pulling crackers and eating festive bao buns.'

'There's a TV in my caravan. The three of us can watch a "Die Hard" movie.'

'I'll be just fine on my own, thanks.'

'You can't live in isolation from the human race.'

'What did I tell you?' said Laura. 'Gunk in the valve. Now we're getting somewhere.'

Ray stood by helplessly. 'Don't you have any desire for close company?'

'The one and only time I let my hair down ended in tears.'

'You're not afraid of men, are you?'

'They should be afraid of me.'

Laura flipped up the digger's armrest, swung it out of her way and climbed into the operator's seat. She needed to drive to the furthermost corner of the gardens where Barry would meet them with shovels and spades.

First she familiarised herself with the cab's gauges, then she gripped the joysticks and moved them about to get the feel of their motion. Finally she pulled on her seatbelt. 'Stand clear.'

'You really up to this?' said Ray, scratching his ear.

'I saw the ignition somewhere…'

'Overhead, to your right.'

'That's it.'

'You need to be careful.'

'I've only just begun.' Laura listened to the engine burst into life. She gripped the large handle in front of the instrument cluster – she gave it a pull to raise the machine's dozer blade off the ground to lift boom and bucket.

Ray stepped back hastily. 'Watch out! You could smash into something.'

'Not if I do this right.'

Now that the mini-digger was free to move, Laura looked down between her legs at two long steel rods with handles – she pushed them both forward, only her machine lurched the other way.

'What did I just tell you!' cried Ray. 'You nearly took my head off.'

'Oops.' Laura checked the tracks. Their blades at the front showed the direction of travel. She had gone forwards all right but it felt backwards. 'Whoever last drove the digger left its cab facing the wrong way.'

'Now you tell me.'

She seized the joystick to rotate and point herself confidently in the direction she wanted to go. The spin was a quick, sharp turn which took some getting used to.

'Where to now?' asked Ray over the noise of the engine.

'Follow me.'

'Watch out for uneven ground.'

'It's not too bad.'

Laura pushed one stick forward and pulled the other back. Each controlled the rotation of the track on the side it was located. That way she could spin the digger half way round. By pushing the levers away from her she sent her machine rumbling over the cobbles beside the coach house and stables.

It was time to get serious about remodelling the garden.

A noisy flock of crows occupied the orchard as she trundled by. They were feasting on thousands of rotting apples, she realised. The greedy, intoxicated birds sat in the leafless trees and pecked at the soft yellow flesh, or they gorged on the sea of worm-eaten fruit already lying on the ground. This garden can be so productive, thought Laura and yet if it weren't for these scavengers its crop would all go to waste. Something about it strikes me as wrong. The garden goes on producing more and more fruit every year while its owner harvests less and less. It's like being in some over-abundant but abandoned Eden.

Barry was already in the field as agreed. 'Lady Ann assures me that a large ornamental lake once existed here, surrounded by a double border of trees. It was a real focal point. As you can see it is pretty much lost to grass now. Our job is to dig out the moat round the island on which stood a lovely summer pavilion long ago. I've convinced her that we should redesign the whole area. Plant new trees. I've marked out the site ready for you. You need to dig inside the ring of pegs I've hammered into the ground.'

'I've been telling Laura that we should have a Christmas party in my caravan,' said Ray.

Barry smiled. 'My mum died days after I was released from prison, so I only have an empty house to go home to. It'll be the first time I've enjoyed Christmas for ages. That's because I didn't celebrate anything while I was in a cell. It'll make a nice change, even if I'm not yet officially designated an innocent man in the eyes of the law.'

'Forget the law,' said Ray. 'The police still want me for all sorts of stupid things. Just because I crashed a brand new motorcycle I hadn't paid for! If it wasn't for this job I'd be totally screwed right now.'

'What about you Laura? Are you running away from the powers-to-be as well?'

'I have no confidence in the authorities. They haven't done one thing to help me. They haven't taken any action. They don't see my... my rape as important. They see me as a nuisance.'

'Rape? What rape?'

She hadn't meant to mention it, she really hadn't. She couldn't understand what had just come over her. It was this weird garden. Something about it made her want to be totally honest about herself. Spill the beans. Come clean. 'It happened at college. I woke up to find someone inside me. That's why I'm here. I've been sent down for a year for skewering him in the balls with a pair of scissors.'

'So you could end up in jail too?'

'So far it has all been hushed up. As if one wrong can cancel another!'

'Good for you.'

'No, it's not good at all. He spent weeks stalking me. Followed me home… to my farm in Lincolnshire. Threw a brick through my window. My father and I chased him away with our shotguns, but I'm still scared of what he might do.'

'I know what I'd do to him.'

'Worst of all, I keep fearing I will meet him again. *Here.*'

'Haunts you, does he?'

'My brain plays tricks on me. I think I see him lurking in every corner.'

'Is that why you've said hardly anything to us since you arrived?'

'I'm sorry if I annoy you.'

'Sorry isn't a word,' said Barry, 'it's an admission of defeat. I wouldn't say sorry for a crime I didn't commit.'

Ray nodded. 'Too bloody right. I didn't crash that £18000 Honda Fireblade on purpose. Some bastard spilt oil on the road. They're the true criminals. Anyway, saying sorry to my guarantor's two homicidal brothers won't do a thing for me – they're still after my blood. So what will it be Laura? Do you want to have some fun?'

'I'm not much fun, I'm really not.'

'You don't want to be alone at this time of year. It's too soulless.'

'I'll think about it.'

'Or are you going home to your parents?'

'Home is the last place I want to be.'

With that Laura restarted the mini-digger's engine with renewed enthusiasm. She lowered the dozer blade firmly to the ground to stabilise her machine. She pushed the right joystick forward to lower the main boom, then moved the same stick to lower the bucket on to the soil. Next she pulled back the left stick to drag the bucket through the field towards her, while she pulled the right stick a different way to scoop earth from the hole. The digger bounced, jolted and roared as she swung her cab halfway round to dump the soil successfully in a heap alongside her.

A second later she lurched violently in her seat. Only her safety belt saved her from being thrown clear in one go. The digger pitched, shook and began to roll with her still in it. Try as she might Laura couldn't release her hands from the levers – she was driving the machine and herself into the mud. A voice in her head urged her to *dig, dig, dig* as the bucket battered the quagmire. Joysticks and levers flew backwards and forwards out of unison – she was caught in a machine gone wild.

'Laura! What are you doing?' It was Barry trying to scale the cab to reach her side, except he got bogged down in mud as well. 'You're in too deep!'

Still she couldn't make her hands do what she wanted. Busy whispers buzzed in her ears but no actual words. They didn't sound like threats, more the dangerous confirmation of vile suggestions. The levers worked her sore fingers of their own volition – they repeatedly rejected what her brain commanded. She was excavating a big hole for herself along with her fears and emotions.

Everything was ready to turn to slime in the swamp.

Next minute Ray mounted the digger and shook her awake. 'Go back. Do it now! Can't you see you're sinking?'

'Oh shit!' Laura snapped out of her daze. The swarm of whispers subsided – they ended in what sounded like a hiss but was also a laugh. The levers froze in her fingers. She sat up with a jolt. Everything came back into focus from some faraway place. 'What did I just do wrong?'

'This ground is a treacherous bog,' said Ray.

Laura raised the dozer blade, boom and bucket. She put the digger's tracks into reverse but the waterlogged field proved just as strong. The tracks lost their grip on the mud and grass that were sucking her down.

Only by opening up the throttle to full power did she manage at last to reverse on to dry land.

She sat there shaking violently.

'I thought you were going to disappear into the bowels of the earth,' said Ray. 'That field may look all grass but its lake has never fully drained.'

Barry scowled. 'It all happened so fast.'

'I'm okay,' said Laura with relief, 'only it means this place is off limits to any machine.'

'I found this in the bucket,' said Ray.

'What is it?'

Barry took a metal plate from his hand. 'It's a weathervane shaped like a fish.'

'There's a bronze wind vane in the form of a freshwater pike on top of the house's octagonal cupula,' said Laura eagerly. 'It's the crest of the Lawrence family who lived here in the 17th century. Look here, there's writing on it which says "ab aeterno".'

'What on earth does that mean?' asked Ray.

'It means "from the eternal". Literally: "from outside of time".'

Barry agreed. 'This vane comes from the island's lost pavilion.'

'We should go back,' said Ray. 'I need a drink.'

Laura restarted the mini-digger ready to retreat. She couldn't help but continue to feel the drag on its tracks where the old lake had risen to try to pull her down. The swamp's power had been odious, malevolent, intelligent. Except she glanced in her cab's bright mirror and saw not some boggy field but an expanse of ruffled water. She looked hard at the reflection and made out the mound that marked where its island had miraculously resurfaced. In the middle of this wonderful vision was a white summerhouse of exceptional beauty. Its fish-shaped weathervane flashed in the sun, while a figure stood at the edge of silvery ripples...

Her jaw dropped. She wanted to dismiss him as another product of her shocked, overwrought imagination...

Fear alone might have created him but he had real substance.

Pretty much.

Whoever he was, he was master of his own form.

Like an avatar.

True, he was not often to be *seen* at work tending the garden, but that didn't mean he wasn't always everywhere in it.

She thought: you're the one who sings me your songs. So who are you really?

21

River Severn

The driver's face was one big, muddy smear through his window.

'That's odd,' said DI Prickett.

'What is?' asked Alison, as she too cast her eye over the salvaged car.

'This Volvo is left-hand drive.'

Alison looked all round to establish a single route into and out of the potential crime scene. 'I can't see any obvious damage. I don't believe it was rammed by another vehicle, not out here, not even by a tractor.'

'Well, something made it tip down the bank.'

'You think the driver *chose* to steer himself into the river?'

'Don't you?'

She pulled on her latex gloves. 'Stand back. I'm going to take a closer look.'

'After you. Be my guest.'

Alison wrenched open the driver's door. Jumped back. A torrent of filthy water gushed past her toes.

'Christ! What a pong!' said Prickett.

'He's been in the water quite a while.'

'His face is like a balloon.'

Alison didn't want to contaminate anything. At the same time she needed to make a preliminary assessment of the scene. Normally she would search the victim's clothes for identification, but the driver was not wearing a single garment under his coating of slime.

'It's on days like this I don't like my job very much,' said Prickett.

'What about you?'

'I'll let you know in a minute.'

Alison scanned the naked corpse for any distinguishing marks. The cadaver's bleached and swollen chest was more manikin than man. He resembled some grossly overinflated doll or disfigured creature from Hell. His skin was all wrinkled. She could barely locate his eyes, nose and mouth where one feature slid into another. Except mud was not all she was looking at. She was staring at a blank, yellow-brown mask akin to soap – his fatty tissue beneath his skin was fast turning into "grave wax".

There was vascular marbling and other dark discolouration of his soft tissues. More skin had begun to slough off his hands and feet where greenish flesh was turning very flimsy and papery.

Prickett held his nose. 'His teeth have turned pink. That suggests he drowned. That would fit with suicide.'

'Actually it's more likely to be due to lividity in the tissues as part of the putrefaction process.'

'Not much to be getting on with then.'

'There's one good thing. Being in the car means no branches or rocks have wreaked havoc on him. No big fish have been able to nibble at him in his watery grave.' When a submerged body was battered by strong currents it could be impossible to tell if its wounds had been inflicted on dry land or underwater.

'Are you done yet sergeant? He's rotting faster now he's in the air.'

She continued to look round the body. 'Can't see any knife or bullet holes in him, but we won't know for sure until we get him out of the vehicle. I can't see his back from here.'

'I'll ring the coroner. I'll get him to authorise a Home Office Registered Pathologist. This death is sufficiently suspicious to warrant their 24/7 service.'

'We should take a quick look in the rear of the vehicle.'

'Can't it wait?'

'Sadly no.'

'Forensics won't like it.'

'Give me a hand, will you?'

'Why?'

'All this water has buggered the tailgate's hydraulics,' said Alison. 'The damned door won't stay up over my head.'

'You're going to get yourself into real trouble one of these days.'

'Do I need your permission?'

'Can't blame me for being cautious.'

'It's by the book…'

'Wait for the experts.'

'…or there's getting the job done.' Alison leaned into the back of the car but touched nothing. She was observing not disturbing. A pair of gloves and wellington boots lay coated with a fine layer of sludge. There were overalls and someone's sodden cloth cap. One end of a filthy black and white bar scarf had stuck itself to the roof. 'There's something under this slurry. I just can't see what it is yet.'

'You care so much, do you?'

'That's me.'

She hooked her finger in a leather strap. Drew a bag with a loud plop from the silt.

'What is it?' said Prickett.

'I'd say it's a body belt full of tools, wouldn't you?'

Together they examined the belt's four green canvas pockets. 'This is one fancy kind of trowel, wouldn't you say?' declared Alison, extricating a heart-shaped blade with sharp sides and pointed end. She dangled it briefly at her fingertips for her boss to see, then chose another pocket. In it was a dart-like metal spike attached to a wooden handle.

'Reminds me of a bolt from a crossbow.'

A third tool proved to be a steam-bent piece of wood with a metal point on one end. 'God knows what this is?'

'My uncle uses one of those to plant his tulip bulbs,' said Prickett. 'He calls it his dibber. It has a slightly offset blade to make the right hole. You grip it in one hand like so and...'

'So our dead man is a gardener?'

'But what's he doing out here?'

'If this isn't suicide then what is it?'

'Save your breath. Forensics have arrived.'

'We'll get to them in a minute.'

'What else do you have?'

'I don't see any ignition key, do you? Where is it, I wonder? Did someone throw it away before the Volvo hit the river? That means they must have pushed, not driven, the car down the slope into the water. Who bothers to do that if they want to kill themselves? Come to that, who puts their seatbelt on? Why prolong the agony? I'd say our deceased has had some help, wouldn't you?'

22

No more sightings of her mysterious prowler.

Whereas Laura had woken up every morning terrified of what people might say about her on social media, she refused now to be obsessed by them hour by hour, minute by minute. I'm not going to play their silly games any more, she thought, I'm not going to text anyone or even look at my phone. I'm not going to live in fear of the threats *he* has sent me.

She was happy to let one day blur into another within the walled garden without any more trouble.

Pretty much.

Even to think of her stalker was to give him oxygen he did not deserve.

Except somebody had just deposited a box of apples outside her caravan door.

'That's weird, I didn't ask Betty for any apples.'

Each week she gave the housekeeper a list of any fresh food she needed and Betty went shopping for her. She did the same for Ray and Barry. While this happy arrangement was clearly designed to discourage them all from leaving the house and its garden, it was also convenient.

Laura went to pick up the fruit only to find that no shop could possibly have sold them.

All apples bar one were bruised, crow-pecked, rotten.

They had come from the garden.

Must be somebody's idea of a bad joke. She threw the windfall away and proceeded to heat tomato soup in a pan on her tiny gas cooker in her caravan. The roof of her Thomson '52 Almond brushed the top of her head as she navigated its cabinets, beds and folding tables. Space everywhere was at a premium. At least the hinged draining board that covered the sink provided some extra room to prepare her meal.

The caravan, already stuffy, became unbearably hot when cooking. If I can just open one of the roof ventilators, she thought and let in the bitterly cold evening.

'Damn it,' said Laura, as she tripped and slopped soup at her feet. 'Now look what I've done.'

She searched around for a cloth, then knelt on all fours on the floor. "House is where the heart is… Fortune favours the bold". She went to clean the linoleum at the base of the bed settee in the forward apartment.

Her new world might be compact, even annoyingly so, but she was still expected to keep it spotless.

'The person who laid this lino did a really bad job,' Laura observed angrily. 'It's all dangerous bubbles and wrinkles. It's not even nailed down.'

She peeled back a corner of the dark green covering ready to flatten it, only to find a big, reddish-brown stain marked the boards underneath. It was nothing to do with her. The crudely fitted lino had been used to cover up something already spilt there.

It didn't look like soup.

She exposed more floor and the same discolouration was all over this end of the gangway.

It did not smell as such.

Someone had failed to scrub the floorboards clean prior to her arrival. She was able to trace rubbed words still recorded in the wood's grain.

Since when did anyone use spilt soup to write a message anyway?

The caravan's last occupant had leaned off their bed to scrawl on the floor with a fingertip…

Four faint letters spelt: H . L P M .

…in their own blood.

Somebody must have been in a very bad way to have done such a thing.

'I won't ask Betty about this,' Laura decided hastily. 'She'll say it's not her job to clean up after anyone. She'll accuse me of wanting her to remove the dead flies from the windowsill next.'

Except this was one secret too many.

She might have to tell someone.

***

Later that night Laura tossed and turned in her bed, when her singer returned.

She sat up and waited while he moved through the garden.

His voice sounded crystal clear on the breeze as he passed by her door:

> Cold are my lips in death, sweet-heart,
>
> My breath is earthy strong.
>
> If you do touch my clay-cold lips,
>
> Your time will not be long.

Laura was expectant, entranced, paralysed. She braced herself, but there came no ugly shouts, no brick through the window...

No one marched up and down outside her door in a proud, stiff and angry manner, shouting obscenities at her.

This was not then.

This was not *him?*

Rather, her serenader's voice was deceptively soft and plaintive. He was keen to lull her back to sleep with his sorrow.

***

Early next morning Laura woke in a panic.

She threw open the caravan's door and almost choked: she had just dreamt she was in a coffin.

She wheezed and gasped in the fresh air.

Suddenly she looked down.

At her feet was a fresh gift of apples from the garden.

23

Police Headquarters
Prism House
Gloucester

'Looks like we were correct about our man in the river,' said Alison, marching uninvited into her boss's office. 'He is almost certainly a gardener.'

'Don't you ever knock?' said Prickett, not without self-importance. He liked to present himself as someone who was always too busy to listen. What irritated him most was an officer who took no notice.

'The bag we found in the car was full of expensive items made in Holland.'

'Don't you ever *listen*?'

'The tool you called a crossbow bolt is a wrotter. That's an old Dutch word for "tough worker". Gardeners use it for precise weeding around herbaceous borders…'

'And your point is sergeant?'

'You use it like an axe on the ground. The heart-shaped trowel is the tool of choice for the annual Keukenhof Exhibition.'

Prickett sniffed loudly. Too much stress triggered his sinusitis. 'Never heard of it.'

'Keukenhof is the world's biggest flower garden. People go there to view eight hundred types of tulips when seven million bulbs blossom every spring. Our corpse just might be a Dutchman?'

'That's nice but probably not true.'

Alison blinked hard. 'Forensics are investigating the bag as we speak. There's a small oval, black and beige logo on its side which says ESSCHERTGARDEN. Esschert Design is a Dutch company that specialises in making all sorts of things relating to gardens and nature. It can be tools or it can be lovely traditional cast iron Dutch cooking pots.'

'Just because he has the bag with him doesn't mean it is his. More to the point, what about the Volvo? Does he own that, I wonder?'

'DVLA says its plate is registered to Anika Janssen in Brighton on the South Coast.'

'I take it that's a no.'

'Her name sounds Dutch to me.'

'It's still a maybe.'

'There's more. On the dead man's back is a lion wielding a sword in one hand and a bunch of arrows in the other.'

'So?'

'It turns out his tattoo is the heraldic coat of arms of the Kingdom of the Netherlands.'

'So your mind is absolutely made up. Our corpse is definitely Dutch?'

'No, I'm not psychic.'

'Not yet anyway. What else do we know?'

Alison handed him the pathologist's report. 'Our man is between the age of thirty and thirty-five. He has salt and pepper stubbly hair to the sides and top of his head and a pointy beard. Dental records should yield more results but not necessarily in this country. No fingerprints were obtainable but DNA samples are being compared with national and international records.'

'What I want to know is what killed him.'

'I'm coming to that. The autopsy reveals a gastric content with plant material, resulting in lung and brain oedema. We are awaiting further test results, but it seems our victim may well have been poisoned with aconite.'

'Aconite?' Prickett cleared his throat. 'As in the garden flower?'

'Weird, isn't it? I've done some research. You can buy aconite root that has been dried and ground as a powder, in shops and online. It also comes in pellets, tablets, capsules and liquid formulas.'

'Christ! Just how lethal is it?'

'Many aconite products come with dosage instructions for adults and children. It's also known as wolfsbane. Shepherds once used it to lace raw meat to bait and kill wolves.'

Prickett shook his head. 'Sounds like something out of Harry Potter to me. You'll be telling me next this is all about magic potions. Sounds a tad fantastic.'

'Don't be so sure,' said Alison firmly. 'In 2010 a British woman was convicted of poisoning someone with spicy aconite curry.'

'Why offer it to the public at all?'

'It's sold in many health-food stores as a homeopathic remedy. You can also find it in pharmacies. That's because many people believe it can help treat various conditions ranging from colds and headaches to heart disease. It's even sold as a "kiddie calmer" to help children overcome their shyness and worry. Some mothers use it to reduce the pain of their babies' teeth. Obviously it's the dosage that matters. A great aunt of mine took it to treat her rheumatism and she was fine. Too much of it will cause fatal haemorrhages in a person's heart and nervous systems, especially if it hasn't been soaked or boiled enough to reduce its toxicity.'

'Anything else?'

'Only this. You can absorb dangerous amounts of aconite through your skin or open wounds. *There is no known antidote.*'

Prickett snapped into action. 'Has no one answered our description of the car yet? Surely somebody sitting on those riverside benches outside The Red Lion Inn at Wainlode saw it go past?'

'Sorry.'

'How long does the pathologist estimate the body has been in the water?'

'She reckons it's been a good few weeks.'

'The sooner we find this Anika Janssen the better. She's our one possible link to the deceased.'

'Okey-doke.'

'You have a better idea?'

Alison walked to his side of the desk. 'May I?'

'You already have.'

She brought up Google Maps on his computer and pointed out the River Severn. She used her finger to trace its course as it wound its way parallel with Wainlode Lane. 'I need to show you something.'

'What am I looking for?'

'The river's ruined lock marks the place where the car went into the water. Now observe how this line of trees snakes inland across these fields.'

'So what?'

'It's barely visible now, but that thin row of trees follows the route of something.'

'You playing games with me?'

'Look again. The trees do a bit of a bend to the left then settle into a more direct line. There comes another turn to the right, but after that the trees run straight as a die for nearly three miles across the wetlands to…'

'Coombe Hill.'

Alison popped a mint in her mouth. 'Those trees follow the line of the abandoned canal. We found our first naked man at the east end of the waterway. Now we have a second naked man at the west end.'

Prickett sniffer louder. 'You know what this means?'

'It means we have to trawl the canal for any more bodies. We also need to establish if anything else links our two dead men to each other. I should get straight on it.'

'So why don't you?'

'You recall there was a fatal hit-and-run incident at the crossroads near Ullenwood five years ago?'

'It's not every day you come across a man with a crushed head lying by the side of the road.'

'It was just before my time. Why *wasn't* the driver ever found?'

Prickett made a face. 'Because we had absolutely nothing to go on. No one saw a damned thing. There was no glass, paint or debris from the damaged vehicle. No skid marks, *nothing*. The pathologist confirmed that the victim had been almost decapitated in one very powerful swipe. That's to say his neck hadn't been sawn or cut with a tool but ripped apart by some great force, more likely by a truck than by a car. We ruled out premeditated murder, more or less.'

'I see. Thanks. I'm going to lunch. Do you want anything?'

'Wait sergeant. You have forgiven me for blocking your transfer to the Avon and Somerset Police last month, haven't you?'

Alison fixed him with her gimlet eye. 'You said you were my friend.'

'I am.'

'Is that true?'

'You really don't know me by now? I didn't want to lose you. I can't do without you on my team.'

'Uh-huh.'

'So you've forgiven me?'

'I have.'

'Really?'

'What else do you want me to do? Say it with flowers?'

She hadn't meant to enquire about the fatal accident five years ago, thought Alison. It had absolutely nothing to with her, so why did it keep coming back to haunt her?

24

Green Way House

'You've found *what* on your caravan floor?' said Barry.

Laura threw more bindweed on the bonfire they were building in the garden. 'Someone tried to hide the evidence under a strip of lino.'

'You sure about this?'

'Absolutely I am.'

'I'd have to see it for myself.'

'I wish you would.'

Barry stared into the crackling flames. They'd had to wait for a suitably windless day to burn this many weeds. That's because they didn't want white smoke to blow over the nearby nurseries that stood at the entrance to Greenway Lane. They couldn't afford to upset the owner when they wished to buy lots of roses from him to fill their new rose beds. 'I don't think we ought to call the police, do you? I've only just come out of prison. It could look bad for me.'

'We should ask Mr Mortimer about it right away,' said Laura firmly.

'We?'

'We can't risk not to.'

'What if he already knows?'

'We can't be sure until we ask him.'

'Perhaps you're right. Does Ray know?'

Laura shook her head. 'Not yet.'

'Probably best.'

She and Barry returned to the front of Green Way House where he unrolled some string to mark out a rectangle ten feet wide on the ground.

Ray leaned against the wall smoking a cigarette. 'What are you two looking so serious about?'

'Nothing,' said Barry hastily and took hold of a spade. 'Once we've excavated this first trench we'll subdivide it so. Then we can fork out the rest of the weeds strip by strip as we progress.'

'Thanks for the rotten apples,' hissed Laura.

'What rotten apples?' replied Ray.

'Come off it. I know it was you. It's your idea of a joke, right?'

'I didn't give you any apples.'

'Well somebody did. They left them outside my caravan.'

'Must be your prowler.'

'As if.'

No sooner had she spoken than Laura saw Mr Mortimer exit the house in a hurry. She mimed to Barry with frantic pointing.

He nodded immediately and thrust his spade at Ray. 'Carry on digging a foot deep. I need Laura to help me plan something. We'll be back in a minute.'

'Do I really have to?' said Ray. 'I can plan things as well. I'm not just brawn, you know.'

Laura smiled. 'Why, what are you normally like?'

'Just because I rebuild stolen motorbikes doesn't mean I don't have a brain. Sometimes I think you underestimate me.'

'Yes, it could be that.'

'You really think I'm not good enough for you?'

'Just teasing.'

'Where'd the butler go?' asked Barry as he marched along.

'He headed that way,' replied Laura and turned left by the knot garden.

Together they entered the cobbled yard, even as Mr Mortimer disappeared into the coach house adjoining the stables.

They saw him step through the wicket cut into one of its big brown gates.

'On second thoughts I'll wait for you here,' said Barry. 'I'll keep watch and give you a whistle if anyone comes.'

'You'd better.'

***

To step inside the coach house was to step into another world, Laura discovered. She was standing next to its cool, whitewashed walls – she breathed the heady smell of its leather and oil. Not a thing was missing apart from the horses. Dust motes flew everywhere as though her own warm breath was sufficient to disturb a place beautifully preserved by time alone. In the tack room there hung collars and hames, leather lines and bridles. There were cruppers and false martingales. She touched the curb bits and they gave a slight jingle. Everything slept rather than decayed.

Next minute she detected voices. The sounds came from a large, rather splendid and self-important carriage that stood idle on the brick floor. Its mud-splashed front wheels were smaller than the rear. It had fancy spiral-shaped spokes and its hinged drawbar was long enough to allow six horses to haul it along at great speed.

She heard the coach creak on its strong leather straps slung between its wheels as someone shifted on its seat inside it.

One of its doors, decorated with polished Venetian mirror glass, stood open to reveal the agitated figure of Mr Mortimer.

His face was as grave as his tone. 'This is the worst he has been. He should see a doctor at once.'

'We both know his condition is not listed in the DSM handbook used to diagnose mental health problems.' The voice was Lady Ann's, Laura realised.

'My wife says he's becoming less and less social.'

'And I say there are no firm rules to guide anyone.'
'What if he stops speaking at all?'
'Trust me, I know as much as any medical expert.'
'He says the songs he hears come out of nowhere.'
'Not from nowhere. Not for nothing.'

Mr Mortimer seized hold of an elaborately sewn hanging-strap that dangled inside the coach – he gripped it as if the carriage were literally moving. He clung on for dear life as though it raced headlong down the road to oblivion, drawn by half a dozen red-eyed steeds from Hell.

'There has to be a good reason why he hears things we don't.'
'Don't keep telling me he's going mad.'
'The same voice tells him he's dead and therefore there's no point eating. It upsets Mrs Mortimer terribly. I don't know how much longer she can stand it.'

'See here John, you know very well his episodes only last a few weeks. Three months at most.'

'This is the longest by far.'
'You tell me this because?'
'Mrs Mortimer is convinced he should go back to hospital.'
'Not before I see what he sees. Not before I hear what he does.'
'My wife is only thinking of what happened in the summer...'
'I couldn't have predicted what would happen back then. No one could.'

'And if it happens again?'
'It won't. You won't let it.'
'Mrs Mortimer has already caught the new girl nosing about in the study. Scared the living daylights out of her, she did. Nearly dropped her tray...'

'Laura is just a child.'

Mr Mortimer stammered. 'M... M... Mrs Mortimer and I can hardly be held responsible for everyone's safety all the time.'

Lady Ann scoffed. 'You do realise I'm on the brink of one of the greatest breakthroughs in the history of psychiatry. My son has glimpsed that day we can all expect to be our last… He has seen what we should neither desire nor fear.'

'Or he's still dangerously paranoid thanks to his addiction…'

'No dealer can reach him here. Nothing so evil as drugs will penetrate these walls ever again.'

'But why try to recreate the old garden? What's different this time?'

'It may be his last chance.'

'Very well, if you say so. Her ladyship can rely on me to do whatever I can. Have I not already proved my loyalty to you in the most trying of circumstances?'

'Tell me John, you do think I'm right, don't you? You don't think I'm being hopelessly morbid?'

'I fear for the poor boy's health terribly too.'

Lady Ann, still largely invisible to Laura on the other side of the coach, raised a warning finger. On it gleamed a diamond engagement ring. 'Don't ever doubt me. We both know what happens to those who doubt me.'

'It hardly seems five years since I helped him shoot rabbits in the garden…'

'And you will do so again! The deceased don't stray far, but they need a safe place to blossom and bloom. They don't appear to this world until we turn the key to uncover their secret. Don't forget how this garden was built to memorialise a dead boy by his grieving father, something of whose spirit still inhabits its walks and lawns. My own son senses it. If he can then so will I. This garden will reunite us both once I have restored its paradise to work its miracle.'

'But can *he* ever be with us again? *Is* such a thing possible?'

'If we dare to hear his song.'

'Your ladyship shouldn't have to grieve much longer.'

'It's bad, isn't it?'

'No, it's only human.'

'Do you know where the word paradise comes from Mortimer?'

'I don't your ladyship.'

'It derives from the Persian word "pairideaza", which literally translated means "encircled with walls".'

***

Laura beat a hasty retreat to rejoin Barry in the stable yard.

'Well?' he asked worriedly. 'What did he say?'

'I didn't speak to him. Mr Mortimer and Lady Ann are sitting in a horse-drawn coach that looks as if it has been there forever.'

'Just as well. It won't do to stir up a hornets' nest.'

'You don't understand. The two of them are talking about her son *as if he is still alive.* To hear Lady Ann talk you'd think William was here with us right now in Green Way House. She hired those gardeners in the summer for the same reason she hired us. She wanted them to create a special garden – a paradise no less, to work some kind of magic she has in mind.'

Barry rearranged his floppy leather hat on his head. 'Who hasn't planted a flower or tree in memory of someone?'

Laura disagreed. 'She didn't say *of* him, she said *for* him.'

'What's the difference?'

'I tell you we're here to establish a place in which the dead can walk within its walls. It's been tried before. Unbearable grief prompted the creation of this sanctuary in the 17th century – if William Lawrence had not lost his wife and son in 1691 he would never have designed the garden how he did. He filled it with all sorts of ways to keep feelings of lost love alive. Because of him this place retains its power to nurture the dead?'

'Whatever that power was, it must be long gone now.'

'No, you've said it yourself. Things from the old garden remain like those "0s" on the gates. Lady Ann thinks the same. Whatever the magic may be, she talks as though it is the key to establishing contact with her missing son. She's obsessed with the idea. She believes she can summon him back to this world. She talks as if she might already have. The question is, how low will she stoop to get what she wants?'

Barry took a long, hard look at her. 'You've got to let this shit go, girl.'

'What I'm telling you is what I heard.'

'You keep going deeper down this road you'll end up in Hell.'

Laura blushed. 'You don't believe me? Then go see what's written in my caravan. Go now!'

'I'd rather not.'

'Something very bad happened there. If we do one thing only, we should find out who wrote their plea for help.'

'When your college sent you down, did they say you were ill?'

'You really got to ask me that now?'

***

All afternoon Laura worked doubly hard weeding more trenches. She felt enraged, roused, energized. Already she had established how the rose walk had been laid out in an heraldic cross to replicate the Lawrence family arms. Since then they had unearthed the bronze weather vane in the shape of a fish. There had to be other amazing things to discover, pointers to the creator's original intention. To uncover more ornamentation would be another step back in time.

It would be akin to the miracle that Lady Ann had just mentioned.

'As such we need to step carefully ourselves,' Laura told herself. 'What we need to decide is where the garden should *not* be changed... *not* disturbed.'

Suddenly there came into her head one of the songs she had heard in the grounds: "In my garden grew plenty of Thyme".

If it had a beginning then it had an end:
>> The willow with branches that weep,
>> The thorn and the cypress tree,
>> O why were the seeds of dolorous weeds,
>> Thus scattered there by thee?

The serious, cerebral words were easily liked, if not altogether to her liking. As with her own heartbeat she sensed them better with her eyes closed. The words were most audible when the singer was invisible.

Barry would have her dismiss her serenader as the traumatic product of her own recent troubles, who could not possibly be genuine.

Except Lady Ann said her son heard him singing too.

25

Brighton

Anika Janssen didn't mince her words. 'I thought we agreed 10 a.m.?'

'My apologies,' said Alison, 'the traffic into Brighton was appalling.'

'You're fortunate I'm still here. You should have rung me.'

They shook hands somewhat perfunctorily. Anika was not about to smile for the sake of it. The subject of her visit struck her as rude or harsh. Either that or everyone from the Netherlands put a premium on punctuality? 'As I said on the phone I'm from the Gloucestershire Constabulary. Normally the local police would interview you, but I'm here in a special capacity.'

Anika invited her into an airy apartment that overlooked the promenade and sea. An empty pink cot stood abandoned in one corner of the room.

'What is it you want exactly, detective?'

'It concerns a green Volvo Estate registered in your name.'

'My partner took my car months ago.'

'Just like that?'

'I haven't seen it or him since.'

'What's his name?'

'Lars Visser.'

'He left Brighton when precisely? Can you be more specific?'

'He took the Volvo at the end of June. I really don't need 'wheels' since I walk to work every day. I'm a waitress in Horatio's Bar opposite the Horror Hotel you can see over there.'

'I'm sorry, the what?'

Anika pointed out the window to the lengthy, wave-washed Victorian pier that stood astride the sea. 'Some rides like the Sizzler, Crazy Mouse and Wild River are shut for maintenance at the moment, but otherwise the pier is open daily except Christmas Day. I've served drinks there for over a year now.'

'What about Lars? Where does he usually work?'

Anika widened her amber eyes. 'Is there something you're not telling me detective?'

'I'm sorry to inform you that we have just recovered your car from the River Severn. In it was the body of a man.'

'Oh mijn God! Don't tell me you think it's Lars?'

'He has a distinctive tattoo between his shoulders. It depicts a lion wielding a sword in one hand and a bunch of arrows in the other...'

'Sounds like the heraldic coat of arms of the Kingdom of the Netherlands.'

'Did Lars Visser have such a tattoo on his back?'

'Yes he did.'

'I'm so sorry...'

'Can you show me a photo of his face? I can easily confirm if it's him.'

'I wish it were that simple.'

'The river?'

'I'm afraid so.'

'Schijt!' Anika hugged herself and walked round the room. Its cleanliness and orderliness were obviously her priority, thought Alison guiltily. Now she had dropped a bombshell into this other person's hardworking, practical and well-organised life.

If Anika could be blunt with her, she had to be blunter. 'More than one person can have the same tattoo. Just because our victim was found in your car doesn't mean he's the driver. However, we also found these. We think they may be significant too.'

'What are you talking about?'

Alison opened her briefcase and took out several photographs in a plastic folder. 'These are pictures of a green canvas tool bag we salvaged from the back of the Volvo. Each image shows a gardening tool manufactured in the Netherlands. The bag has the Dutch brand name Esschert on its side.'

'Lars owns a bag like that,' said Anika at once. 'He brought it with him from Holland.'

Alison's heart beat faster. 'So Lars is a gardener.'

'Yes he is. But you already know that, don't you.'

'I have to follow every line of enquiry.'

'Every year Lars had a job planting bulbs for the Keukenhof Exhibition. After we moved to England he had trouble finding employment he liked nearly so much.'

'You all right?' asked Alison anxiously, as Anika flung open a door overlooking the sea. A stark white light glared back at her from the water. She gripped the ornate iron rail of the balcony with both hands and let the wind blow her black hair over her eyes while she gazed towards the cloudy horizon. If she had come across as loud and opinionated just now, she was in reality a very private person.

'I was sick. I was afraid for my baby. I told him not to go.'

'Go where Anika?'

'Something about it didn't sound right… It was too good to be true.'

Alison stepped after her on to the balcony. Her host might be very down-to-earth and not easily swayed by emotion, but six months ago something had caused her heart to overrule her head. 'Tell me what happened. Start from the beginning.'

'There was an advertisement in a gardening magazine: "Workers wanted for special project. Initial twelve months' contract. Bed and board provided. Contact Lady…". I forget the name.'

'So what worried you?'

Anika sighed. The fierce glow of the sea was hurting her eyes, or she was blinking back tears. 'Who creates a whole garden in a year?'

'Go on.'

'The owner wanted to establish a "hortus conclusus", which I thought very odd.'

'A "hortus conclusus"?'

'It's a garden within walls. In medieval times such places represented an intensely private and impregnable, even divine space. Not worldly. The way she spoke of it in her Zoom meeting with Lars made it sound almost supernatural. Of course he was excited. The "hortus conclusus" figures large in the history of gardening. It is a place of miracles. As such it represents the Virgin Mary's closed off womb and a place of immaculate conception. Such a garden is without original sin. You can expect to see in it such things as a cedar tree, an olive tree, a fountain and rosebush. That's why two pilgrimage sites are dedicated to "Mary of the Enclosed Garden" in the Dutch-Flemish region of the Netherlands where I come from. One is the statue at the hermitage-chapel in Warfhuizen: "Our Lady of the Enclosed Garden". The second, Onze Lieve Vrouw van Tuine – literally "Our Lady of the Garden", is venerated in the cathedral of Ypres. People who are very ill or in desperate situations go there to invoke her help, which is what I said we should do…'

'Why is that?'

'I was pregnant and ill with pre-eclampsia.'

'Go on.'

'Instead he got it into his head that he could save me and our child by creating something worthy of the Virgin Mary right here in England. He hoped God might spare our son if he did good work in an almost sacred project. I proposed that we move back to Holland permanently but Lars wouldn't agree. He saw it as failure with a big F. We rowed horribly about it. I told him that the new job sounded like a snare and delusion.'

'You smelt a rat?'

'I blame myself.'

'How is any of this your fault?'

'I didn't prevent him.'

'Why *didn't* you stop him taking the job?' asked Alison, sensing something else.

'It was hopeless. He was totally spell-bound by it right from the start. It's hard to explain. I couldn't get through to him. In the end I threw the car keys at him and told him to go wherever he liked.'

'When did you last hear from him?'

'It was early to mid-August. Since then nothing. I suffered a seizure and lost my baby. I nearly died but Lars didn't come home. He stopped ringing me. I thought that was it… that it was all over between us. It never occurred to me that he might be missing.'

'I'll need anything you have of his – a brush, comb or some item of clothing. I need to check them for DNA.'

Anika buried her head in her hands. 'I should never have said what I did to him. It meant nothing.'

'Here's my card. Ring me if you think of anything else.'

'He left a comb behind in the bathroom. And he didn't take his slippers.'

It took a few minutes to find and bag the evidence. 'Do you want me to arrange for a Family Liaison Officer to support you during the investigation?'

'You said it yourself. We don't yet know if it's Lars. We can't say for sure he's dead. Now I want you to leave.'

'Of course,' said Alison. 'I'll inform you of the results of the DNA test as soon as possible.'

But Anika turned back to her balcony. 'Looks like a storm is coming. You can always tell by the smell of the sea – those waves are building to something big.'

'One last thing,' said Alison, before she let herself out. 'What address did Lars give you?'

'It's where you come from. It's in Gloucestershire. He had to drive to a place called Green Way House in the village of Shurdington, near Cheltenham.'

'Was the owner's name Frost by any chance? Lady Ann Frost?'

'That's it. That's the name he mentioned.'

'Are you sure?'

'Her ladyship might not be willing to pay him as much as he would like, he said, but he wanted to help her with her vision of a perfect garden. Lars told me his life needed new purpose. As if a baby wasn't enough!'

***

Alison sat in her car by Brighton's busy promenade and Googled "Our Lady of the Enclosed Garden" on her mobile phone. The Sorrowful Mother of Warfhuizen appeared on its screen holding a white handkerchief. She looked resplendent in her gold crown and jewellery and richly embroidered mantle. She held the handkerchief to wipe away her tears.

It was all slightly odd and not a little alien to her own eyes since she had stopped attending church very often, but that didn't detract from the genuine hope, longing, desperation. 'Anika is right,' said Alison to herself. '"Our Lady of the Enclosed Garden" represents Mary's pity for her Son. Pilgrims concerned for their sick relatives go to her for her blessing. They record their heartfelt pleas on behalf of their ill or injured children in the book of intentions. Whoever wants a walled garden at Green Way House shares Lars Visser's faith in divine intervention? They need a miracle of their own?'

26

Zac's Nurseries
Greenway Lane

'Do you sing old ballads?' asked Laura.

The good-looking plantsman with long pink hair eyed her rather casually. Almost too casually. This was the first time she had ventured out of the garden since her arrival. His vast airy glasshouse with its view of the hills might only be a few yards from Green Way House but it was like a different world. He struck her as very laid back and unconcerned. He was probably happiest with a spliff in one hand and a pot plant in the other, she decided.

He shot her a toothy smile. 'I do sometimes sing to my plants, I must admit. I do it when I'm working late at night trying to catch up on orders. Why do you ask?'

'I might have heard you. My caravan is just across the lane on the other side of the wall.'

'Sorry if I get a bit carried away.'

'Do you ever sing songs about gardens?'

'I'm more of a Country fan.'

'It can't have been you then. My name's Laura.'

'Howdy. What can I do for you?'

'Lady Ann Frost sent me.'

'So it's true? She really has hired new help? What does the witch want this time?'

'You should have some Rosa Mundi for her,' said Laura, doing her

138

best to ignore his barb.

'You've left it a bit late in the season. It's the winter solstice tonight.'

'We've dug new beds by the house ready for planting.'

'We?'

'I'm staying at Green Way House with two other gardeners.'

'There were three of you last time. I'm Zac by the way…'

'Pleased to meet you.'

'Well Laura, you're in luck. I have those Rosa Mundi for you. It's easily the most popular of the old roses.'

Zac obviously enjoyed his own flamboyance – he didn't mind that his garish bow tie in daffodil yellow might not be to everyone's taste. 'Lady Ann usually buys her plants from you, does she?'

'I thought she'd abandoned any attempt to remake her garden… on account of what happened.'

'She told me somebody suffered an accident.'

'Which one?'

'You mean there was more than one?'

'I've heard screams come from the garden.'

'What screams? When?'

Zac flinched. 'All these questions!'

'What about them?'

'I only got to know the girl. She was your age but prettier. She lived in an ancient yellow caravan in the grounds.'

'Did you get her name?'

'Lolly Hooper. She told me she liked to paint pictures in her spare time.'

'Lolly Hooper?' said Laura promptly. 'Are you quite sure that's who she was?'

'I quite fancied her to be honest. She wears sexy little scarves like the one you're wearing now. Lovely long red hair! I offered to buy her a drink in the local pub, but she said Lady Ann wouldn't approve. Lolly wasn't supposed to stray too far from Green Way House during the evenings. No one was.'

'That I can believe.'

'Then you'll know by now that Lady Ann is a great one for rules. She doesn't want her staff wasting her time, I suppose, though what business it is of hers what people do after work hours, I can't say. Everyone should be able to enjoy themselves once in a while. But no, she wants perfect workers for her perfect garden.'

'Where is Lolly now? Have you any idea?'

'Search me. All I can say is that she left Green Way House without telling me goodbye. She just did a runner one day. Very rude! I put aside the Rosa Mundi for her at her request and charged them to Lady Ann's account as instructed.'

'Lady Ann didn't think to collect them herself?'

Zac shrugged. 'Her ladyship has bought a great many plants for her garden over the years, but nothing much ever seems to thrive. That's what happens when you try to impose the new on the bones of the old.'

'Why do you say that?'

'A garden that old knows what it does and doesn't like. Plants live there without disturbance, it has been reseeding and regenerating itself for so long.'

'You've seen behind the walls then?'

'Yes, but it's none of my business.'

'Don't worry, I won't ask you to act as informant.'

Zac gave her another toothy grin. 'You'll realise what I mean in a few weeks' time. Wait until the snowdrops flower. What a sight! Like snow! Big Dutch crocuses come along a month later and crowd them out, but not before you'll see something quite extraordinary. You'll find winter aconites by the thousand. When they're all in full bloom the garden shines like gold.'

'I wish I had your faith.'

'Is that what you think?'

'Frankly I find Green Way House a little sad somehow. A bittersweet shadow hangs over it. Things have happened there and not just long ago.'

'People will tell you that its over-zealous creator set out to express his grief at the loss of his wife and son, but surely he meant it to be a celebration of their worth as much as their demise? Then again, any garden is the repository of our greatest emotions. Think of it as a glorious act of perpetual reawakening. Okay, so you might not be able to see much above ground yet, but believe me it is full of bulbs and tubers. Those fleshy roots are stores of moisture and food for the plants' hibernation – everything is quietly continuing unseen, ready for spring's great revival.'

'I guess any garden can surprise us.'

'Better still, it can give us hope.'

Laura nodded with a zeal of her own. Nothing wholly described the unpredictable feelings she felt, ever since starting work in Green Way House's secluded grounds. The garden stimulated heart-felt sympathies and sensations. Not for the first time she found herself wanting to ascribe to it the word 'passion'. 'You're very enthusiastic about gardening, aren't you?'

'Plants are my way of expressing what I feel. They make me come alive.'

'I'm sorry, I should have brought a wheelbarrow with me. I'll never carry all these plants back to the house in one go by myself.'

'I still have the wheelbarrow that Lolly left behind.'

'One quick question. Did you mean it when you said she did a runner?'

'None of my business is what I said.'

'Except the garden did seriously hurt someone?'

'Something like that.'

'What did you witness?'

'Shit happens, I guess.'

'If I told you I don't feel entirely safe there, would you believe me?'
'That's too bad.'
'You'd tell me if something really awful occurred, wouldn't you? You'd tell me if the garden maimed or killed someone?'
'All I know is that Lady Ann is never satisfied. No gardener can give her what she wants, because what she wants does not exist outside paradise.'
'So tell me, what is it she has been unable to create so far, in your opinion?'
'Lolly told me she feared her ladyship won't rest until she has a haven that is pure, spotless, without fault. In her own mind it has to be free from all flaws and mistakes.'
'No wonder everyone leaves.'
'You should too…'
'I hardly think so.'
'If you still can.'
Laura suddenly disapproved of Zac even more than before. She had no confidence in him. He was too ready to dismiss her as a fraud just like those detractors and doubters at her university? He looked at her as if he could see straight through her bluff and pretention, just because nobody knew as much about his beloved plants as he did. 'Lady Ann is perfectly entitled to create what she likes, no matter how immaculate.'
'Good luck with that.'
'You'll see, I might just help her do it this time.'
'And if she's delusional?'
'I'll be the judge of that.'
'Don't do anything foolish. Don't listen to her siren voice.'

27

'You do realise that today is Christmas Eve, don't you detective?' said Lady Ann Frost sharply. Dressed in a shocking pink dress embroidered with red roses, she did her best to block Green Way House's front door.

Alison shivered in the shadows.

'I called before, but the gates were locked and I couldn't make anyone hear me.'

'I only allow visitors by appointment.'

This was the first time she had managed to view the house this close. She could only say she could feel it resist her. She took a step forward and sensed at once how prepared the old mansion was to foil, thwart and forestall her? At the same time Green Way House stood proud within the high brick walls of its extensive garden. 'As I said on the phone, I need to ask you a few questions about one of your gardeners.'

'Very well detective, if you insist. Follow me.'

'You have a very impressive home, if I may say so? It must date back hundreds of years.'

'My husband is dead but he bequeathed me his fortune.'

'You must miss him?'

Lady Ann bridled. She was slightly neurotic, uptight and twitchy today. 'Why would you say that? I never said that. Just because people are dead doesn't mean I can't have the place to myself.' It was her rebuff, her block, her parry.

They passed by the hall's wrought iron fireplace, with its cracked motifs of leaves and grapes, to enter the drawing room. Her reluctant host picked up a black enamelled cigarette case with a red rose in its centre – she flicked it open to offer Alison one of three cocktail cigarettes, but she declined. 'No thank you. I don't smoke.'

'Neither do I, but I pretend I do because my mother said it was more sophisticated.'

Alison warmed herself at the fireplace. She watched its flames illuminate carnation-like flowers carved on the chimney piece's columns as well as its grotesque human heads and dragons. That chill she had felt at the front door had not gone away. 'The person I'm enquiring after is called Lars Visser.'

'I was afraid you were going to say that.'

'So you admit he was here?'

Lady Ann fingered a brooch on its safety catch. Fiddled with its pink and white everlasting flowers set under a Perspex dome. 'I hired him as my gardener along with two others in the summer.'

'Why Lars Visser especially? Was it because you and he were already acquainted?'

'I didn't know him from Adam. He simply answered my advertisement in "Gardening News". I thought it was meant to be. Being Dutch fitted the bill. Call it divine intervention.'

'What do you mean exactly?'

'I'm engaged on a project to restore Green Way House's grounds to their former splendour. You're right about it being old. Did you know its garden was originally laid out to a Dutch design in the 1690s?'

'I did not.'

'I thought a 21st century Dutchman like Lars might sympathise with the original creator's intentions.'

'Sounds ambitious. You are clearly very serious about it.'

'Have you ever lost someone very dear to you detective?'

'Excuse me?'

'If you saw the opportunity to bring someone you loved back from the dead, you would, wouldn't you?'

Alison looked at the fire and its hideous faces grinned at her. Their bulging eyes gleamed in the flames until they turned positively mischievous. 'Thanks to Covid-19 my father died all alone in a care home. I wasn't allowed to visit him in his final hours, I could only watch him through a window. It's hard to accept he has gone forever, I must admit.'

'If death were the end of the story we wouldn't still be trapped in it.'

'I'm not sufficiently religious if that's what you mean.'

Lady Ann walked to a chair and picked up a stone-coloured plastic bag by its handle. Two roses in shades of pink and heliotrope bloomed in its panel of hand-stitched wool tapestry at her fingertips. 'Tell me, what would you wish for if you had one wish only?'

'I'd wish my father was still alive.'

'Of course you would. Losing those close and dear to us is always a tragedy.' Next minute Lady Ann took out a photograph and brought it back to the light of the fire. She offered it to Alison. 'The young man in this picture is my son William. He came home for a weekend to celebrate my birthday shortly before Christmas five years ago… He decided to go for a quick stroll before returning to college. Instead he was virtually decapitated by a hit-and-run driver at the crossroads at the top of Greenway Lane. He died instantly.'

'It's a very dangerous junction.'

'What else do you know about it?'

'I know the driver was never caught.'

'Then you'll understand my frustration with people like you.'

'What's your son got to do with Lars Visser?'

'I hired Lars to remake the garden in his memory.'

Alison studied the good-looking student clad in enormous wig, coat, large black tricorne hat and red-heeled shoes. She turned the print over and a few words were written on its back. 'It says here that this picture was taken on stage in Bristol?'

'William died before he could begin his PHD on seventeenth century drama at Bristol University. He loved Restoration comedy plays. He did his first degree in the history of British drama. That's him playing Count Verole in "Sir Anthony Love" by Irish playwright Thomas Southerne. It premiered at the Theatre Royal in Drury Lane in London in 1690.'

Alison pointed to another, framed picture propped on the mantelpiece. 'Is that him too?'

'What? No. I mean yes.'

The boy in the second photograph bore an uncanny resemblance to his mother. It was not just the small nose and grey-blue eyes, it was like looking at Lady Ann reborn as the child she so dearly wished to have back in her life again. 'He looks different without his wig and costume.'

Lady Ann snatched the first picture back to avoid any more comparisons. She ducked Alison's gaze and her voice was evasive too. 'I really can't agree.'

'Did Lars Visser have enemies that you know of? Did he ever confide in you?'

'I'm not in the habit of trading secrets with people who work for me detective. Suppose you tell me why you're really here?'

'I'm sorry to say a body has been recovered from the River Severn. His partner has since supplied us with his comb and slippers. DNA testing indicates it is Mr Visser.'

Lady Ann's face set hard. 'A difficult man! He could be very direct, even brusque. He was a hard worker, but in the end he let me down.'

'How so?'

'I don't want to talk about it.'

'You must have been one of the last people to see him alive?'

'All I can say is that Lars failed to fully grasp what I wanted him to do. He couldn't love the garden the same way I love it. He wanted to do everything according to the latest fashion, whereas I see its restoration as an act of historical enquiry and homage – I wish to lay bare its point of inception in all its glory. Gardens back then were laid out according to certain rules that should be respected.'

Alison gazed at the hideous heads on the fireplace and they were all shuddering cries suddenly. 'A garden of mourning is an emotive subject. It would be wonderful to believe in something like that, but it's very personal. *To you.* Perhaps Lars felt your passion for it was a bit too much for him? Maybe he felt overwhelmed by the task you set him?'

'You can never tell a garden it is loved too much.'

'So you didn't fall out over it? He didn't depart Green Way House in a huff about anything?'

Lady Ann fiddled with her brooch. Turned and twisted it. 'One day he said something that made me think he might have quarrelled with somebody. It was preying on his mind all right. He said, "I shouldn't be here. I regret ever coming. I'm not wanted. None of us is." Soon afterwards his car was gone and he with it. Of course I assumed he had rushed home to his partner who was expecting his baby. The other gardeners had already left. Without them I've been at a loss what to do, until now.'

Alison glanced again at the ugly faces by the fire and they were watchful, wary, full of lies. 'You say you hired three gardeners for the summer. Who were the other two?'

'The young woman was Lolly Hooper. She claims to be a painter. Gardening is just one of her ways of financing her ambition to get into Art College. I asked her to paint me a picture of Green Way House and its garden, but she never has. Not that I've seen. Now I'm not sure where she is. It's as though she has decided to vanish from the face of the earth.'

'And the other?'

'His name is Paul Carter. In his Zoom interview he informed me that he had worked for two years as a scaffolder. A nasty fall on a building site in Bristol saw him break his leg. It left him with a bad back which meant he could no longer climb ladders very easily. I felt sorry for him. He couldn't bear to work indoors, he said, so he decided to try his hand at gardening. Pain still got the better of him, unfortunately, which is maybe why he chose to leave Green Way House so suddenly. Or he never did like hard work.'

'He didn't give any other reason?'

'No he didn't, but he has… how shall I put it… a serious weakness.'

'What weakness?'

'He is too fond of cannabis.'

'I see.'

'It's the reason why I was going to fire him. I can't abide that sort of thing. Don't get me wrong detective. Paul isn't all bad. He's a lively person with a keen sense of mischief. You'll recognise him when you meet him if I tell you he has a great cackle of a laugh. Come to think of it, I have a parcel for him. It arrived a week ago from a bookseller in Redland in Bristol.'

'May I see it?'

'Really?'

'That would be useful.'

'I've been meaning to return it to the sender's address written on the back of the package.'

Alison glanced out of the window. Through its tangled ivy she saw someone walk by carrying a spade on their shoulder. She failed to observe their features, on account of the large black hat they wore on their head. She might or might not have just heard them whistle a song:

> O think upon the garden, love,
> Where you and I did walk.
> The fairest flower that blossomed there
> Is withered on its stalk.

'I'm glad to see the garden's restoration has resumed in earnest.'

'What's that?' asked Lady Ann and rushed to see for herself who was in the grounds. The person in the hat was already gone round a corner. Or the ivy was too thick for her to see that far. She shivered, then frowned. 'Vital work must go on detective.'

'Absolutely.'

Next minute Lady Ann opened a drawer in a desk and held out a white jiffy bag. 'I find it strange Paul hasn't asked me for it.'

'Have you tried ringing him?' asked Alison.

'His phone won't answer.'

'I'd like to keep this parcel if I may. The sender might help me find him. I need to ask Paul about Lars.'

'Be my guest.'

'I'm sorry about your son, your ladyship. I'd like to think one day I'll catch the driver that ran him down. Perhaps then I might hope to put your mind at rest.'

'And if hope is not enough?'

'What else is there?'

Lady Ann led the way to the door. 'Do you trust in miracles detective?'

'I'd like to.'

'You should. It's what we believe in that matters most. I'm not just talking about good intentions, I mean to make it happen. I like to think I've already begun.'

'I wish it were that simple.'

'Believe me detective, the garden I'm creating will be my son's perfect memorial.'

Alison stepped out of the house into the grounds strewn with weeds and rubble. 'You have certainly got your work cut out.'

'Who doesn't adore a beautiful garden?' said Lady Ann, looking intently all round. Her lip twitched nervously. 'Only a garden can make you feel nothing bad will ever happen again. Good luck with your enquiries. I'm sorry I can't tell you more about Mr Visser. My butler John Mortimer will meet you at the same gate you came in. He'll let you out with his skeleton key.'

***

Alison stood alone on the steps of Green Way House and surveyed its grounds. There had to be up to eight gated plots within the walls, resembling rooms in a house. All were in varying states of decay. The knot garden was railed off from the upper court, the court from some fruit trees, the fruit trees from a rose walk, the walk from another orchard, the orchard from a wild wood et cetera… and that was just what she could see.

The layout was definitely to a Dutch design. She could say this with some accuracy, since the parcel from Bristol turned out to be a book detailing the history of Green Way House and its garden from 1636 to 1697. Inside was a large, fold-out reproduction of a contemporary engraving that showed house and grounds as they had been more than three hundred years ago. The resemblance to today's plan was uncanny.

What's more, the book's flyleaf depicted the original owner dressed in his gold waistcoat and long black wig. His portrait showed him seated in the entrance to his garden edged with tall cypresses. It was William Lawrence.

She was suddenly back in the Restoration England that Lady Ann's dead son had so adored.

28

Mr Mortimer, on high alert, let Laura back into the garden. Hastily re-locked the gate. 'You took your time. My feet are freezing.'

'Give me the key and I can come and go as I please.'

'No one keeps keys to Green Way House except me. Her ladyship is most particular about it. She has stated quite categorically that this gate is to be kept…'

'*Locked at all times.* I know.'

Mr Mortimer shot her a sharp look. 'There wasn't any trouble at the nursery, I hope.'

'It seems Lady Ann paid for these roses months ago.'

'So what kept you?'

'I was chatting to Zac,' admitted Laura blithely and pushed her wheelbarrow full of plants past the grumpy butler. 'He was telling me about the red-haired girl who worked here in the summer.'

'Oh he was, was he?'

'Her name is Lolly Hooper. You must remember her.'

'That girl deceived us all. Her ladyship should never have hired her. She was a liar and a fantasist. But how do you tell? None of us could have predicted she would go so crazy, could we?'

'Are you saying Lady Ann and Lolly quarrelled?'

His smile was full of regret but also spite. 'That girl didn't deserve to be here.'

'Sounds harsh.'

'The fool went around saying the garden "deserved better".'

'Fool is a strong word,' said Laura. *Girl* was downright insulting.

'Lolly kept asking: "What if the garden already has a gardener of its own?"'

Laura's heart missed a beat. She pushed her barrow with increased gusto. 'Who might that be?'

'In the end she shut herself in her caravan. Went on strike. She objected to working anywhere in the grounds by herself. "Did we not know what lay in store for us?" she kept asking. "Why didn't someone tell her before she arrived? Somebody must have heard things about this place". That girl went off her head, I tell you.'

'Doesn't sound very scientific.'

'How would you put it? She kept trying to tell us she heard someone singing outside her door.'

'You did say Lady Ann lives here all alone, didn't you?'

'Who else should there be?' snapped Mr Mortimer. It was a plea, a protest, almost a profanity.

Laura watched him storm off back to the house, when the wildest thought occurred to her: whoever you saw, dear Lolly, is still here no matter how much our resentful butler pretends otherwise?

***

'Where's Ray?' asked Laura, the second she met Barry in front of the house.

'He's fixing a cold frame somewhere.'

'Good. It's you I want to talk to, not him.'

Barry indicated he was busy as well. 'I did hope to place these rose bushes in one of these trenches we've dug – we need to heel them in with soil so their roots can't dry out while we wait for better weather. Trouble is, the temperature last night was too severe. The frozen ground has set rock solid. Besides, the soil needs time to settle.'

'Please, I don't know what to do…'

'Luckily I've found this excellent potting shed where we can keep them frost-free.'

'Forget the damned roses, will you?'

'Follow me and I'll show you.'

'I've just been told the name of one of the gardeners who worked here during the summer. She's called Lolly Hooper.'

Barry paused at the shed's door. 'Not what I was expecting.'

'Zac met her at the nurseries. Guess what, she lived in the same caravan I'm living in.'

'And why not?'

'Don't you see? That blood on the floor could belong to her?'

Next minute Barry led the way past hundreds of red terracotta pots, big and small, that had been stored on shelves and floor. 'Let me make myself clear Laura. I'm here to create a garden. Whatever else you think you've found will have a quite innocent explanation, you'll see.'

'Not if it was Lolly who wrote HELP ME before she vanished?'

'No one but you is implying she has come to any harm.'

'Why else should I sense such a strong connection?'

'What connection?'

'Lolly met a prowler too.'

'I thought we agreed there's no such thing?'

'She shut herself in her caravan and wouldn't come out. She refused to work alone in the garden. She must have feared she wasn't going to leave this place alive.'

'Don't be ridiculous.'

'Who saw her go? Zac didn't.'

'So?'

'She didn't even tell him goodbye.'

'I have a suggestion.'

'What?'

Barry waved his hand about. 'Help me put sacks over these roses and forget all about her.'

'I would but for one thing. Do you know Lolly is a nickname for Laura? Since I have the same name, will I suffer the same fate?'

'Not likely. This cruel and savage attack you are imagining never happened. It's only in your head.'

'It's like this. Ever since coming here I've started to think the worst thoughts ever, which also happen to be the best ones.'

'Whatever do you mean?'

'I keep imagining how good it would be to do what I liked to that rich boy who took my virginity while I slept. He violated me. It's the sense of entitlement I can't forgive. Instead I feel as if nothing can ever be perfect again... My whole life is measured against one base act, when before I was so full of hope. How do I get that back? How do I lay the spectre of it to rest? How does anyone? Where do I go to find out?'

'That's funny,' said Barry, 'because I've been having some pretty wild thoughts too. I've found myself wishing I could strangle the person who got me convicted of a murder I didn't commit. I've just spent years in prison for some killer whose name I don't even know. It's not a desire for revenge per se, it's about restarting the clock – I want back that innocent person I used to be before all the injustice, vilification and shame that I endured behind bars.'

'Admit it. There's something about this place that would have us feel complete again. Perhaps Lolly felt it too. It would have us be like Adam and Eve in their first hours, naked and alone? To get back to our own beginning we have to weed out the ugly parts of ourselves and start over?'

'La-di-da! Aren't you the seer!'

'You and I deserve better, Barry. We are due some happiness. Neither of us should have to fear false accusations ever again, not if we are pure of heart. "Sticks and stones may break my bones, but words will never hurt me".'

'There you are then! What are you worrying about?'
'Except it only takes one little bit of malice to make it murder.'
'Don't be stupid. Stop trying to play the detective.'
'Hallo, who's that over there?' said Laura, looking up quickly.
'Where?'
'Walking past the house.'
'Oh her? She's here to visit her ladyship.'
'What for?'
Barry pulled a face. 'She's from the police.'
'The police? Really?'
'Hey, where are you going?'
'There's something I must do.'
'What's that?'
'If you won't take me seriously then perhaps someone else will.'

29

With the book came a handwritten note.

Alison flattened the piece of paper in the palm of her hand. It was a few words from the Bristol bookseller: "Dear Mr Carter, herewith the item you requested relating to "Shurdington", the seat of William Lawrence (now called Green Way House.) I'm sorry it has taken so long to obtain it, but not many copies survive. It may give credence to what you and your friends have been seeing? The garden you plan to restore is the morbid construction of an obsessive recluse. It is mired in deep melancholy. This is the product of a man who conceived it while shut up alone with his most violent sorrows. He was deranged. Lost. Obsessed. Totally out of control. You should get away while you still can."

No sooner did Alison finish reading the message when she heard a shout.

She looked up: a breathless young woman was hurrying towards her along the side of the house.

She hugged its wall like a thief. 'Is it true you're from the police?'

'Who's asking?' said Alison.

'I thought I saw your car parked in the lane… My name is Laura Bloom. I'm one of Green Way House's new gardeners.'

'I'm Detective Sergeant Alison Ellis from the Gloucestershire Constabulary. Is something wrong?'

The girl was pale, nervous, shifty. 'I need to show you something.'

'The butler is waiting for me at the gate…'

'You are here about the murder, aren't you?'

'What are you calling a murder?'

'This way. We'd better hurry.'

The girl struck Alison as very earnest. Apart from her jeans she wore a baggy cardigan and spectacles that were almost too large for her rather plain face, like a scholar's. The heavy glasses kept slipping down her nose as she marched speedily along. Yet what drove her now was more physical than mental – she was caught up in the force of the moment.

They soon arrived at a shabby yellow caravan parked in the grounds. Laura opened the door and pointed inside. 'I can't sleep at night for thinking about it.'

'What is it?'

'Go past the gas cooker to the forward apartment.'

'I don't see anything.'

'Look on the floor by the bed-settee. Lift the loose corner of lino.'

'Where?'

Laura hurried aboard the caravan after her. 'What do you mean *where?*'

'There's nothing.'

'You can't miss it.'

'You sure about this?'

'It was written right there, I tell you.'

'All I see is a piece of new board.'

'Can't be!'

'It's a new patch of floor all right.'

'Somebody has been in here while I've been at work in the garden,' said Laura with dismay. 'Lady Ann must have put them up to it.'

'Why Lady Ann?'

'She spies on us from her glass lantern high on top of Green Way House. From up there she can see into every corner of the garden.'

'Whatever was here is gone now.'

'I know what I saw. Someone wrote HELP ME in blood in the aisle.'

Alison wanted to believe her. 'Have you told anyone else about this?'

'Only Barry, my fellow gardener.'

'So you haven't mentioned it to her ladyship?'

Laura blanched. 'How can I say anything when she might have a hand in it too?'

'What makes you so certain there is a killer?'

'I've seen somebody. Here. In the grounds.'

'Can you describe him?'

'Lady Ann must know who he is. She patrols the garden with her gun.'

'So you can't tell me what he looks like?'

'The only way you'll make this right, detective, is to interview her as soon as possible. Do it today under caution at the police station.'

'I can't do that when there's no crime.'

'Are you even listening to me?'

'Show me the evidence.'

'Why won't anyone ever believe me?'

'Look, here's my card. Ring me if you find anything else suspicious.'

'It's pathetic.'

'No, it's lack of proof.'

'Same thing.'

That moment Mr Mortimer arrived at the caravan's open door. 'Oh there you are detective. I thought I'd lost you.'

'What do you know about blood on the floor of this caravan?' Alison asked him immediately.

Mr Mortimer looked vacant. His blind white eye professed ignorance. His casual indifference shocked her. She had asked him an important question but his aloofness bordered on dismissal. 'Her ladyship likes to shoot rabbits and foxes from her balcony. One night a badly wounded vixen crawled in here and expired on the bare wooden floor. I covered the bloodstains temporarily with lino, but part of the chipboard was so badly stained that I decided to rip it up and replace it this morning. It's more hygienic. I should have done it weeks ago except I've been too busy.'

Laura nearly choked. 'What vixen writes HELP ME in her own blood?'

'Is that what you saw: HELP ME?'

'As good as.'

'Meaning what exactly?'

'The letters were very faint because someone had done their best to erase them with bleach. They spelt H . L P M .'

'So they didn't actually spell HELP ME, did they?'

'What else?' said Laura, wavering.

'You saw what you wanted to see,' declared Mr Mortimer. 'Nothing more.'

Alison stepped outside. 'There's an easy way to settle this. Please show me the piece of chipboard that you took from the floor.'

'I just burnt it.'

'Out of my way,' said Laura. 'You've done enough to discredit me as it is.' She jumped back in the caravan and slammed its door shut behind her.

'Strange girl,' said Mr Mortimer, with regret. 'She doesn't realise what a privilege it is to work for Green Way House. But don't worry, she'll come around to her ladyship's way of thinking. They all do. Either that or they have to leave.'

***

As the butler walked away he sang a ditty in the garden. Laura sat on the edge of her bed-settee and tried not to listen.

There was something mocking about it. His voice called to mind the sad voice she had resisted so far, except his rendition struck her as altogether too vile and clever.

The way he sang it sounded a warning:
>   Now if you were not true in word,
>   As now I know you be,
>   I'd tear you as the withered leaves,
>   Are torn from off the tree.

30

That night Laura kept careful watch from her caravan's window.

She lay in wait for whoever would sing to her again – this time she would catch them red-handed.

Either Mr Mortimer was her stalker or he was in league with who was. He had chosen to imitate someone in order to cow her, only she was not prepared to be silenced that easily. When the police wouldn't take her seriously she must act by herself. Something odd was going on in Green Way House. Bad things happened to people here and she wasn't about to be one of them.

It was not easy at first to distinguish anyone from the darkness.

Just then the moonlight lit the rhinestone flowers on a person's black, long-sleeved sweater.

It wasn't Mr Mortimer.

Laura buttoned up her denim jacket in a hurry.

Listened for a song.

Instead Lady Ann passed by silently on her nocturnal round – she stopped every few yards to observe the ground…

Laura waited while she shone a torch at her feet.

…as she looked for signs of someone's recent passage.

Then Laura grabbed her scarf and beanie and slipped out of the caravan's door to go in pursuit.

Her ladyship's whole demeanour suggested someone hungry for almost scientific answers – she treated each possible clue like a person conducting experiments. She carried a loaded shotgun over one arm as usual.

Twice the chatelaine retraced the tracks of her quarry. "Seek, and ye shall find", thought Laura. "Patience is a virtue". Next minute Lady Ann steered for the chicken run situated beyond the south-east range. She walked right round its wire fence where she stooped to search for more clues.

Anyone else might suppose she was hunting foxes.

But when Laura did the same she found no trace of anything living.

Still her ladyship deployed all her powers of concentration – she behaved as if there was definitely someone to be detected.

Laura suddenly snapped a twig underfoot. Froze in the gloom. That crack of breaking wood sounded, to her ears, absolutely deafening.

Like a gunshot.

'You know where I am,' cried Lady Ann defiantly. 'Come find me.'

Laura did not move. Held her breath. To her right a long line of trees stretched to the foot of the hill at the garden's south-eastern boundary. Open countryside lay beyond that, up the slope to the tree-topped escarpment. She was caught in the open? Except she was not the one being addressed...

Lady Ann uttered a deep sigh. Consulted her wristwatch. She behaved in a way that suggested someone or some*thing* had just failed to rise to her challenge.

It wasn't a fox.

No animal set foot on lawns grown so wild.

That's not to say her ladyship was all angry frustration, Laura noted. On the contrary, she suddenly beat a hasty retreat back to the house. She rushed to bolt its front door top and bottom.

Lady Ann locked herself in as if greatly relieved to prove her worst fears unfounded – she too had feared to be serenaded tonight by some beautiful melody that was even older than the words?

31

Next day Lady Ann Frost was all nerves. She clutched her coat tight across her chest while she shivered in the chilly air. Her grey-blue eyes were as cool as her name. She was distressed, worried, fretful. If it was on account of her failure to discover anything last night she didn't say so. Instead she simply fretted. 'That wretched police officer had no right to ask so many questions. No right at all. Did Detective Sergeant Ellis mention if she was coming back at all?'

Barry glanced at Laura. She did the same to Ray. 'Any reason why she should?'

'Mr Mortimer says he found her poking about inside your caravan, Laura.'

'It was a silly misunderstanding.'

'I trust you will not have reason to speak to her again.'

'Can't say I will,' lied Laura promptly.

'Me neither,' said Ray, 'I'm keeping out of her way.'

'Just to be clear, did DS Ellis go anywhere else in the garden before she departed?'

'Anywhere else?' asked Laura. Her ladyship was using one thing to distract from another.

'Was she looking for something? Here for instance? At this tree?'

'As I say your ladyship, there was a bit of a mis…'

'If it's all right with you,' said Barry, eager to change the subject, 'but we have a lot of couch grass to dig up this morning.'

'Not so fast,' said Lady Ann and paced about rubbing her hands. She chewed her bottom lip and her eyes looked set to pop out of her head. 'As you can see, this tree leans over the wall into Green Way Lane in a most dangerous manner. I want it felled right now, do you hear? You can use this ladder I've brought you.'

'Are you sure?' asked Laura, taken aback.

'I want it chopped! Axed! Burnt!'

'But why destroy such a fine specimen?' Laura objected. The formerly smooth trunk, so characteristic of beeches, had acquired the rough bark of antiquity. Trees were like people: they could grow impressive wrinkles.

Lady Ann instantly ran out of patience. 'Do you think I don't know my own mind? Can't you see it has outgrown its usefulness? Those great balls of mistletoe hanging off its branches have sucked the life out of it.'

'It may look half dead,' said Barry, 'but this beech is a pillar of the garden. True, it's forked…'

'Like the Devil's tail.'

'…and each fork has its own crown which has strained the trunk where the two divide.'

'Like the Devil's tongue.'

'A tree will always break at its weakest point, but that may never happen.'

'Since when do you make all the decisions?'

'See here where the rain has washed away the soil. Its roots are densely entwined with those of its brothers and sisters. They have grown up together and will most likely die together. To fell such a titan will expose the others to storms and drought. A family of trees is like a family of people – each one can only be as strong as those around it.'

'The hateful, evil thing disgusts me,' said Lady Ann. She began to trample on its thousands of beechnuts in a tantrum – she stamped and smashed their crunchy brown mast to destroy its bumper crop and legacy.

'Barry's right, this tree is king of the garden,' said Laura with enthusiasm.

'You disobeying me too?'

'No, but…'

'Can't I trust any of you at all?'

'Of course, only…'

'Then finish what others have failed to do. Kill the damned thing before it kills us all.'

***

As soon as Lady Ann had stormed off, Laura approached the beech and embraced it. 'She really has got it in for you, old chum. She speaks as if you and she are mortal enemies.'

'Her ladyship meant what she said,' said Ray. 'Someone has tried to fell this tree once already.'

Barry nodded sadly. 'They've half girdled it with a saw not too long ago. They've begun to remove a strip of bark to stop its growth. Had they succeeded they would have condemned the poor thing to a slow death over several years.'

'You saying it's badly wounded?' asked Laura.

'A tear in its bark is like a tear in our skin. This tree is in pain. It needs its bark to take sugar from its leaves to its roots. Without food the roots can't pump water back up to the crown. Break the continuity of its bark and the whole tree will dry out.'

'We must assume it was the previous gardeners?'

'Who else?'

'Who or what caused them to stop their murderous mission, I wonder?'

'Maybe the tree bit back,' said Ray and laughed. 'Maybe that's why Lady Ann hates to go near it?'

Laura gently placed her hand on the expanse of exposed trunk. She felt the festering wound. This was no rotting cadaver, not yet, but she recoiled from slimy black fungi that wept like poison from the hideous gash. Some might say the beech, not she, recoiled with pain. Not everything was lost: some kind hand had smeared tar on the bare wood to save and seal it. 'I don't think we should do anything more to it, do you? It's not fair.'

'We do what we're paid to do,' said Ray. 'Besides, felling half a tree is more fun than digging new rose beds. I'm all for it.'

'I don't think the garden will like it.'

'What do you mean *like*?'

'Nothing.'

Barry straightened his cap on his head. Picked up the ladder. 'We'd better start by cutting off that big branch that overhangs the lane.'

'Is this ladder sound?' asked Laura, still hoping to stave off disaster.

'Looks sound enough to me.'

'What do you say I climb up and take a look first?'

'Meanwhile I'll fetch another saw from the stables,' said Ray, sloping off.

Laura propped the ladder against the trunk and set about mounting its wooden rungs. "Nothing ventured, nothing gained… Cowards may die many times before their death". She ascended most of the way up the fork that was to be lopped, only to stop at the sight of something cut in its bark. 'Guess what?'

'What can you see?' called Barry from below.

'Someone has carved a couple of words and a date up here. It says "cor unum 1697".'

'I'm familiar with the Latin names of plants but I'm not sure what that says.'

'It says "one heart 1697".'

'Are you joking?'

'How fast do beech trees grow, do you reckon?'

Barry thought a minute. 'They can take ten years to get to two feet high. To reach fifty feet will take eighty years. Why do you ask?'

'So it would only have been a sapling in 1697.'

'I see what you mean.'

'Betty told me this garden wasn't created until 1696 or so. Does it look that ancient to you?'

'Usually only pollarded trees last that long.'

'Is that a yes?'

'Well, our tree has definitely been pollarded, hence the fork in its trunk.'

'Or someone climbed up here and carved "one heart" a lot more recently. But why carve 1697? Why pretend to belong to so long ago?'

'Whatever the truth, Lady Ann wants it gone. We should hurry. The sky's getting darker. It will rain soon.'

'There's something else up here,' said Laura.

'Be careful.'

'I can see something on a branch over there. I might just be able to reach it if I lean sideways...' Next minute she wobbled very badly. She felt the ladder glide away invisibly beneath her. She rocked... lost her grip on its wooden struts. The tree spun as she spiralled. The ground rushed up and suddenly she was heading straight for it. With a burst of sky it was like being blinded, but then the drop was so quick there was only a sense of darkness descending. She went to scream but no scream sounded...

She felt certain she was going to die when a branch broke her fall.

That's when she landed.

Her head tore up the ground and it was all soft beech mast and roots. She heard a voice shouting. She thought she detected gasps, sighs, wails. She tried to move but something else stopped her. There was a great blow to her head and she saw the tree's black, bare branches lift and dance violently before she heard Barry say, 'For heaven's sake Laura!

Are you okay? What the hell did you think you were doing?'

'I found this.'

Barry prised open her grazed fingers. 'Where did you get it?'

'It was snagged on a branch.'

'It's a lock of red hair.'

Laura sat up painfully but triumphantly. 'Lolly Hooper had red hair.'

'Never mind her. Are you quite sure you haven't broken any bones?'

'I reckon she climbed up to view the same carving I did.'

'Better call it a day.'

'What if she slipped like me as she tried to make sense of it?'

'You're going to have some pretty impressive bruises.'

'Lolly might not have been so lucky.'

'Just forget it.'

'No, this is evidence.'

***

That evening Laura sat listening to the wind and sleet. It was only five o'clock but already the day had ended in darkness. The snowy blasts coated the caravan's windows in white ice before she realised: it was not the rattle of the frozen rain that had her full attention.

She listened harder to identify a subdued, continuous whispering as of waves. The murmur of scratchy twigs was a barely audible expression of discontent. Low tones complained, grumbled and emitted mournful calls borne to her by the breeze.

Laura wrapped herself in a blanket and opened the caravan's door. She did so as gusts of wind bent the trees in the garden. At first they all swayed together, but some swung back faster than others. Bare branches clashed, rose and fell again, but not so violently. Instead the biggest tree of all used its bulk to quell its companions, ready to have every one of them bow again on the next squall. Meanwhile the wind whipped up wet, dead leaves from the garden and hurled them in the air. They plastered the caravan and her. One leaf glued itself to her cheek, another stuck to her mouth…

With the flurry of leaves came a plaintive cry. It wasn't human exactly, but appealed to something human in her.

'It's the old beech tree,' thought Laura. 'I recognise its forked trunk against the night sky.'

The sleet hit the tree's cold branches and turned them instantly to ice as the temperature plummeted. The beech was soon strung with white pearls that shone like eyes. It had to be one of the most magical things she had ever seen. Its call was less a cry of pain than a paean.

She felt humbled yet honoured. "A cat may look at a king… Adversity makes strange bedfellows". If she didn't know better she'd say her arboreal friend was thanking her for winning its reprieve this afternoon.

She was thinking about the carving on its trunk. She remembered what Betty had told her: 1697 was the year William Lawrence died.

Next moment a song sounded:

> Then through the mould he heaved his head,
> And through the herbage green,
> There fell a frosted bramble leaf,
> It came their lips between.
>
> And well for you that bramble-leaf
> Betwixt our lips was flung.
> The living to the living hold,
> Dead to the dead belong.

Laura looked everywhere to see Mr Mortimer engaged in more nefarious business on behalf of his mistress.

He came bearing his gift of worm-eaten apples?

Gift or not, she would throw it back in his face this time.

But bitter blew the wind and biting were the drops of rain.

32

Police Headquarters
Prism House
Gloucester

'What do you mean, there's no going back now?' said DI Prickett, after Alison kicked open his office door with her heel. She always chose to work between Christmas Day and New Year. She had finally bought cards and presents for everyone in the nick of time, but any festive goodwill was already beginning to feel a distant memory. Instead her boss was like a bear with a sore head this morning. Unlike her, he didn't want to be here. His grumpiness was all the more unnerving because he looked so genial – he was wearing a startling, new green tie. 'I have a resolution for you sergeant. It's the same as last year. Please knock before you enter my office.'

She dropped a pile of files on his desk. 'It concerns our naked body in the refrigerator.'

'What of it?'

'I have here more notes from the pathologist. They confirm our man suffered a distal fibula fracture about a year before he died. Surgeons fixed a break in one of his bones between his knee and ankle parallel with his tibia. They used a metal plate.'

'I don't have time for this. The SIO wants me to catch whoever stole a three-foot-high illuminated reindeer from outside her house. It appears they snatched it first thing on Boxing Day morning...'

'The plate has a part and serial number on its side: SN2107257 Zephyr XLDR LOT S5615. S6625 2010.09.30. St Jude Medical.'

'You're annoying me now.'

'Let me finish. St Jude's is a private hospital in Bristol. I rang them. The serial numbers appear in their medical files all right. Surgeons fitted the plate to a Paul Carter.'

'And?'

'It so happens that someone of that name worked for Lady Ann Frost at Green Way House last summer. It might not be a coincidence.'

Prickett scratched his badly shaven chin. 'There are any number of Pauls in this world. Your own brother is a Paul. Also Carter is a common enough name…'

'The thing is this. Lady Ann told me that Paul Carter had a serious fall while erecting scaffolding on a building site in Bristol. She said he broke his leg.'

'I didn't tell you to question any lady.'

'I did what I had to.'

'Unbelievable.'

'She gave me the name of a second-hand bookseller. Paul bought a book from him. Unfortunately he doesn't have any address for him other than Green Way House. He did give me Paul's telephone number but no one is answering.'

'What book are you talking about?'

'It details the early history of Green Way House and the creation of its garden.'

'How is that relevant?'

'Don't you see?' said Alison, resting both hands on his desk. She hunched her shoulders. Leaned his way. 'It can't be mere chance that Paul and Lars both end up dead about the same time after working in the same place.'

'It's a serious accusation.'

'Nothing makes sense without Green Way House.'

'You can't talk like that.'

'You're right. I need proof.'

Prickett growled. 'Any other news? Has no one reported seeing Anika Janssen's car near the River Severn yet?'

'Not yet.'

'What about Coombe Hill? What about the canal? Someone must have noticed something around the time our man went into bulrushes, surely?'

'There is something. A birdwatcher reports spotting a Volvo Estate parked at the wharf in August.'

'Meaning what exactly?'

'It was the same colour car that Anika lent to Lars.'

'Probably means nothing.'

'Except it might.'

'Why's that?'

'Our keen-eyed twitcher said it was a left-hand drive vehicle. Anika told me that she and Lars brought their car with them from Holland. The Dutch drive on the opposite side of the road from us.'

Prickett growled again. 'Better ask her if her partner was a bird lover.'

'He wasn't.'

'So what was Lars doing at Coombe Hill Nature Reserve?'

'His car may have been there but that doesn't mean he was.'

'Our trawl of the canal hasn't dredged up any more bodies.'

'But we have found a very old garden cart marked WL which was almost certainly used to dump the refrigerator in the water.'

'Okay sergeant. Go back to the house. Take another look around. Try to establish any more links between our two dead men.'

'I dare say Lady Ann will tell me the same pack of lies she told me before. I should never have listened to her.'

'You really think she knows more than she's telling?'

'I'm afraid for the girl.'

Prickett glared. 'What girl?'

'Laura Bloom. She's one of Lady Ann's new gardeners hired to replace Carter and Visser. She tried to tell me someone had been seriously hurt at Green Way House but I didn't believe her.'

'And you tell me this now?'

'Nothing came of my enquiry.'

'And?'

'It's quite possible Laura Bloom has stumbled upon some tragic story. If so, she is now part of it and so are we.'

33

Green Way House

'You missed all the excitement,' said Ray. 'I hammered on your caravan door for ages last night. Did you really not want to see in the New Year with us? I came bearing gifts of beer and fireworks.'

'You were drunk,' said Laura matter-of-factly.

'I brought you mistletoe.'

'That makes me so happy.'

'All I wanted was a kiss.'

'Yeah, I'm sure you did.'

'I've never met anyone so suspicious.'

'Spare me the agenda.'

'Don't you think we're made for each other?'

'The twist is, I hardly know you.'

'You never will if you don't have a drink with me.'

Laura's hackles rose. She didn't have time for this. She couldn't get Lolly Hooper out of her head. That prowler she saw had killed her? Instead Ray was trying to shame her because she hadn't unlocked her door for him. It was a crime to be so little fun. He only intended to befriend her because he fancied his chances... now he was implying she was abnormal because she didn't like drunken parties. He was trying to make her feel small because he was disappointed that he hadn't got what he wanted. Liked to think of them as Adam and Eve in their very own walled garden. The only difference was that he had dangled a bottle of beer in front of her instead of an apple. 'How did you come by the alcohol and fireworks anyway?' she asked.

'I climbed over the gate and hitched a ride into town.'

'Mr Mortimer won't be pleased.'

'This place gets on my nerves. I think Lady Ann Frost might be the new Scrooge. Her house is like a mausoleum.'

'I told you. Her beloved William died around Christmas time, which is why she won't celebrate it anymore.'

'Who says?'

'Betty says.'

'Well I think it's stupid.'

'It doesn't matter what you think.'

'What are you two kicking off about now?' asked Barry, as he walked into the greenhouse carrying packets of seeds.

'*You* think Laura should have seen in the New Year with us, don't you?' asked Ray with a flick of his blond fringe. 'Anyone else would have. She should have come to our party.'

'It was hardly a party, it was two lonely men getting tipsy in a caravan.'

'That's not the point. We're supposed to be a team. We should all muck in.'

'Leave Laura alone and help me sow these sweet peas in pots. Now we're able to heat the greenhouse with this paraffin stove we can do the same for the antirrhinums and begonias.'

'What about these?' said Ray, pointing to two long lines of plants arranged on a bench. 'They look pretty dead to me.'

'Don't be silly,' said Laura enthusiastically, 'those are oleanders. My grandmother has one.'

'They're losing their leaves.'

'That's because they've been allowed to get too cold.'

'Do we even want them?'

'*Somebody* does.'

'How can you tell?'

'They've been watering them.'

Ray turned up his nose at her. 'You think?'

'It won't be Mr and Mrs Mortimer. You won't ever see them getting their hands dirty. They don't do any gardening.'

'Can't see Lady Ann with a watering can either, can you? She even forgets to top up her vases of roses.'

'Someone visits this greenhouse when we're not here.'

'To hell with our phantom gardener. We should empty every pot and be done with it.'

'Don't be silly, they'll grow back in spring. You'll see lovely red, pink or peach blossoms in the summer.'

'Someone must like them, I suppose. The tatty things are everywhere.'

Laura laughed. 'You don't know a weed from a flower, do you Ray? You'll never make a gardener. You're hopeless.'

'Oh no I'm not, you are.'

'I'm not going to answer that.'

Ray snarled and looked resentful. It did not help that she refused to back down or show any regret, thought Laura. She was not afraid to win their spats of which there were bound to be more. Actually she surprised herself. She suddenly felt very protective of the garden. To stand up for it was to stand up for herself which was oddly heartening. She liked to think that whoever was watering the oleanders without their knowledge was the same person who had done their best to heal the damaged beech tree. Just because she could not yet put a name to someone so incalculable didn't mean she didn't secretly applaud them. Meanwhile she smashed a cracked terracotta pot and placed its fragments in her plant containers for drainage. She filled everything with seed compost and pressed it firmly down. She did it with aggressive silence.

'Try mixing the begonia seeds with a little bit of this silver sand,' said Barry. 'It'll make it easier to distribute them more evenly.'

Already the greenhouse was a vital hub of their operations. What they germinated here would determine what they could plant out in April.

Laura sifted a shallow layer of compost over the seeds, then placed a sheet of glass on their pot and covered it with paper. She liked the work best when it was just her and the plants. She wanted to pay attention to them, cherish them and see them spring up and bloom. With flowers she could be her true self.

'Someone ought to take a look at the plants we've chosen to overwinter in the garden,' said Barry. 'They might have been lifted by last night's frost.'

'I'll go,' said Ray.

'Let me,' said Laura cheerfully.

'Why you?'

'I know what to look for.'

'Very funny!'

'Check the wallflowers, sweet williams and polyanthus,' said Barry. 'Firm them back in the ground as well as you can if they've shifted.'

'At least let me help you,' said Ray.

'No thanks,' said Laura, 'I work better by myself.'

***

A brisk walk took her through the derelict kitchen garden where she very much hoped they might yet grow herbs and vegetables, to the knot garden at the front of Green Way House. "A rolling stone gathers no moss... All good things come to she who waits", thought Laura as she set about inspecting plants in the square beds. Barry was right, the previous night the garden had been subjected to dangerously cold temperatures. At the same time everything was very damp. The alternating freezing and thawing had lifted the soil and plants out of the ground. Some biennials were in a bad way. Where cold air had sunk into the earth she found ice at her fingertips. Large frozen cracks had left some plants to dry out and die from exposure. 'So much goes on in this garden that we simply fail to appreciate. It's a constant life and death struggle for its very existence. It's happening under our very noses.'

She broke up more frosty soil with her trowel when Lady Ann marched out of Green Way House carrying her shotgun. Betty rushed down the steps after her. 'I'm so sorry your ladyship.'

'I don't want any excuses.'

'But it happened so fast.'

Lady Ann took two brass-capped cartridges from her pocket…

'Should I fetch Mr Mortimer?' asked Betty.

…and pressed them side by side into her weapon.

'Perhaps that would be best.'

'All outer gates are locked, your ladyship. There can be no easy escape from the grounds.'

'Let's keep it that way.'

'I did everything you said. I was very careful.'

'But you didn't prevent it.'

'Should I warn the gardeners?'

'That won't be necessary.'

'They deserve to know.'

'That's what you said last time.'

'What'll we do if something happens?'

'You mustn't talk like that.'

'It happened before.'

'I did what I had to.'

'Please your ladyship, let Mr Mortimer handle it.'

'There's no going back anymore. Leave me alone.'

Laura watched Betty run into the house to inform her husband. Meanwhile Lady Ann snapped shut her gun in the loaded position.

Laura diligently pretended to firm more soil with her boot at the base of a sweet william.

Then she followed…

34

'No one orders me about,' thought Ray, stomping through the garden in his ill-fitting overalls and heavy boots.

He unlatched the iron gate into the orchard and wove his way past apple and plum trees.

'It's "Ray dig a trench", "Ray prune the roses", "Ray fix the greenhouse",' he thought, even as a large red bowsaw bounced about noisily in the bottom of his wheelbarrow. 'All the time it's "Ray do this" and "Ray do that".'

It wouldn't be so bad, but Laura wouldn't give him the time of day. 'Just because she talks posh! Well, I'll show her what a real man can do.'

He had been sent on another fool's errand, this time to fetch a sieve for sifting stony soil, but he had a better idea. His bossy co-worker could put the rest of the seeds in pots by himself. 'What makes Barry think *he* can successfully sow anything in this garden anyway? Haven't I said nothing much ever grows in clay?'

Instead he set his eyes on tidying the wood gone wild. The impulse came out of the blue – the garden itself might as well have just hissed it snake-like in his ear. Secretly. Seductively. Now he couldn't let it go. Urge was as good as command… he was obeying instructions. *To kill.* Liana-like ivy climbed the ash trees ready to throttle them. The bulky vine threatened to bring many of them crashing down in the next big storm with the sheer weight of its tendrils. 'I need to saw through the creeper just above ground level,' he told himself happily and set to work on the thick woody stems. 'That way I'll leave the rest to die off in the treetops. I'll strip and burn as much as I can, so help me God, in one big bonfire in that little glade over there.'

Already he was out of sight from the rest of the garden as he worked his way deeper into the dense grove.

If he suddenly felt horribly lost and lonely in his solitary work then he was unapologetic.

'This is my decision and I stand by it,' Ray thought defiantly.

He might not entirely recognise everything he ripped from the bark with his bare fingers, but he was content to indulge his ignorance. Most of the hurtful growth was glossy, evergreen leaves, but other barer threads bore no leaves at all, only clusters of pretty white berries. He picked and rolled a few of them in the palm of his hand. The clusters of small, circular fruit looked almost edible. Killing years of unchecked growth satisfied the new, destructive urge in him. He tore at foliage and fruit alike, then dragged everything to his bonfire which soon began to smoke prodigiously.

He coughed as its thick white clouds penetrated his throat right into his lungs, causing him to wheeze and splutter terribly…

'What the hell?'

Ray retreated in a hurry, but already the smoke surrounded him – its plume of suffocating fumes wound itself about him like a full-blown serpent. He had never encountered anything like it. The whole wood was lost to view in seconds.

He looked this way and that, except there was no obvious route back, no visible path to follow…

'Damn it. Can't see a thing.'

He rubbed his stinging eyes and stumbled through the trees quite randomly.

Next minute he found his way blocked by a wall of delicate white flowers. Each tubular blossom with prominent yellow anthers gave off a heady, sickly perfume. He was looking at one enormous bush which had to be some sort of honeysuckle.

The coiling vine had taken the shape of the thing it smothered.

It was a black door.

Ray immediately began to claw at the mass of flowery stems like a madman. 'If I can just get inside and out of this smoke for a few minutes?'

He was coughing and spluttering, spitting and wheezing... More acrid smog ate at his lungs – it blocked his airways to make his breathing impossibly painful.

He couldn't take another step for gasping.

It felt like drowning.

He sliced, hacked and cut at the door's disguise with his bare hands...

'It's no good. This smoke is something else,' thought Ray. 'I can't breathe. I must make a run for it while I still can.'

But when he looked back he saw the door stood open.

Something told him his first decision had been the right one.

He should leave well alone.

So why did he feel he was invited?

35

Laura saw Lady Ann scour the upper court then search the nearest orchard.

She went via the statue of Old Father Time in the rose walk. She saw her wrench open its iron gate in a great hurry.

Her ladyship was being vigorous, resolute, unsparing in her circuit of house and grounds. This was no timid, nocturnal foray when she was too afraid to face what she found. Instead she held her shotgun ready to fire: 'You might as well come out now. You can be sure you won't get away from me today.'

To whom are you talking, Laura wondered?

'What will it be this time?' cried Lady Ann. 'Will you break into the stables to steal the ladder?'

Laura waited. Held her breath.

'Will you climb your tree to skip over the wall via one of its branches? Do you think I haven't thought of that? That tree is coming down.'

She means the prowler…

'It does no good to add insult to injury. You can't keep worrying and obsessing the way you do.'

I should go another way…

'Maybe you're upset by the new gardeners?'

To get closer.

'The truth is, they need never meet you. It doesn't have to be like last summer. You don't really think I will permit it again, do you?'

Lady Ann's words recalled her conversation with John Mortimer in the coach house, thought Laura and broke cover. 'Stop! Who is it you're after?'

Except her ladyship vanished behind the nearest hedge.

'Lady Ann? Wait! Who hurt Lolly Hooper? What happened to her?'

Seconds later Laura felt a sharp shove into nothing. She trod empty air. *Dropped like a stone.* She went to exhale but her lungs were empty.

Her stomach rolled over…

She fell back against compacted rock and earth in the grassy field.

…as she hit the ground.

Her first thought was a big hole. She covered her head with her hands before everything collapsed on her?

But nothing happened after she opened her eyes.

She wasn't in a pit exactly.

Instead there rose behind her a four-foot-high wall down which she had just tumbled. She couldn't yet see how far it extended right and left of her.

First she had to unfold her leg where she lay at an awkward angle… She felt so winded she tried to vomit.

The pain was excruciating but nothing was broken. She stood up slowly and gazed blurrily all round her. Then she realised. She might feel she had just stepped off the edge of the world, but she was only at the bottom of a ha-ha. The earth rampart was designed to prevent sheep from invading the rose walk and lawns while enabling them to graze the rest of the grounds.

The ditch, high on one side and low on the other, stretched both ways into the distance as if Green Way House had its own dry moat. No warning fence or grill obstructed the drop, which was why she hadn't seen it gape under her toes.

Had her ladyship just replied to her cry with a push? If so, there was no sign of her. It was as though she had just stepped into infinity too?

That's because the garden, in spite of its iron gates, suddenly opened into a broad avenue of sycamore trees that stretched right to the horizon. Like a trick of the eye. Thanks to the ha-ha, Laura was standing at a cleverly designed vantage point where the view from the lawns, courts, parterres and orchards extended up the hill seemingly without a break in one seamless vista. The avenue directed her gaze to the foot of the hill for a purpose. She could see a series of steps to a space on the hilltop of many feet square. Some missing building was meant to rest there on the vacant foundations? Had she not just taken a tumble she might never have noticed it so far away.

Some splendid folly or monument should be standing in sight of the valley visible for miles as the avenue's main focal point?

She dusted herself down. Prepared to limp back to the house. Lady Ann had left her to suffer and wonder, only she was not alone, Laura realised.

Someone lay curled in the ditch only yards from where she was standing. His dark embroidered coat reached as far as his breeches just below his knees. His sleeves were full with deep cuffs of plain silk satin as he carried a tricorne hat tucked under one arm. Laura could see the hat's edge of metal galloon and its interior fringe of ostrich feather round its brim. Stockings covered his lower legs. He wore high-heeled shoes made of black leather with crimson heels. The shoes were cut square at the toe and covered each foot to the ankle, giving the appearance of boots dipped in blood. If his clothes greatly surprised her, so did his glossy black wig – it was parted in the centre in two high peaks that swept upwards from his forehead. He was slightly built, not at all muscular, flat about the waist but not the chest. There was a scared look in his grey-blue eyes with extra-long lashes.

He had taken refuge at the foot of the ha-ha's retaining wall to hide from his pursuer? He had dropped out of her sight even as she stood on the edge of the ditch directly above him. When he spoke his voice was high-pitched, full of panic. 'Don't come any nearer! My arms and legs are rotting away. That's why I smell so awful.'

'What's your name?' asked Laura warily. 'Do you live in Green Way House?'

'How can you say that when nothing has any value or meaning?'

'I know that feeling.'

'Then you must be dead inside too.'

Laura made to move towards the fugitive when he jumped up and ran.

'Hey! Come back! Who are you?'

'I'm the son my mother should never have had.'

Laura looked on helplessly as he set off along the ha-ha's ditch to the wood that had grown so wild. He bounded into it like a deer. There she lost sight of him completely as if the trees swallowed him whole. His outfit called to mind the figure she had seen on the day she nearly drowned in the lake.

She had just talked to her killer?

***

That evening a winter moth flew into Laura's caravan. It fluttered about most annoyingly before it settled on the plate rack by the washbasin. She did her best to ignore it as she went on heating vegetables in a saucepan on her tiny gas cooker. Actually she was not very hungry. Her thoughts were still totally taken up with the events at the ha-ha.

Suddenly the moth took off again – it drew attention to itself with its bouncy, erratic flight. It hovered over her, then worked its wings frantically in her hair.

'Damn it,' said Laura. 'You're going back outside where you belong.'

She jumped on a bed and used her hand to fan the moth across the ceiling, when something fell off the top of the roof locker and hit her head.

It was a roll of canvas about two feet long.

Laura forgot the moth and sat down to spread her find across her knees.

'This is a picture of Green Way House and its grounds,' she realised immediately. She would recognise its great gables, stone-mullioned windows and ashlar chimneys anywhere. Here were its pebble-dashed walls, stone slate roof and arched doorway. The artist had included the extension to the library on the south side as well as the distinctive glass lantern high above the gables very accurately.

The same could not be said of the garden. Rather than depict a present-day ruined landscape strewn with rubble, the artist had used their imagination to colour it with greens, reds and whites like a painter's palette. The bird's-eye view of Green Way House and its surroundings showed an abundance of orchards and flowerbeds in full bloom.

'The signature at the foot of the picture says Lolly Hooper,' Laura noted. 'Did you mean to leave it behind or did you deliberately abandon it?'

So detailed was the image that it showed someone standing beside Old Father Time in the centre of the rose walk.

Her breathing quickened.

'You!' said Laura with alarm. 'You're wearing your coiffured black wig. You are carrying your tricorne hat under your arm and you are wearing black leather shoes with red heels. You look just like the person I met at the ha-ha!'

Was this the man Lolly had been so frightened of seeing? Presumably it was. Whatever the facts, she hadn't dared to omit him from his own house and grounds?

Or she wanted to leave a clue behind?

Point to her murderer?

Night and day he was forever patrolling his garden.

'How long,' Laura wondered, 'before you decide to call at my door again? What will it take to make you do it? More to the point, where do you go to hide?'

At that moment her heart swelled and her head filled with song:

>Within a garden a maiden lingered,
>When soft the shades of evening fell,
>Expecting, fearing,
>A footstep hearing,
>Her love appearing,
>To say farewell.

Laura rushed to open her caravan's door ready to defend herself, but met no one.

Only the moth saw its chance to escape into the dark day.

36

The Round House
Mercombe Wood

'You're very quiet tonight. What are you reading?' said Ravi, feeding a log into the hot stove. He might miss the comforts of his own flat, but this former toll house had one redeeming feature: it was small and easy to heat. That didn't mean he didn't jump every time an owl screeched like a banshee as it flew past the window. 'Please tell me it's not more ghost stories.'

Alison turned up the wick on her oil lamp. She rotated its little brass knob at the base of its glass chimney to get a brighter, less smoky flame. 'This book came addressed to one of Lady Ann Frost's gardeners at Green Way House. Unfortunately, he left her employment before she could give it to him. She hasn't heard from him since. She says she doesn't know where he is or what happened to him.'

'Who are you talking about?'

'His name is Paul Carter. There's a good chance he's our man in the fridge at Coombe Hill.'

'So?'

'I've spoken to the second-hand bookseller in Bristol and he says that Paul was eager to discover all he could about Green Way House's garden. He was especially anxious to know about its creator William Lawrence.'

'Hoped to make friends, did he?'

'Oh no, didn't I say? This book details the history of the house and grounds only from 1636 to 1697. William died over three hundred years ago.'

'So what's the problem?'

'Something isn't quite right about Green Way House. It is very different from anywhere else I've ever visited.'

'Different how?'

'Save it. Let's just say that whatever Paul hoped to prove probably never happened.'

Ravi passed her a glass of wine. 'Now you have the book and it's all set to make you regret it. But you already knew that.'

'It says here that William Lawrence likened the doctors to murderers for not saving his wife and his son in 1691…'

'Let's face it, modern medicine was still in its infancy back then.'

'Anne and Will died within months of each other, sadly.'

'The poor patient was usually bled half to death with leeches. It must have left him feeling very embittered.'

Alison continued to summarise. 'This book says Lawrence holed up at home for several years with only empty hopes to console him. It was while he was a recluse that he set about establishing his paradisal garden to honour his dearly departed. He placed funereal urns on pillars shaped like pyramids and added Latin inscriptions to iron gates to recall his dead family. Paths, flowers, walls and statues were meant to commemorate them both by marking the different stages of life from birth to oblivion.'

'So?'

'What are the chances that Paul uncovered a pyramid, or some words of Latin, with which he sought to unlock their secret?'

'Well, we both know that's not true,' said Ravi. 'No garden lasts for three hundred years.'

'Not so. I know for a fact that a seventeenth century garden exists very much in its original form at Chastleton House in Oxfordshire. It can't be the only one.'

'I rather expect Lawrence's dream died with him, don't you?'

Alison smiled. 'In fact he chose to remarry – to someone called Dulcibella – not long before he passed away.'

'So the garden *did* outlive its creator?'

'He certainly made Dulcibella promise to finish what he'd started.'

'And did she?'

'Alas no.'

'What did I tell you!'

'This, despite the fact that Lawrence left her instructions to build a chapel on a hill at the edge of the grounds. He intended to rehouse Anne's and Will's bones from the local churchyard – he wanted them to rest in their very own garden. Look here. This book's reproduction of a contemporary engraving shows where an avenue of trees on the southeast side of Green Way House ends in a flight of steps partway up the escarpment. On its summit is the place where the dead should have been reburied.'

'Clearly the new wife was jealous of the old?'

'We'll never know why Dulcibella didn't do as her dead husband wanted. What we can say is the garden has never seen its purpose fulfilled.'

Ravi took a closer look at the large, fold-out picture to which Alison pointed. 'It's a very fine and detailed engraving, I must say. Who drew it?'

'His name was Johannes Kip. He was a Dutchman who set out to record every major country house in Gloucestershire in the early 1700s. You can find his work in Sir Robert Atkyns's "The Ancient and Present State of Glostershire".'

'Such an odd perspective!'

'The elongated panorama is deliberate. It's a bird's-eye view showing the full extent of house and estate to the hills and fields beyond. It has been done to flatter the owner by making the estate look much bigger than it is. Perspectives have been stretched to the limit while the garden has been captured in the round.'

'Who's the man on the balcony?' asked Ravi.

'What man? Where?'

Alison had already noted a few people and animals dotted about the print. She particularly liked the six grey horses that drew a carriage with spiral spokes along the main road that led to Green Way House's front gates. Its driver could be seen waving his whip while a man rode his rearing horse alongside. Four stags with large antlers grazed in a neighbouring field. Such extras brought the scene to life, but this figure was the only one depicted in the house itself. He looked down on all he owned. His stance, cryptic yet deliberate, had an air of finality that was almost unanswerable. Tall and lithe, he looked proprietorial and stubborn. Here was a gentleman of some standing in provincial society who was intent on defending his beliefs and who was unafraid to fight his corner.

'What are the chances it's William Lawrence?' asked Ravi.

'No, you're wrong. Look at the title of the engraving. It says: "Shurdington the Seat of Dulcibella Laurence Relict of WM Laurence." Relict means widow. Laurence – they spelt it then with a 'u' not a 'w' – died in 1697. Kip didn't tour Gloucestershire until 1707 at the earliest. If that is William Lawrence then Kip drew a dead man.'

'Must be Dulcibella's new beau? Did she have one?'

'She never remarried.'

'It may be nobody.'

'Wait while I fetch my magnifying glass,' said Alison.

'Don't waste your time.'

'Won't take a minute.'

'Who cares who he is?'

'I do.'

***

Alison quickly returned to her book. Moved it closer to her lamp's yellow glow. 'That's odd.'

'What is?' asked Ravi.

'Kip has sketched Green Way House's formal lawns and parterres with lots of dashes and dots to better suit the process of engraving. It's crude but efficient. That makes our gentleman rather special.'

'How so?'

'His far more realistic reproduction is an anomaly in a picture meant for general show, not accuracy.'

'Not even going to ask!'

'He's standing outside the rooftop study that Lawrence built for his son before he died from fever. He's carrying his hat in one hand and holding his walking cane with the other as he looks over the balcony's iron rail.'

'Whoever he is, he's not of our world.'

'You're right. His wig is parted in the centre in two high peaks swept upward from his forehead.'

'Anybody of any importance wore wigs in the 1700s,' said Ravi, pulling a face.

'He's not from the 1700s.'

'Are you serious? How can you possibly know when he's from so precisely?'

'Look at his hair,' said Alison.

'I just did.'

'By the time this engraving was done most well-to-do men liked to powder their wigs to kill the lice, as did their wives and children. This man's hair is jet black, not a fashionable white. Also his coat is mostly buttoned up to reveal very little of his shirt's ruffled frill, unlike later dress styles.'

'You'll be telling me next he was a Cavalier in the English Civil War.'

'Too early. Note the black hat that he carries under his arm – it doesn't have any extravagant plumes. All it has is a discreet white fringe around the rim made of ostrich feather. We're talking about men's fashion in transition. I'd say he is wearing clothes from the 1680s or 90s.'

'Can I be frank?'

'What?'

'The clock just struck eleven. It's our bedtime.'

Alison held her glass to her eye again. 'I'll be along in a moment.'

'I know you. You'll be here 'til 2 a.m.'

'Okey-doke.' She wasn't about to say it to his face, but Ravi could be correct after all. If this really was William Lawrence, original creator of the garden, then he was not merely admiring its flowers, trees and shrubs.

The proprietorial figure on the balcony stood at the very centre of the picture of Green Way House. He displayed a natural distrust of intruders and enjoyed keeping them at a distance.

Now he had made his presence known it was impossible to ignore him, even in death.

The larger Alison magnified his face the longer its slit shaped his smile. It was less mouth than gash.

He was grinning straight at her.

37

Green Way House

'A man in red-heeled shoes?' said Barry, inhaling sharply. 'In the ditch? Are you sure?'

Laura snapped back. 'Do you really think I'd invent something like that?'

'Seems to me you've begun to 'see' all sorts lately.'

'I've never seen him before in my life.'

'And?'

'The moment we met I could see he was terrified. Lady Ann was hunting him down with her loaded gun. It's on account of him that she patrols this place like a prison.'

'Really? Is that what you think?'

'She pushed me off a cliff, damn it.'

'How do you know it was her?'

'Who else could it have been?'

'What did this man in fancy dress do? What did you say to him?'

Laura raked and shovelled drifts of dead brown needles into a wheelbarrow. 'He ran off into the wood before I could say anything.' They were trimming one of the garden's overgrown hedges now that the weather had turned milder. Normally a yew was best left alone, but this one needed cutting back to encourage several thin patches to grow again in the spring.

Barry leaned in and pruned crowded shoots to within six inches of the main stem. 'Tell me more about his weird clothes.'

'What can I say? They were like William Lawrence's.'

'How do you know that?'

'His portrait hangs on the wall partway up Green Way House's main staircase.'

'I haven't seen any portrait.'

'Take it from me, I could have been looking at a fashionable seventeenth century English squire.'

'You'll be saying next you've seen a ghost?'

'That was no ghost,' said Laura. 'He just dressed like one.'

'What then?'

'I think I might have met Lady Ann's son.'

'You can't have. William died five years ago.'

'It was something he said. Also he has her same grey-blue eyes.'

'His death is the only reason we're here, to remake the garden in his memory.'

'We only have her word for it he ever died.'

'I dare say it was all over the local newspaper at the time.'

'We only have her word for it that it was *he* who was killed?'

'Has anything else happened?' asked Barry. 'Have you seen any sign of him since?'

'It's all gone quiet.'

'The important thing now is you do nothing.'

'That woman is capable of anything.'

'You're back to your first theory?'

'Trust me, that crazy witch is keeping something from us. If that is William, he almost certainly murdered Lolly?'

'Who says he did?'

'Blood is blood,' said Laura. 'I know what I saw on the floor of my caravan.'

'If that was true why didn't he attack you?'

'Maybe he intended to when Lady Ann stopped him.'

'Now you're being ridiculous.'

'I feel absolutely sure he hurt Lolly and that's why her ladyship is hiding him in the house or grounds.'

'If there's an explanation we'll soon get to the bottom of it,' said Barry, 'but you're not the one who has to find the answer. It was embarrassing enough when you buttonholed the police last time…'

'Only because you refused to back me up.'

'Let's face it, there was nothing.'

'This is different. He spoke to me.' She should show Barry the canvas that she had discovered in her caravan, thought Laura. She should make him aware of the costumed figure that Lolly Hooper had depicted strolling along the rose walk. If this was their prowler then he had been imprisoned here a lot longer than they had. Her clue was much more than a warning.

***

Laura worked on in painful silence. Took care not to betray any more fear. It was enough that Barry had not laughed in her face. He was right: they had to bide their time before the whole world got to hear of things they had yet to explain.

She had to hope nothing else bad happened while she secretly investigated. Most importantly of all she owed it to Lolly to get to the truth. In the meantime she had to act normally so as not to arouse any suspicion.

'So what are we going to do in the garden today?'

'See how these roots have undermined the pillars of this lovely gateway,' said Barry, lifting his floppy hat to scratch his hot brow.

'I marvel its gate is still on its hinges.'

'Use your spade. Do as I do. We need to cut the roots back before they do any more damage.'

Laura took up position a little less than two feet from the centre of the yew hedge. She thrust her spade vertically into the ground to the full depths of its blade.

But it was not roots she struck but something more solid. 'Shit.'

'Have you hit a brick or what?'

'I'm not sure.'

Barry used his trowel to excavate the sunken object. 'It's no brick, it's some sort of statue.'

Together they dragged a stone woman from her shallow grave. On her head was an urn.

'She's very heavy,' said Laura.

'Help me set her upright…'

'Not what I was expecting.'

'She's a sundial. A very old one.'

'Why bury a perfectly good statue?' Laura scraped mud off the sculpture's face and its blank eyes looked back at her with intent. Its smile became meaner as it became cleaner. 'All this dirt tells me she has been down here a while.'

'She guarded the gate before the hedge grew too wide.'

The reader of shadows stood no higher than their chests. Carved curls on her head matched the acanthus leaves on her dress. She had fallen where she had once stood perfectly vertical on the local latitude in line with the true North. 'She looks pretty much intact,' said Laura, dusting neck and shoulders.

They took it in turns to scratch dirty, blueish green verdigris from the metal gnomon mounted on top of the urn. The gnomon immediately began to cast a shadow on the hour-line inscribed round the dial – its style likewise started telling the time.

'I remember when I was a child at the seaside,' said Barry. 'I stuck a stick in the sand and drew all the hours around it. Then I watched the sun work its magic with its shadowy finger.'

'How old is she, do you think?'

'Go back far enough and sun-dials represented real time. People even used them to correct the first clocks. It wasn't until about 1800 that anything mechanical was regarded as more accurate. I've seen some very old dials in some very old gardens. This one is almost certainly 17th century.'

'Then she's as old as the house and grounds.'

'I'd say so, yes.'

'Is that some sort of saying inscribed round the dial's rim?'

Barry picked at a line of letters with his fingernail. 'It says "mors certa".'

'"Death is certain."'

'I've seen a motto like this on a sundial before. There should be more to it, from what I recall.'

Laura's spade rang loudly again in the hard ground. 'There's something else down here.'

It took another fifteen minutes to free a second figure from the mass of roots which bound her like shackles.

'Stand her up straight,' said Barry, very excited.

'She completes the pair all right.'

'There should be more writing on the dial. Here it is. It says "hora incerta". Put together the complete saying states: "Death is certain, its hour is uncertain".'

'What do you think William Lawrence meant by it?' asked Laura. 'Why place matching statues either side of this particular gateway?'

'He's telling us the way to the future is via the past.'

'Is that what you reckon?'

'I reckon we've just restarted the garden's clock, don't you?'

As with the first dial the sun cast a living shadow that aligned with the hour. The gnomon's broad finger pointed to XI while the narrower style marked the minutes. The garden could once more divide itself into past, present and future. Good and bad times would no longer come and go unrecorded.

'What will William Lawrence have us find next, I wonder?' asked Laura.

'Did I not say one garden rests on top of another?'

'However you look at it, it's like following a trail.'

'Lady Ann will be delighted.'

'Knowing her, she might not be.'

'Why not?' queried Barry. 'Has she not made it abundantly clear that she favours some marvellous *resurrection* rather than anything more modern? She rejects all my novel suggestions.'

'Let's face it, digging out the lake was a step too far.'

'Her stubbornness drove the previous gardeners away for sure.'

'It's true her ladyship would have the garden preserve her love for someone as though he were still alive, but the heart can only live in the present.'

'It's almost impossible to get anything done because of her.'

'Now we know why.'

'Can it be true?'

'You said it yourself: *if* her son isn't dead, why does she need a garden in his memory?'

'I think you're exaggerating.'

'Why else do you think she's too scared to take your advice? Why else won't she ever see her grand project through?'

'Surely she lives for happier days?' said Barry.

'I did think that, but this is certain: she hasn't been straight with us about things that have happened here. Lolly discovered it and paid the price.'

'Not this again.'

'She has cast a dark spell over this whole enterprise.'

'If she pays us our wages on time, why worry?'

'Lady Ann is not to be trusted, I tell you. She has hired us to do something she doesn't need or dare not finish. Someone has to confront her or this will end very badly. I can feel it in my bones. She may go around dressed in pretty floral dresses covered in roses, but it's only for show. In reality she's all deadly nightshade and hemlock. She had hired us for some darker purpose.'

'You literally don't trust her anymore, do you?'

'Do you?'

Next minute there came a sickening howl.

'That was close,' said Laura, alarmed. The cry was less lament than loud protest. It was the sort of noise a person might make when they discovered a terrible crime. The garden had wailed at something it deplored, as though it had just sustained a terrible wound – it filled it with great misery?

Barry stopped to listen. 'It's only a dog going by in the lane.'

'I know what I heard.' Next minute Laura kicked open the gate of statues… 'It came from the wild wood. I should take a look.'

'I'm going with you.'

***

The wood's densely growing ash trees left little room to follow anyone else's narrow trail, Laura soon discovered. Hundreds of spindly trunks had seeded themselves far too close together. They were poor, deformed specimens which would never reach their full potential as they competed to crowd each other out from the sun.

'We should fetch Ray,' said Barry. 'Where is the wretched man anyway? I haven't seen him all day. He's busy drinking beer in his caravan again, I suppose?'

Laura shook her head. 'We need to do this ourselves.' The fierce howl might have faded but not its echo. How stupid Barry and Ray are, she thought. They understand nothing. They are so dim, wilfully blind, so *tainted* by the world – they lumber about the grounds, digging, wrenching, twisting. It's so special here, she told herself. I alone appreciate what it means to be pricked, prodded, stabbed against your will. Only I feel the outrage and pain that come when someone stamps and stomps all over you...

A miniature house stood before her. She had never seen such a strange dwelling – it was buried in a mound of earth whose winter honeysuckle grew all over it. The tiny abode stood not much higher than her head and had no windows.

Such a hideout might suit a killer.

Just then Barry caught hold of her arm. 'I thought I'd lost you back there for a minute.'

A classical triangular pediment capped a black door. 'Not many people know about this place, to be sure.'

'In which case I think we should leave now.'

'Too late, I'm going in.'

Laura went to turn the door's handle, while high on the roof of Green Way House Lady Ann looked down and shivered as she observed everything from her lofty lantern...

38

Police Headquarters
Prism House
Gloucester

'We definitely can't rule out suicide,' said DI Prickett, barely looking up from his desk. 'It turns out Lars Visser had serious marital problems. Anika was ill and wanted to give birth to their baby back home in Holland. He was depressed. He may well have regretted going to Green Way House as Lady Ann Frost said. He told her he was "not wanted". Soon after, he was gone. Either that or Anika lied to you and she's covering for him.'

Alison cracked a mint. 'She's no liar. I saw the empty cot in her flat.'

'You agree then? Lars killed himself?'

'She and Lars did quarrel about leaving England.' Her voice was sceptical, pre-occupied. 'Also Anika let Lars go away to work at Green Way House. Only later did she miscarry her baby. She wrote to tell him the sad news…'

'And he couldn't bear the loss of his child!'

'Except she heard nothing back.'

'We only have her word for the timing of it all.'

'Anika *assumed* Lars had deserted her, but by then he was dead. The point I want to make is this: they might have fought but they were still committed to each other.'

Prickett looked up at last. 'Says who?'

'Lars was prone to fits of depression but he was also very religious. Harming himself would have been a heinous sin in his eyes.'

'How do you know?'

'He and Anika made pilgrimages to "Mary of the Enclosed Garden" in the Dutch-Flemish part of the Netherlands.'

'And your point is?'

'People who suffer marital problems, or who have a sick person in their family, go to Mary to invoke her help. Right from the beginning when Lady Ann Frost hired Lars to remodel her garden at Green Way House, she envisaged it as her very own "hortus conclusus" or walled garden.'

'You've lost me.'

Alison took a deep breath. 'Lars was going to create the perfect garden here in England. It would – in his mind's eye – be dedicated to the Virgin Mary, in so far as it would be a spiritual place of great beauty, peace and reflection. Lady Ann planned it as a garden of mourning in memory of her son, but Lars also thought of it in terms of saving his own child. Like a real "hortus conclusus", no less. Either way, he would help Lady Ann do good work and be rewarded with God's blessing in return. He died before the miracle could happen.'

'Or he was as deluded as she is.'

'Not at all. It's about purity of motive.'

'Not something we police usually come across.'

'It's an odd tale but not suicide.'

Prickett pulled a face. 'You can't ignore the facts. Lars and his partner had a fight. Their baby died. He was far from home.'

Alison pointed to the latest report from the pathologist. 'I had Forensics run further tests on him. The aconite caused his kidneys to fail, not least because they were already displaying signs of disease. He was dead before he hit the water.'

'Lars was a gardener. He knew how to do himself in.'

'Or someone else at Green Way House is going around poisoning people.'

'Admit it sergeant, you know you're wrong.'

'Am I? Am I really?' She slapped a second file on his desk. 'The pathologist has analysed Paul Carter's blood. Guess what? Our man in the refrigerator was poisoned too.'

Prickett listened at last. 'You don't say?'

'The lab has detected traces of non-digitalis cardiac glycosides from the oleander plant. It's an ornamental shrub or small tree…'

'I know what it is.'

'You have to grow it in a greenhouse, though it will sometimes thrive in more balmy parts of Cornwall or in the warm, inner city gardens of London.'

'Say what you have to sergeant.'

'There is the Nerium oleander or its yellow relative the Cascabela thevetia. Both are extremely toxic. Oleandrin and neriine are potent cardenolides found in all parts of the plant. The red flowered varieties of oleander are the most poisonous.'

'Surely you have to eat it in some quantity to come to any harm?'

'One leaf can kill an adult.'

'A pro wouldn't make such a mistake, surely.'

'Lady Ann may have hired Paul Carter to help restore the grounds of Green Way House, but he definitely wasn't a professional gardener.'

'So it got into his system by accident!'

'You'd think so, wouldn't you. Except people do often use oleander leaves in folk remedies. Not only that, but oleander remains toxic when dry. A lethal dose is only 4 grams. I've found one case of a woman who took it to help her get pregnant. She was lucky to survive. Often it results in vomiting, light-headedness and heart attack. Is it not probable that both men were killed by plants grown in the same garden?'

Prickett shook his head. 'Are you really trying to suggest the garden is poisoning people?'

'Two deaths can't be a coincidence.'

'And I'm Agatha Christie.'

'All the more reason not to rule out foul play,' said Alison firmly.

'In that case I have a few things to add. Lars Visser and Paul Carter had no serious enemies. No one stood to gain by their deaths, nor have we established any previous connection with Lady Ann or anyone else in Green Way House.'

'Not so far.'

'Paul and Lars had not met each other until then?'

'Not that we can tell.'

'You see my point. What possible motive could anyone from Green Way House have to murder them just weeks after their arrival? What motive did they have to kill each other for that matter?'

Alison made a face. 'The poisonings are not the mystery, it's why someone chose to cover up their deaths by throwing both bodies in the water.'

'Yet nobody saw a thing.'

'Two people have told me they heard screams coming from the garden.'

'Any CCTV?'

'Security cameras at Zac's nurseries don't cover the lane. The same goes for Cherry Tree Farm.'

'You literally believe we have two cases we can link together?'

'But nothing yet to indicate any person of interest.'

'There is one thing,' said Prickett and pulled a picture from a drawer in his desk.

'What is it?' asked Alison.

'This is a 3D satellite image of Green Way House that I've printed from Google Maps.'

'Not entirely sure what you want me to see.'

'What we have here is a compilation of innumerable photographs combined together every second of every day. Have you ever seen a man with no legs on your computer screen?'

'I once saw a horse with two tails.'

'When Google Maps stitch together new photos of the same scene, not everything always lines up quite right. This is particularly true when things are in motion, like a horse trotting or a plane flying.'

'It's not so terrible.'

'Look carefully at the person strolling in the garden. Who do you see?'

'I see Lady Ann Frost. Her face may be blurred, but I'd recognise her ladyship's bright flowery dress anywhere.'

'I thought as much. Who else do you see? Is that someone walking behind her in the rose walk? They're shadowing her every movement, don't you think?'

Alison studied the picture again. A dark figure was not so much a patch of shade projected by Lady Ann's own body, as her appendage. He was her inseparable attendant or companion.

'That was an hour ago,' added Prickett. 'We'll have to wait for more substantive updates to see it again.'

'But what does it mean?'

'I won't know until you tell me.'

'You think there is someone else living at Green Way House that we don't know about?'

Prickett scowled at her. 'I doubt it's your mysterious poisoner, but....'

'You want me to find out who?'

'Someone has to.'

Alison stared again at the blurred, ghostly figure caught unawares on film from space.

His representation might be faint in the strong sunlight, but it was still extravagantly fanciful, grotesque, eccentric. He walked like a gentleman from another age. Nothing so unsubstantial ought to make her shiver… No trick of light should feel like a premonition when it had already happened.

Because their paths had crossed before? She had already studied him through her magnifying glass as he stood on the balcony of Green Way House? Hat and coat struck her as the same. This was the man depicted in the book that the bookseller had mailed to Paul Carter from Bristol.

39

'Whatever this place is, it has been here a while,' said Laura. She ducked through the diminutive house's low doorway to find herself in a narrow passage that smelt of cold earth and stone.

Barry hung back at the entrance. 'I don't like it. I have a bad feeling about it.'

'I bet it started out as an ancient burial barrow in the Bronze Age? People laid their dead to rest here centuries ago.'

'Might have, for all you know.'

Laura expected the air to be stuffy, unhealthy, low on oxygen, but she breathed freely. 'It's the sort of place you might expect a goblin or hobbit to inhabit. Any second now we're going to meet some diminutive, mischievous imp with hairy feet.'

'Best be careful.'

'Damn, I left my phone in my caravan...'

'Watch where you're walking.'

'...I could do with a light.'

'I might have a match on me.'

'How far does this go, do you think?'

'Did you hear what I just said?'

'There's some sort of...'

'Laura, stop right there.' Barry sounded serious this time.

She was standing at a curve in the tunnel with only blackness beyond. 'What is it?'

'Don't take another step.'

It was true there had been a sudden change in the atmosphere. The last glimmer of light from the door died just as the subterranean dwelling seemed to inhale – it responded to an abrupt external change in barometric pressure. 'Don't worry, I can feel my way from here.'

'No!' Barry gripped her arm.

She wriggled: 'What's wrong?'

'If this is what I think it is then you're about to break your neck.' He struck a match from the box he used to light bonfires.

'I'm not afraid of the dark. Are you?'

'Do as you're told, look at your toes.'

'What about them?'

'You're standing on the edge of a pit.'

Laura glanced down. The floor was suddenly blacker, colder, deeper. All round her the cool subterranean air rose to caress her face and hair as it invited her to step into its void.

'What the hell?' she cried.

Barry dropped his burning match and it descended into a large, demijohn shaped hole. The yellow flame flared and went out halfway into the gloom. 'God knows how deep it is.'

'What is it?'

'You're looking at a snow-conserve. Many big estates had one in their grounds. This is where the first owners of Green Way House stored their ice long before anyone invented refrigerators. Most pits are filled in now because they're so dangerous. This one should at least have a lid on it.'

'The garden is playing some sort of game with us,' said Laura and shrank from the thought of what could have just happened.

'See here,' said Barry. 'This second pit is where people placed their ladder.'

'It is?'

Another hole.

'This is how they climbed down to extract the ice from the main well.'

Another trap.

'But where did the ice originate?' asked Laura.

'It came from that lake we uncovered in the grounds. People waited until its water froze solid in winter, then they sawed through the ice and brought it here piece by piece in wheelbarrows to their ice mound. They packed everything tightly together to slow any thaw.'

'Suppose they did, yeah.'

'Ice would stay solid all summer because the insulation was so good.'

Laura took another peek over the edge. Her eyes adjusted to the new level of darkness. She did what the creator of the garden had done before – she followed in his footsteps. In here something could potentially last forever, she decided with enthusiasm. It was like arresting death itself. 'There are some rusty tins and someone's leather bag on the ground.'

'People have used it as a general cold store.'

'Or this is someone's secret den.'

'Some ice houses made handy air-raid shelters during World War II…'

'There are some old tools here,' said Laura, exploring the corridor.

'This bill hook with its bone handle is very old. The same goes for these dibbers, forks and trowels.'

'Leave those. Look at this.' Laura held up a cane. Its wooden top had been skilfully fashioned into a crow's head with a berry stuck fast in its beak. 'Whose is this, in your opinion?'

'I'd say it was once the fashion accessory of some discerning gentleman,' said Barry with a grin. 'It's someone's fancy walking stick.' His own find continued to interest him more. 'Never have I seen such beautiful, wrought iron gardening tools. These look pristine as if they were used and cleaned yesterday. I could use them today, since spades and trowels haven't changed much in the last three hundred years.'

'On the stick are the initials WL. What are the chances they stand for

William Lawrence?'

'Can't answer that.'

Laura waved the cane about like a wand. Its original owner would have wielded it as a weapon and symbol of power. Certainly it evoked a bygone age of gold waistcoats and red-heeled shoes, but no more such apparel appeared out of the darkness.

Barry lit another match and threw it down the well. This time it didn't go out until it hit the bottom. He gave a loud gasp. Traded looks with Laura. 'I suppose you'll say this explains the prowler you keep seeing in the garden?'

'No, but it's enough for you to believe me.'

In the pit lay Ray Knight.

40

'And I'm telling you someone wants to kill us,' said Laura, as she pushed her thick brown spectacles higher on her nose. 'It will be me or Barry next, detective.'

DS Alison Ellis stood by the fireplace in the drawing room of Green Way House. Four grotesque figures eyed her intently from their Greek and Rome pillars high on the chimney piece. Since her last visit all the carvings had, if anything, grown more fantastical – their wooden statues, blackened by soot and age, were an almost blasphemous interweaving of human and animal form. They wore bizarre and outlandish head-dresses. One held up a crooked arm as if in sombre warning, another rubbed their bony hands together with great relish. All four resembled misbegotten and deformed devils. Their fish-like pupils, polished cheeks and pot-bellies were not only unpleasant, bordering on the repulsive, but were morally revolting to mind and senses. 'You did right to call me,' she said with a shudder.

'I told you what would happen if you did nothing. I told you about **HELP ME** written on the floor of my caravan. Now Ray Knight has died too.'

'Please sit down. Do you want a glass of water?'

'Can you blame me for panicking?'

'I've confirmed it with Lady Frost. It appears the ice house's pit once had a metal grating for protection.'

'What more proof do you need?' said Laura.

'Whoever uncovered the hole may be hard to determine. It might have been done recently or it might date back years…'

'Forget the grating. What I want to know is when you're going to arrest her.'

'Her?'

'Lady Ann knows who pushed Ray into the pit, or she did it herself. I hate to think what else that woman is capable of. It's my belief she poisoned her husband years ago…'

'Why would she do that?'

'You should speak to Zac.'

'Zac who?'

'He runs the nurseries in Greenway Lane. You should ask him what happened to Lolly Hooper. He'll confirm she stayed in my caravan. That blood on its floor will be hers for sure…'

'So you've said.'

'…since when I've found a lock of red hair snagged in a tree.'

'I'm trying to trace her right now.'

'Lolly's hair was red.'

'As I say, I'm looking into…'

'Oh my God! So she is dead?'

'Not Lolly, her two co-workers.'

'I knew it. How did they die?'

'Lars Visser and Paul Carter were both poisoned.'

'So what are you waiting for?'

'No one is suggesting their deaths are connected to Ray Knight's.'

Laura looked contemptuous. 'How else do you think he came to end up down that hole?'

'Nothing suggests he did anything other than fall and break his neck.'

'That's not what happened at all.' Laura was beside herself with anger and worry. Her eyes blazed. Her voice choked as she struggled to convey her certainty. 'Lady Ann even keeps her own son a secret!'

'What son?'

'Ask her!'

Alison stepped sharply away from the fire. It was not its heat that bothered her but the sudden chill. No amount of roaring flame could warm Green Way House today. 'You think someone else is living here apart from her ladyship? Are you quite sure this person is her son?'

'He told me so himself. As good as.'

'You've met William?'

'It wasn't the first time. He was trying to escape from his mother via the ha-ha.'

'What ha-ha? Where?'

'It's an earth and stone ditch in the grounds.'

'You're absolutely sure he said he was her son?'

'Lady Ann keeps him shut up like a dangerous animal.'

'Did he *say* he was William Frost?'

'He has her colour eyes.'

'What happened exactly?'

'He ran off before I could get any more sense out of him.'

'So you could be wrong?'

'Will you stay blind to the consequences of her craziness, or will you wake up detective? She's concealing some awful crime? Must there be another tragedy before you do something about her?'

'Don't worry, I will ask Lady Ann everything. Meanwhile let's go back over the facts, shall we?' said Alison. There might be a malevolent presence at work in Green Way House, but there was a difference between knowing and feeling. 'You last spoke to Mr Knight when exactly?'

'He and I had a bit of a spat in the greenhouse on New Year's Day. He had a hangover and was in a bad mood. He was miffed because I hadn't joined him and Barry for a drink the night before.'

'Why did that bother him especially?'

'He keeps – kept – coming on to me. I can't bear that sort of thing. Why must some people ruin everything for others? When I was ten I thought love was perfect but the adult world is so ugly. Ray was an awkward lout. An oaf. Worst of all he didn't respect the garden.'

'Meaning what?'

'He literally rode roughshod over it on his moped. He beat and battered it. No living thing should be taken by storm, wrecked, violated… That's especially true of people? Do you believe, as I do, that the soul as well as the body is *propagated* detective? We are born with a budding capacity to love that is very fragile and needs careful nurturing – it is our secret place which is to be enraptured, charmed, entranced, filled with delight if we have the courage.'

'So you're saying Ray Knight forfeited his right to work in the garden? You saying it got him killed?'

'I don't know detective. Do you?'

'Please go to the police van in the courtyard. An officer is waiting there to take a written statement from you.'

Laura paused on her way out. Looked round. 'I didn't wish Ray any harm, I really didn't.'

'I was wondering what you meant.'

***

Alison stared through the drawing room's window and watched medics stretcher Ray Knight's body to a waiting ambulance. Laura also observed the proceedings, she noted, as she crossed the courtyard. A pained expression filled her face. Ray was not someone Laura had known very long but she recoiled physically with fear, horror and disgust as the blanket slipped from his chin. He looked stiff, grey, cold. Laura covered her eyes with both hands. She stood for a while with her head bowed. She was like a snail that retracted its horns. She was like a cat that concealed its claws.

Most of all she was like a flower that shut its petals at night when the day ended.

***

'So sorry to keep you waiting,' said Alison and directed Barry Barnes to a chair by the drawing room's fire. 'You wished to talk to me?'

'It concerns Laura Bloom.'

'Sounds urgent.'

'Nothing that girl says can be taken at face value detective. Not by a long shot. I believe she is a bit of a romantic.'

'Why's that?'

'Laura is convinced she has met someone lurking in the garden.'

'And you haven't?'

'Never. Neither did Ray.'

'I see.'

'I don't think you do detective. Fact is, Laura is only here because she is in trouble at university.'

'What kind of trouble?'

'Someone sexually assaulted her at college then followed her home. He harassed and stalked her. It's hardly surprising if she still feels jumpy.'

Alison stepped closer to the fire and its line of fleshy, sinuous serpents slithered sideways along the top of the chimney piece. From there they lashed their thin tongues at her like dragons. She was looking at hideous, slimy creatures which dated back to the beginning of time itself. They mocked her very origins. 'You honestly think Laura is in perpetual fear of some imaginary intruder, rapist or burglar?'

'All of those.'

'She seems certain he's Lady Ann's son, William.'

'As I say she has a tendency to create encounters. Things. *People* especially.'

'Or there really is someone else living in Green Way House?'

'Don't believe a word she says. She has some increasingly strange ideas about her ladyship.'

'You believe that too, do you?'

Barry sighed sadly. 'I had hoped to mention it before she got to speak to you – before she put any *falsehoods* into your head.'

'Go on.'

'No matter what Laura says, no matter what she has told you has happened, Ray Knight was not murdered by her ladyship's son or anyone else. That much I know.'

Alison blinked rapidly. 'What do you know?'

'Ray should never have gone near those ash trees with his bare hands. He did wrong to touch them.'

'How so?'

'That ivy he stripped and burnt from their bark was poison ivy. It contains an oil called urushiol in its leaves, stems, roots and berries. It gives you a nasty rash and when swallowed can kill a child.'

'The pathologist will report back in due course…'

'Tell them to check Ray's throat. Burning ivy like that can produce a deadly smoke that causes an extreme allergic reaction in some people. I should know because I saw it happen to a friend of mine when I was a head gardener years ago. His airways swelled until he couldn't breathe. He was lucky. I rushed him to hospital where they injected him with epinephrine in his thigh in the nick of time.'

'As I say, the pathologist will…'

'You've seen Ray's face. It's all puffed up. That's because he has the poison in his eyes. That'll be why he sought refuge in the ice house to get away from the fumes. Whatever he hoped to achieve by going in there, he could barely have seen what he was doing or where he was stepping.'

Alison frowned. Barry's agitation was to be expected. On the other hand he seemed desperately keen to dispel any notion that Ray had been pushed into the pit – he was anxious to deny even the possibility of foul play. 'You say Laura Bloom has invented her story about an intruder?

You think she is reliving her own recent past? Is there anything else about her I should know?'

'According to her, she has seen someone dressed in seventeenth century clothes. That's how disturbed she is.'

'Really? She didn't tell me that.'

'The clothes match those of William Lawrence whose portrait hangs in the house.'

'*The* William Lawrence, creator of the garden?'

'You know about him?'

'Yes, but why should he trouble Laura so?'

'She'll be saying next he haunts the place.'

***

Lady Ann Frost was never one to feel the cold, thought Alison, as she swept into the drawing room and sat down. She dressed for perpetual summer in a pink, short-sleeved dress that was printed with dazzlingly bright blue hydrangeas on a white background. Her greying hair was tied back in a ponytail.

'Really detective, I don't think I should have to be interviewed all over again. I feel like a criminal in my own home.'

'These things take time,' said Alison and did not move from her place by the fire. At once the sea serpents stopped wriggling as their grotesque, half human figures grew suddenly expressionless. They ceased to hiss in the heat. Each sharp, sibilant sound was no longer a sign of disapproval and derision. They would not drive her away as they writhed. Instead their grinning faces reverted to inscrutable wooden masks that were mere likenesses of their true selves – *they watched and listened.* 'Please bear with me while I try to establish the exact sequence of events over the last forty-eight hours. It's very important.'

'Isn't that why I'm here?'

'Laura Bloom says she quarrelled with Ray Knight in the greenhouse on the morning of New Year's Day. After that she didn't see him alive again.'

'But I did.'

'When? Where?'

'I was in the lantern study at the top of the house. I was standing on its balcony at about 12 noon. I looked down and saw Ray Knight cross the garden and enter the wood.'

Alison made urgent notes in her notebook. 'Did you see what happened next?'

'The foolish man set about tearing ivy off the ash trees like a mad thing. I'd say he was in a bit of a temper. He felt better for doing something bad I suppose.'

'Was he alone?'

'As far as I know.'

'You definitely didn't notice anyone go into the wood after him? No... *prowler*?'

'All I know is that he lit a very large bonfire. He shouldn't have done that. He can't have been thinking straight. Might have set us alight! As it was, the day was damp which turned everything to an awful fog. Covered half the garden! I had to shut the lantern's door in a great hurry because of the smell.'

'You can see the ice house from your balcony?'

'I'm afraid the fire went from smoke into smother in a matter of minutes.'

'You hadn't thought to lock the ice house's door?'

'I'd forgotten its very existence. Everyone had.'

Alison scratched her ear. 'Not everyone, surely?'

'You've seen the honeysuckle. The ice house is buried in it. Like a jungle! If Mr Knight hadn't deliberately gone poking about in there none of this would have happened. He is a victim of his own insatiable curiosity.'

'Thank you your ladyship. That'll be all for now.'

'I am so sorry the poor man is dead. I do feel responsible. Will you inform his family or shall I?'

'Leave it to me,' said Alison. 'Someone will call you in a minute to make a written statement. Now if you'll excuse me I must interview Mr and Mrs Mortimer. I do have one more question though. Who else lives at Green Way House? Do you have another son?'

'I already told you that my poor William died in a road accident five years ago.'

'No other friend or relative resides here with you?'

'Good grief detective, to whom have you been talking?'

'So no, then? I have to be sure.'

Lady Ann shot her a brief smile. Over the fire the hideous figures were all eyes again. They were wary, watchful, guarded. A serpent jerked its tail. 'Of course you must be sure detective. There can be no more secrets in Green Way House.'

'No more secrets?' queried Alison as she escorted her ladyship to the door.

Lady Ann passed the police officer posted outside with perfect poise. Her fierce gaze fixed his for a lot longer than he could endure, dared him to look away a fraction too soon. 'Every old house has its mysteries, detective. We simply have to learn to live with them.'

She might not be ready to blame anyone for Ray Knight's death, thought Alison, but something stuck in her mind. Her ladyship had just uttered an odd turn of phrase. When describing the bonfire that Ray had so foolishly lit in the middle of the wood, she had said "from smoke into smother". She had used the words to describe the smoke's progress when they were more often used to mean "from one *evil* to another".

***

'I'll always be here for her ladyship,' said Betty. 'That goes for my husband too, doesn't it John?'

Mr Mortimer declined to sit down in the drawing room as Alison flipped a new page in her notebook. 'Did either of you see Ray Knight go to the ice house yesterday?'

'No I didn't,' said Betty, 'but that wretched bonfire of his is still smoking now. I do wish Lady Ann wouldn't hire such... amateurs. I keep telling her we can't live like this every day, every minute, can we John?'

'To be fair dear,' Mr Mortimer replied darkly, 'her ladyship does have great plans. Her garden is her labour of love.'

'Love's not working, is it?'

Alison intervened. 'Neither of you lives in Green Way House?'

'Oh no detective,' said Betty. 'We wouldn't *live* here for all the money in the world. Green Way House is too dark, too cold, too *unforgiving*.'

'How about a relative of Lady Ann's? Some visiting cousin is staying here perhaps?'

Mr Mortimer quickly shook his head. 'No relative ever stays in this house.'

'You sure about that, because I've been told otherwise.'

'Then you've been told wrong.'

'You've not come across anyone in the grounds?'

'Lady Ann won't allow any visitors of any kind, not since her son killed himself.'

'Killed himself?' said Alison, startled. 'Lady Ann insists he was fatally injured in a hit-and-run accident.'

'She shouldn't lie to you.'

'That's what she told me.'

'She isn't always in her right mind.'

'But she was very specific: William died at the crossroads at the top of Greenway Lane five years ago. The driver was never identified.'

'Rumour has it that's where he *chose* to end it all.'

'You really think it was suicide, do you?' asked Alison.

'Who am I to say?' replied Mr Mortimer. 'There were no witnesses. The driver drove off because they believed they had knocked someone down in an act of gross carelessness? Then again, perhaps they were drunk or driving too fast? One thing's for sure, even if they had reported the crash they would not have saved his life. Half poor William's head was smashed with one blow.'

'I thought her ladyship was being straight with me.'

'She can't accept he's gone, is all.'

'Truth is everything.'

'It's been too long.'

Alison stared at the grotesque faces carved above the fire and they were quietly resentful, sullen, ill-tempered. 'So Lady Ann is something of a recluse on account of her son's demise?'

'Just like Green Way House's original owner,' said Betty. 'Just like William Lawrence in the 1690s. He couldn't bear to leave this house much after his wife and son died. He kept to the garden – made it his whole world until the day he passed.'

'That doesn't put you off? You're not frightened to work here? You don't think this place has bad vibes?'

'It's not as if my husband and I *need* to work in Green Way House, is it John?'

'No dear.'

'*We* are in too much demand. No one can get servants these days: things are so bad that some people are closing down their country houses completely. They have to cancel dinner because they can't find enough staff to cover weekends. Fact is, working for Lady Ann suits us, doesn't it John?'

'Well…'

'*She* doesn't make me change the sheets every day. *She* doesn't make me polish the silver too often.'

'I'm sorry,' said Alison, 'but what does this have to do with Ray Knight's death?'

Betty sat up and sniffed. 'That man was a disgrace. A real ruffian. Green Way House deserves only the best. As I say, Mr Mortimer and I could work in far better places than this. Top recruitment agencies like Polo & Tweed are desperate for people with our experience. We could go to a house with a swimming pool, cinema, gym, laundry block and dry cleaning machines, only we are loyal to Lady Ann because *she is a good person*. You don't meet many of those these days. She's pure in heart. Has a strong spirit. Ray Knight was neither good nor honest. He was not worthy of this house and its garden. His presence defiled and tarnished it.'

'That'll do dear,' said Mr Mortimer hastily. 'I'm sure Detective Sergeant Ellis would prefer not to hear our personal opinion of Mr Knight.'

'You aren't sorry he's dead then?' said Alison.

'Of course we're *sorry*,' replied Betty, 'only I'm glad he's not here to do any more damage. One reason my husband and I choose to work at Green Way House is because we both respect its history. We tell Lady Ann so every day. What would happen to it if it were ever to change hands? What if someone saw our departure as the chance to change everything forever? As I say detective, these other country houses all have their swimming pools, tennis courts and helipads, but not a walled garden. I couldn't bear it. What about you dear?'

'I feel the same.'

'Makes sense,' said Alison. The Mortimers' reverential enthusiasm for Green Way House and its grounds bordered on the fanatical. Or Betty was intentionally derailing her line of questioning to suit her own purposes. 'When did you last see Ray Knight alive?'

'To put it another way detective, I didn't see him finish work as usual.'

'Neither did I,' said Mr Mortimer, breaking into a sweat. 'Normally he's kicking fallen apples about the garden or throwing stones at empty beer cans, but yesterday he was nowhere to be seen.'

'The pathologist will confirm time of death, but what you say fits my initial thoughts – Ray died on New Year's Day. It just took a while to find him.'

'Will that be all detective?' said Mr Mortimer. 'Her ladyship wants me to clean out the gutters.'

'One last thing,' said Alison. 'Did you see Ray and Laura together at all? Would you say they actively disliked each other?'

'There's no room for discord in this place,' said Betty sternly. 'There can be no nastiness at Green Way House. It's a garden of mourning. I'd sooner blaspheme in a church or fornicate in its graveyard…'

41

'What else was I supposed to say?' said Laura angrily. 'Someone had to tell her – Detective Sergeant Ellis needs to investigate Ray's murder this minute.'

'And I have explained to her that he was killed by poison ivy, not by some mysterious prowler.... especially not by her ladyship's son!'

'You said what?'

'You saw how swollen his face was. Believe me, he poisoned himself.'

'Forget the ivy.' She was helping Barry inspect rhododendrons which ranged in size from bushes to trees. They grew so thickly in this part of the grounds that she felt lost in their maze. Leaves on one bush were a pleasant green on top and a pretty rusty-red underneath. By contrast another variety had shed all its foliage but was still coming into flower – their perfectly exquisite, rose-red purple petals showed to full advantage in the winter sunshine. Laura wanted to reach out and pick one particularly tempting bloom. She wished to bury her nose in its scent and nectar and dream of spring. 'Ray didn't break his neck down that pit by chance. Believe me, Ray met William in the ice house when he uncovered his hiding place. You and I are next. Meanwhile Lady Ann is covering for him by denying he even exists. Did you know her ladyship's husband died years ago in suspicious circumstances too? A farmer told me so in The Air Balloon.'

'We hardly know the woman,' said Barry.

'Seriously? You don't think she gave Ray a push, the same way she pushed me off the ha-ha?'

'Why would she?'

'Because she panicked.'

'Admit it Laura, you didn't actually see who pushed you into the ditch, did you?'

'Poor Ray fell into a trap someone laid for him. You were in the ice house. You know I'm not making it up, right?'

'It's not that.'

'I can't stop now.'

'I think you can.'

'Ha!'

'Take my advice,' said Barry, 'and leave well alone.'

'Ray deserves justice.'

'Not him, the flower. That rhododendron you're sniffing can be dangerous.'

'What about it?'

'Rhododendrons contain a nasty toxin in their branches, leaves and flowers. In 2008 nine famished North Korean children perished eating petals from a plant such as this.'

'But it looks so beautiful when so little is in bloom.'

'Farmers call it "lambkill" because young, inexperienced animals die when they consume it. Never keep bees near rhododendrons. The honey made from their nectar can make you very ill.'

'Thanks for the warning.' Far from satisfied, Laura began to pull up unwanted suckers that had grown from the rootstock. These were relatively easy to recognise because of their different leaf shape and colour. She had to remove them as far back as possible in order to discourage similar shoots sprouting again.

Barry passed her his pair of secateurs. 'That's odd. Someone has been doing our work for us. That's to say quite recently.'

'What makes you think that?'

'See here, a low branch on this rhododendron has been bent down into the soil and held in place with a peg.'

'What about it?'

'That's what we call layering. Whoever did this has made a nick in the underside of the shoot below ground level, from which roots will emerge.'

'Lolly Hooper and her friends must have done it last summer?'

'It's not a method much used by nurserymen these days.'

'Admit it, someone else tends this garden.'

'Whoever did it knows how to do a good job.'

'What do I keep telling you!'

'I'm not talking about your fictitious stalker.'

'These secateurs are blunt,' said Laura bitterly. 'What do you say I go back to the stables and fetch a saw?'

'You do that,' said Barry, unable to hide his irritation. Ray's demise had left him badly shaken. The last thing he needed today was Laura stirring things up. *Again.* He hadn't told anybody yet, but he was seriously considering leaving. He couldn't bear her planting any more seeds of doubt and suspicion.

***

Laura walked through the coach house and breathed the familiar smell of straw and horses. The animals were long gone from the stalls, yet the very old carriage had fresh mud on its spoked wheels. It was as though its wheels could spin round without a sound, as if the coach had been newly drawn along by invisible steeds with flowing manes and tails… She grimaced as an old song sprang to mind:

>My Ladye hath a sable coach,
>And horses two and four,
>My Ladye hath a gaunt blood-hound,
>That runneth on before.

Her duplicitous ladyship didn't deserve to be the chatelaine of Green

Way House when she let her son skulk in the grounds:

> My Ladye's coach hath nodding plumes,
> The driver hath no head,
> My Ladye is an ashen white,
> As one that long is dead.

She might not like it but Lady Ann's protection of him was twisted, depraved, vile... almost to be pitied. You and I share a fear of hostile shadows that is like a maggot in the brain, thought Laura, which was no whimsical fancy. It was imperative she discover the truth about William without delay. Her own life depended on it. She ought really to carry a knife or something. "Through truth, strength... Forewarned is forearmed... If you want peace, prepare for war".

Next second something brushed her face. She looked up to see a shower of dirt fall from the floor above. Oak boards leaked hay and straw as someone moved about directly over her. She didn't hear any scraping or sliding, but the silent plumes of dust and debris were enough to betray their progress through gaps and holes. They were quietly sliding one foot over the other as they advanced with cat-like steps along the length of the loft.

'Hallo?' cried Laura, as her hot breath condensed in the cold air. 'Come down whoever you are.'

She grabbed a pitchfork for her own safety.

Next minute she started up a set of rickety wooden stairs.

No one had reason to visit this part of the coach house-cum-stables any more, yet somebody had just disturbed its air of gentle abandonment.

They were padding about on creaky floorboards.

'I said where are you?' demanded Laura and used her fork's sharp prongs to prod a rotting haybale. A spider scuttled out. It was as big as her hand and ghost-white. The albino arachnid teetered on the tips of its toes. She saw it feel its way very gingerly, not like an ordinary spider at all. It had lived for so long between the hayloft's dark floorboards that she wondered if it had gone blind.

She kicked aside a second bale. 'I said come out, damn you.'

Slowly a young man extended a long, white spidery leg of his own. He came up for air from behind the stacked hay – he trained one grey-blue eye on her as he hid half his head with his arm. 'Did mummy send you? I bet she did.'

Laura levelled her pitchfork at his face. 'By that you mean Lady Ann, I assume.'

'What do you care?'

She got ready to stab him in both eyes. 'Stay back.'

'What are you afraid of?'

'Don't make any sudden moves.'

'Please don't hurt me.'

Dark shadows circled his eye sockets and he looked famished. All he had on was his grubby nightshirt. She watched him sweep handfuls of crumbling yellow hay from his naked thighs. He was cowed, defeated, *reduced* in stature. Mere skin and bone. 'I'm Laura. We met at the ha-ha.'

'I'm sorry I ran away.'

'Why did you?'

'You'd do the same if you knew somebody was after you with a gun.'

'Why was she?'

'She gets in such a temper.'

'For all she cares I could have ended up dead too.'

He hung his head in his hands. 'I'm that already.'

'No you're not. You're here with me.'

'Perhaps you're dead too.'

'What happened to your clothes? It's the middle of winter, for heaven's sake. You'll die of frostbite.'

'Tell her that.'

'If you don't have clothes you can't go outside the garden, is that it?'

'Not if she can help it.'

'Why won't Lady Ann let you leave?'

'It's on account of her son's death five years ago.'

'But you're him! You're William!'

'I'm his twin brother Liam.'

Laura froze. 'Lady Anne never said she had two sons.'

'Now she won't allow me out of her sight in case anything else bad occurs.'

Her pulse raced. Her head reeled. Despite everything, her heart went out to him. He appeared lost and innocent in his state of undress, like another Adam. *He didn't look like a killer.* 'So why hasn't Lady Ann introduced you to anyone?'

'It's on account of the things that have happened… '

'What mother pursues her own son with a loaded gun? Anyone else would say she is afraid of you?'

'That's because she believes I talk to those beyond the grave.'

'Only mediums can do that.'

Liam shook his head. 'She's convinced I can talk for my dead brother. She thinks William speaks through me.'

'Why would he?'

'Look at me. I belong in the grave too. My bones are rotting. I have no insides left. I stink of decay.'

'You really don't.'

'My heart, kidneys and liver are irreversibly injured. I have neurological damage and I frequently suffer from secondary infections. Everyone can see that any long-term prospects are out of the question.'

Laura had absolutely no idea what she was dealing with here, but she decided to play along. 'I don't know what nonsense this is,' she said sternly, 'but I'm inclined to think your mother has filled your head with all sorts of things that aren't true. She's using her skills as a psychiatrist to bamboozle you.'

'I wish it was that simple.'

'You say you're dead? I can't get my head around that. What does that even feel like?'

'It gets really scary.'

'You don't seem that scared.'

'I always feel on edge.'

'I don't know a thing about your medical history…'

'I 'died' when William did.'

'You suffer hallucinations?'

'Yes.'

'How's it going otherwise?'

'It's like some sort of chronic fatigue.'

Laura kept firm hold of her pitchfork. 'Hasn't your GP prescribed you any medicine?'

'There is none. You can't cure the dead. Doctors are in the same uncharted territory I am.'

She was inclined to help but not touch him. There were no cuts or bruises visible anywhere on his dirty skin. It was all psychological. 'Why hide here? What have you done that's so wrong?'

Liam hugged his bare chest as he rocked to and fro. If he had seemed better a moment ago, now his symptoms bounced back. He could not shake off the fearful fatigue that hindered him getting to his feet. His bones felt broken, his stomach shrivelled and his senses dulled. He was in the grip of some terrible dilemma… 'Truth is, William isn't dead. I am.'

'That's impossible. You just said it yourself, he was killed five years ago.'

'Have you not seen him prowling about in the garden dressed in his theatrical clothes? You've seen him in his coat and tricorne hat… '

'That's you.'

'You think?'

'Have you told your mother?'

'She already knows.'

'Of course she does.'

'She alone can say what really happened to him.'

'What do you think happened?'

Next minute there was a shout. 'Liam? You in here? Come out now.'

'Not a word,' signalled Laura and placed her finger on her lips.

She crouched low and peeked through a gap in the floorboards. Directly beneath her stood Lady Ann.

She saw her snap shut the barrels of her shotgun ready to fire…

42

Police Headquarters
Prism House
Gloucester

'It turns out Barry Barnes was correct all along,' said Alison. 'Ray Knight broke his neck but not before he was poisoned by poison ivy.'

DI Prickett looked up from his desk. 'Go ahead. Depress me with the details.'

'The pathologist has found swollen airways in his throat. Ray lit a bonfire whose smoke triggered an extreme allergic reaction – he must have suspected he was in danger of dying when he sought shelter in the ice house. He could have been dead in minutes.'

'Never heard of a bonfire killing anyone before.'

'It wasn't just the smoke that contained deadly urushiol. The same toxic oil was in the woody stems and berries that he touched with his bare hands. His palms have acquired a tell-tale rash and blisters.'

'So Ray Knight thought he was destroying everyday ivy, when he was really destroying something more deadly?'

'Ordinary ivy keeps its foliage all year but the poisonous variety doesn't.'

'I never knew gardening could be so lethal.'

'In summer poison ivy has fewer leaves.'

'Since when did you become the expert?'

'My grandma taught me: "Leaves of three, let it be".'

Prickett drummed his fingers on his desk. 'So Ray Knight has an attack of anaphylaxis and seeks shelter in the ice house, where he falls down its well. The SIO will be pleased. We can go ahead and close his case at least.'

Alison leaned in. 'Not yet we can't. I have fresh evidence.'

'What?'

'Ray must have met someone because he has left us a clue.'

'He has?'

'He died clutching somebody's silvery gold button.'

'You mean the poisonous smoke wasn't the only reason he sought shelter in the ice house? He was trying to escape from somebody?'

'Or they were already inside when he entered. He surprised them. There was an argument. The result was a struggle and a fall?'

'You really think they threw Ray into the pit?'

'More likely Ray was so surprised by what he saw that he didn't have time to look where he was stepping. It's possible no one actually laid a hand on him as such. Rather he lashed out to save himself from falling. We're checking for another person's DNA. Nothing so far.'

'You really believe somebody else was in the ice house?'

'We should find the owner of this button, don't you think? We should do it urgently,' said Alison and passed him the photographic evidence.

'That's not like any button I've ever seen before.'

'I agree. A modern fastener has two or four holes in it for attachment. This one is a cast pewter button. It fixes to the garment by way of a single hole through the shank on its back.'

'You know something about that?'

'As you can see, it has been wrapped in silver and gold thread which suggests its wearer was well-to-do.'

'Was? Why the past tense?'

'I've had it dated. This style of button was used on gentlemen's coats and waistcoat in the 17th century.'

'I'm sorry, you've lost me. What is a button like that doing in an ice house?'

'There was a walking cane in there too, with the initials WL burned into the wood. As it happens they stand for William Lawrence who was the house's original owner. Whoever left it behind is most likely interested in the theatre or historical re-enactments.'

Prickett snarled. 'What re-enactments?'

'Hobbyists get together to recreate the past by dressing up in the clothes from a particular period. They buy them from speciality stores or stitch them together themselves. It's a very old tradition. In 1674 King Charles II staged a recreation of the siege of Maastrict in which his illegitimate son James, Duke of Monmouth, had been a key commander. Samuel Pepys wrote all about it in his famous diary. Some people take it very seriously and strive to make every detail exactly right. They create a "living" history. First-person interpreters will feign previous folk from past ages – they pretend not to know anything of the events outside their epoch. Such people talk in antiquated dialects and use old-fashioned mannerisms. Highly visual things like buttons have to be just right.'

'So we're looking for someone who likes dressing up as William Lawrence?'

'I don't have any other explanation, do you?'

'It may be nothing.'

'I know something very wrong happened in that ice house. I can feel it.'

'Any news yet on Lolly Hooper?'

'Thanks to Laura Bloom I've spoken to Zac who runs the nurseries opposite Green Way House. He remembers Lolly well. Says she is a keen painter. I'm about to contact the SAA about her…'

'By that you mean the Society for All Artists?' said Prickett.

'Their online directory says it has over 1500 UK based affiliated clubs. Lolly may have joined it to hold exhibitions and meet others in her local area who share her passion for art. Once I have details of the clubs it's just a case of working through their membership list to find anyone who knows her. They might give us a clue as to where she is now. The SAA site should enable me to look for all local art clubs in a five, ten, twenty, fifty and one hundred miles radius of here. The first thing I have to do is enter Green Way House's postcode. That's if she isn't already dead.'

'God forbid Laura Bloom is right and someone is targeting everyone who works at Green Way House.'

'We can't rule it out.'

'Better do the same with the local re-enactment clubs while you're at it. Better see if anyone from Green Way House has ever been involved in anything theatrical.'

'That's just it, they have. Lady Ann's dead son William studied seventeenth century drama at university.'

'I mean anyone *living*.'

'Okey-doke.'

'By the way sergeant, where are we on the facial reconstruction of our man in the refrigerator?'

'Good news. The lab has come up with a high-resolution, three-dimensional computer image. It's our Paul Carter all right. I've already had Lady Ann positively ID him.'

43

Laura gestured frantically to Liam. Waved at him in complete silence. At the same time she bent her knees lower and lower as she mimed descending the stairs in slow motion from the hayloft. She meant her, not him. Instead Liam took fright. Went to run. She furrowed her eyebrows at him and placed her hands on her hips to demonstrate her annoyance. When he went to sidestep her again she raised both palms flat in front of her face. She acted as if they had to find a way out of an invisible box – she identified its corner and sides. She slid her fingers across the "edges" of the imaginary prison as she warned him to stay put or else. She mouthed at him: leave this to me.

Seconds later she grabbed an armful of mouldy hay and started down the wooden steps as bold as brass. 'Good morning your ladyship.'

'Laura? What on earth are you doing in the hayloft?'

'I'm collecting old fodder to place on the flowerbeds to protect them from any more frosts. Hope you don't mind?'

'I'd say felling that beech tree overhanging Greenway Lane deserves more attention, wouldn't you?'

'Uh-huh.'

'*How* is it you've not done what you were told?'

'Have you seen the daffodils? They're a foot high already in the middle of the knot garden. They'll bloom very soon if the weather permits.'

Lady Ann frowned suspiciously. 'Never mind about that! Who were you talking to just now?'

'No one,' lied Laura cheerfully. 'Why do you ask? Is something wrong?'

'There was a break-in at Zac's nurseries recently. I'm worried about intruders.'

'Could Ray have met a prowler too?'

'What's it got to do with you?'

'I think about him all the time.'

'Let's rely on the police. Let them come up with the answer.'

'But it's so upsetting and mysterious.'

'Death changes everything and nothing at all.'

'How can somebody be with us one minute and gone the next? Does nothing now separate our life from his?'

Lady Ann frowned. 'It's really borderline, isn't it?'

'What if we never find out exactly why he fell into the pit?'

'You're not far wrong.'

'Why would anyone go to a place so dark?' asked Laura. 'Why take the risk?'

'The same reason you did. He wanted to know what lay beyond its black door.'

'I fear I wasn't very nice to him.'

'Don't worry, regret is our lifeline. Regret is how we keep hold of our lost friends and loved ones.'

'Betty warned me the garden is a dangerous place.'

'From now on the door to the ice house will be kept firmly locked.'

'Good. That place is a danger to anyone who goes poking about where they're not wanted.'

Lady Ann shot Laura a steely look. 'You might want to remember that.'

'Oh I will, don't you worry.'

'Come to the house tomorrow after you finish work. Bring Barry with you. We'll drink a toast to Ray one last time while he is physically if not spiritually still in this world. We'll discuss the next phase of the garden.

I have exciting new plans to show you.'

***

Lady Ann did not ascend into the hayloft after all, Laura observed thankfully. Instead she took her word for it that there was no one upstairs and marched off to inspect the carriage in the coach house. After that she looked in every stall on her way out.

Laura watched her return to Green Way House empty-handed before she called to Liam.

'It's okay. You can come down now. Your mother has gone.'

Total silence greeted her from the dusty loft.

'I said the coast is clear.'

But Liam was no nowhere to be seen after she mounted the stairs. 'Damn it,' she thought, 'where have you gone to?'

Laura arrived at an open doorway where fodder had once been unloaded from horse-drawn carts parked in the yard below. Liam had slid down a drainpipe and disappeared in the cat and mouse game he liked to play with his warder. He had been ready to reveal some vital truth about his brother.

Unless the dead really did walk in the garden.

Lady Ann hunted Liam day and night.

Unless that man was not this one?

One brother had to be the dead ringer for the other.

Was not Liam simply a nickname for William?

44

Cathedral Close
Gloucester

'Yes, I'm Lolly Hooper. What of it? Who wants to know?' The red-haired young woman kept the door on its chain. Peered round it. A smudge of cadmium yellow oil paint marked her chin. 'If this is about the rent again, you'll just have to wait…'

'I'm Detective Sergeant Ellis from the Gloucestershire Constabulary,' said Alison, holding up her police warrant card.

'How did you find me? I've ditched my phone. I've even erased all presence on social media. As far as the world is concerned I'm as good as dead.'

'Another painter suggested this address.'

'What do you want?'

'I need to question you about Paul Carter and Lars Visser.'

Her long slim paintbrush slipped through Lolly's fingers. Her face fell. 'Please don't tell me something bad has happened?'

'I wish I had better news.'

'Wait while I let you in.'

'Thank you,' said Alison and took her foot from the door.

Lolly led the way into a conservatory-cum-studio. Its sliding glass windows faced a small yard that lay in the shadow of Gloucester Cathedral. 'I'm sorry about just now. I thought you were a church bailiff. The diocese is doing its best to evict me because I'm three months behind on my payments for this place.'

'It can't be easy selling paintings these days.'

'I've had nothing but bad luck lately. A shadow hangs over me somehow – I can feel it dogging my footsteps. *Someone* won't be happy until I'm dead or destitute, that's for sure.'

'Since when did anybody want to do you harm?'

'What if they still do?'

Alison came to a halt beside an easel and canvas. 'I see you're painting a picture of Green Way House?'

'Its owner asked me to do it, but I can't seem to get it right.'

'What is it that bothers you?'

'Lady Ann Frost will only take it if it's perfect.'

'But it looks perfect to me.'

Lolly wrung her hands. 'You don't understand. Only bad things ever happen there.'

'What's that got to do with painting its picture?'

'I can't paint it if I don't feel right.'

'That I can understand. Anything truly creative has to come from the heart?'

'The trouble is, Green Way House has left me with too many troubling memories.'

'For instance?'

Lolly paled. 'You mustn't tell anyone if I tell you.'

'That bad, is it?'

'One day the three of us – Lars, Paul and me – were instructed to lop a very old, very big beech at the edge of the garden.'

'I think I know the one.'

'The tree's forked trunk grows out over Greenway Lane and Lady Ann Frost wanted it cut down in a hurry, so I climbed a ladder to begin sawing off its branches. That's when I saw something carved in the bark. It read "cor unum 1697". I gave Lady Ann a shout because I thought she might want to preserve it. Instead she became very angry. Cut it down and burn it at once she said, because it was hideous, ghastly, evil. The minute I set to work a bough broke under me. I fell fifteen feet to the ground. Cracked my skull on a stone…'

'Stop right there. Did you write HELP ME in blood on the floor of a caravan parked in the grounds?'

'You know about that?'

'It's another line of enquiry.'

'I really thought I would bleed to death from the cut on my head.'

'Lady Ann did all she could to help you?'

Lolly scoffed. 'She did what she had to and no more. She made Lars carry me to my caravan's bed and said I was not to move. I was left to drift in and out of consciousness for what seemed like ages… It might have been days.'

'And that didn't strike you as strange?'

'Not then. Not at first.'

'Did someone not send for a doctor immediately?'

'I have blurred memories of a man bending over me to examine my wound one night. I can still picture his dark coat, gold waistcoat and yellow teeth… I heard the rap of his cane on the caravan floor, although I might have been hallucinating. Who knows?'

'Sounds like you were terribly unlucky?'

'Not to Lars I wasn't.'

'Excuse me?'

'There was no luck involved he said, only malice. That branch I broke had been half sawn through already. He accused Lady Ann of deliberate sabotage.'

'What did she say to that?' asked Alison.

'She said something very odd. She said, "Sometimes you have to let something die to let something live."'

'She was of course talking about the tree?'

'Maybe.'

'Sabotage is an odd accusation to make? What made Lars choose that particular word, do you think?'

'Because we both saw Lady Ann's son in the vicinity when it happened.'

'I know for a fact that William died in a road accident at a crossroads near Ullenwood…'

'He has a twin brother who lives.'

'What brother?'

'Lady Ann keeps him confined to the house and garden.'

'She has told me otherwise.'

'He's her sick Liam.'

'There is someone called Liam who lives at Green Way House?'

'As I say, she does her best to keep him hidden from the rest of the world.'

'What happened exactly?' asked Alison.

'We were digging in the former kitchen garden when a section of high brick wall collapsed right next to us. Another step sideways and we might have been killed.'

'I've seen those walls. They're very old. The mortar securing the bricks is mostly missing. It wouldn't surprise me if they didn't all collapse one day soon.'

'Either the wall fell or it was pushed. There's a difference.'

'Do you have any evidence?'

'I found fresh shoe-prints behind it. I saw toes and heels. Some weeks later Lars was drinking tea as usual during his ten a.m. break in the greenhouse, after which he was violently ill. Despite Lady Ann's objections Paul drove him to hospital in Lars's own car, where doctors said he had ingested some highly poisonous aconite. They had to flush out his stomach as they fought to save his kidneys. Any more and he would have died that day for sure.'

'Aconite is about right. The pathologist's report has identified its presence in his body.'

'Lars has died? Oh God. Doctors did all they could.'

'Sorry.'

'Only Lars took sugar in his tea. He reckoned its jar had been tampered with.'

'Or the poison got into a cut on his hands when he was digging up roots in the garden?'

'Let's just say Lars and Liam hated each other from then on.'

'What else do you know about this Liam?'

'I know he helped Paul smoke his stock of cannabis. They met in the former brewhouse behind the south range at the back of the house. That's where Lady Ann caught them puffing on spliffs and kissing.'

'Not what I was expecting.'

'He and Lady Ann had a big row about it.'

'Keep going.'

'Paul thought Liam was being mistreated, as did we all. For her part Lady Ann threatened to blow his head off with her shotgun for supplying the weed.'

'I see.'

'Wait detective. Is that the only news you have or is there something else you have to tell me?'

'Please take a look at this,' said Alison, producing a picture from her pocket.

'What is it?'

'It's a facial reconstruction of a person we recently pulled from the Coombe Hill canal.'

'Why show me this now?'

'Is he one of your fellow gardeners?'

'That's Paul all right.'

'Are you quite sure?'

'Of course I am. Why do you ask?'

'He's dead too.'

Lolly hunched over her stool. Uttered a groan. 'How can this be?'

'Paul Carter died from non-digitalis cardiac glycosides present in oleander plants.'

'You'll find plenty of those in Green Way House's greenhouse.'

'If Lars and Paul argued with Lady Ann about Liam, it can't have made for a very pleasant atmosphere?' said Alison.

'It didn't help that Lars had such a violent temper.'

'How bad was he?'

'The poisoning brought out the worst in him. He wasn't well, but he insisted on going back to work in the grounds. It was as though he had been bewitched by a spell. Everyone had trouble staying on the right side of him. We were all under suspicion. Even the garden didn't like him, according to Paul. He became more and more paranoid about it.'

'What about Paul?' asked Alison. 'When did you last see him alive?'

'Paul vanished soon after the episode with Liam in the brewhouse. Lady Ann professed to know nothing about it. Denied she wanted him to leave.'

'That's not what she told me. She said she had decided to fire him.'

'She and Lars rowed about it. One thing led to another. Next minute Lars brings up the subject of the aconite again. He blames her son for setting traps for us in the garden. He accuses her of knowing all about it. Says it to her face. Her son wanted them all dead or gone, he said.'

'I doubt Liam wanted that.'

'Someone did.'

'But not Liam?'

'I wouldn't rule it out.'

'How can you be so sure?'

Lolly rubbed her brow. She did it intensely, angrily, painfully. 'Because there's something very strange about Liam.'

'Strange, how?'

'He's too repressed. Quiet. He doesn't wash much. He once said he should die for the awful things he had contemplated doing, such as murdering his father and raping his mother. He felt scared and thought one of us should report him to the police for all his bad thoughts and that he would go to prison.'

'What happened then?' asked Alison.

'The last I heard of him he was refusing to eat. He said the food was as rotten as he was. He said someone would kill him if he didn't kill them first.'

'Did you believe him?'

'Of course not. No one did, but he was already a shadow of his former self.'

'Did Liam ever threaten you directly?'

'No, but I quit Green Way House the first day I was well enough to leave my caravan. I wish to God I hadn't. I should never have left Lars to face him alone.'

'You seriously think Liam killed Lars?'

'*I* never said that. Lars was paranoid, is what I said. He was convinced someone was trying to kill him. If it wasn't Liam it was somebody else. He talked about it every day. Said he'd seen someone prowling about in the grounds. But you're right, Lars most likely poisoned himself with aconite by accident.'

'Only we have a pattern.'

'What pattern?'

'Someone called Ray Knight has just been found dead at the bottom of a pit in Green Way House's ice house. He was a gardener too. In light of what you've just told me I will have to talk to Liam as soon as possible…'

Lolly didn't trust the sound of her own voice. Spoke in whispers. 'Just to be clear, I never said I saw Liam hurt anyone, detective. I don't know why he would do anything like that. He vehemently denied it was him we saw in the glasshouse or by the fallen wall. For all I know he was telling the truth when he said he was being followed too.'

'*Followed?*'

'You won't believe me if I tell you.'

'Please try.'

'It's hopeless,' said Lolly. 'I saw too much and now I can never run too far, no matter how much I try to hide…'

'Who did Liam see follow him?'

'He said he saw William.'

45

'What do you mean, he *saw* his dead brother?' asked Alison, appalled. 'That makes no sense?'

Lolly's voice became a whisper. 'Liam had taken to wearing William's stage clothes. He dressed for his part in a play from his days at college. Shortly after that he began to see him everywhere.'

'It's true William played roles in seventeenth century dramas, but…'

'It's more than that.'

'Grief plays cruel tricks. I can quite understand one brother might want to dress up as the other to remember him by…'

'What if Liam was mistaken? What if the person he saw only looked like William in his period clothes?'

'Are you trying to tell me he saw someone else?'

'If you were in my shoes you'd say the same.'

'What shoes are those?'

'Trying to blot it all out does no good.'

'Then it's time to face facts.'

'You don't understand detective, you really don't.'

'Let me be the judge of that.'

'We are not alone.'

'Hurry up and explain.'

'I've seen him too.'

'Him?'

'He likes to sit on a white metal seat in the rose walk.' As she spoke Lolly walked over to a row of paintings that stood propped against the wall on the floor. Suddenly she pulled a cloth from their frames. Each picture showed Green Way House finished in all its detail, where she had obsessively striven to capture some elusive quality of light and shadow. The great number of oil paintings – as many as fifteen – had the same forced perspective and foreshortened horizons, the same bird's-eye view of house and grounds.

They reminded Alison of the early eighteenth century engraving by Johannes Kip. That's when her heart gave a leap. If one painting depicted a bewigged figure in one part of its composition, then the next did the same in another part. She blinked hard. From some angles the occupier was totally invisible. On one canvas the contrasts between pale and dark were all hard edges, in another they were softer, while in a third the transitions were so smooth that she could barely see where they blurred. Yet there could be no mistake. Every colour – green, red, blue, purple – had an underlying value somewhere between black and white: it was only where the colour contrasted along this edge of light and dark that he emerged from the shadows. 'Why paint the same view so many times?'

Lolly wiped away a tear. 'Have I not said? I haven't a choice. Lady Ann has commissioned me to paint something perfect. Trouble is, *he* won't let me alone. *He* won't let me paint anything without him.'

The bewigged, black-coated figure was to be seen standing in the knot garden, upper court, orchard and rose walk. He walked by the sunken lake or he emerged from the stables in his red-heeled shoes. He was the focal point of Lolly's attempts to depict Green Way House in all its glory. All leading lines led to him – he was the centre of the picture's harmony, rhythm, movement and balance despite all her efforts to the contrary. He smiled just enough to show his teeth with a hideous grin.

'Can't you simply take a brush and paint him out?'

Lolly almost choked. 'How do you obliterate someone who has no brain, nerves, stomach or soul? He doesn't exist because he's dead, yet here he is. House and grounds *are* him. If I'm wrong and Liam did hurt Lars, it would only be because he was made to do it? By this man?'

'What man in fancy dress can make anyone do anything?' replied Alison flatly.

'All I know is that I led a perfectly happy life until I went to work at Green Way House. Once you try to change things there, *he* won't let you go. *He* won't forgive you.'

'Are you really trying to tell me this is not Liam in his brother's stage outfit?'

'More likely it's somebody like him.'

'It doesn't sound very plausible.'

'What do you know?'

'I know you should help me solve this.'

'I doubt he wants that.'

'What does he want?'

'He wants to be left alone to tend his garden.'

Alison looked Lolly straight in the face. 'What is it you're not telling me?'

'You can see his portrait in Green Way House.'

'I'm aware of such a portrait.'

'You are? Then you must know the garden has a very strange history. Its creator died before he could complete it. His name is…'

'He *was* William Lawrence.'

Alison pointed again to the man's black wig, coat and red-heeled shoes. In one painting he doffed his tricorne hat at her, in the next he leaned on his cane. 'Clearly the sight of this centuries' old gentleman has made a great impression on you. He has become your muse.'

'Muse and nemesis. They're not the same.'

'That's no reason to fear a portrait.'

'Let's stop trying to kid each other, shall we? You looked shocked when

I uncovered my paintings just now. You half *expected* to see someone present in the garden, only now you want to deny it?'

'Well, I...' Alison recalled Paul Carter's history book and its engraving. It was true, she did want to refute what she had seen with her own eyes. She especially did not want to think of the man depicted on its balcony as William Lawrence.

'Admit it detective, you believe he inhabits the garden as much as I do.'

'I believe no such thing.'

'All I know is this. Whoever or whatever prowls its paths will borrow your soul to show you Hell. He has done it to the rest of us and he'll do it to you.'

***

Alison felt a chill run down her spine. Lolly struck her as a very capable, talented person but a terrible urgency gripped her now. She watched the artist hastily conceal her paintings under their cloth again as their spectral witness threatened to hold them both spell-bound. Who was she to deny the garden's creator had some malign influence over people's lives? Nor did it seem to her that Lolly overreacted, as each imperfect depiction of Green Way House and its garden hinted at infinite powers of wickedness? And yet a flickering voice in her head said *'Beware should you believe in him too!'*

'Help me out here Lolly. Did you, or did you not, see any actual criminal activity at Green Way House while you worked there? What real evidence do you have to think that anyone intended to harm anyone else?'

Lolly looked horrified. 'You're the one who says three people have been poisoned.'

'That doesn't make it murder.'

'Then why are you here?'

'Because somebody has gone to a lot of trouble to cover up their deaths.'

'It's the garden, I tell you. Something about it gets into your head. Makes you think terrible thoughts. *Do* awful things.'

'There must be a more logical explanation for it all.'

'Why does that feel worse?'

'I don't think it's you.'

'Am I that transparent?'

'Please Lolly, think hard. Can you remember anything else that struck you as odd while you stayed at Green Way House? Any detail might help me.'

'Says you.'

'This could be very important. Who would want you believe the unbelievable? Who would have Liam believe the same?'

Lolly's panic did not desert her. 'There is someone.'

'In your own time.'

'The night Paul disappeared I saw him drive away from the house with a passenger beside him in Lars's car. He turned right out of a gate close by me, which was when I saw his face behind the wheel. There had been a lot of talk about getting rid of a large broken refrigerator. Lady Ann didn't want to pay for its disposal at a council depot. She may be very rich but she is also very mean – she wanted them to dump it in a field or ditch instead.'

'How was Paul?' asked Alison eagerly.

'That's just it detective, he was deathly pale. He looked like he'd seen a ghost himself. He stared straight ahead as they swept by. Either that or he was high on something… in a trance.'

'You say 'they'. Did Lars go with him?'

'No, he was back in hospital.'

'Who then?'

'I can't be absolutely certain, but it looked to me a lot like John Mortimer.'

46

Green Way House

This evening Lady Ann Frost was all glitter and glaze like her name, thought Laura enviously. She appeared resplendent in her sleeveless cocktail dress. Spirals of white nylon braid brightened its milky net material, which was stitched with crushed plastic tape that sparkled like specks of ice. Its high neckline and front bodice dripped clear, rimy dewdrops sewn in a 'V' to her waist. Meanwhile two red plastic rosebuds were pinned above her left breast. It was not the first time her ladyship, a person of great intensity and blessed with large cold eyes, resembled a winter wonder.

'Spring is just around the corner when we can look forward to great things,' declared Lady Ann happily. Their host clearly meant what she said, even if dark circles round her eyes indicated more insomnia. 'Already the snowdrops are beginning to flower. I may have failed before but I won't do so again. By this time next year the "hortus conclusus" will be firmly re-established. We will have restored it to its former glory.'

'Poor Ray,' agreed Laura, 'he did his best, but he was totally out of his depths. We'll get on faster without him.' The drawing room, an elaborate floral composition of red and pink roses, was filled with flickering firelight from the blaze in the hearth. The chimney piece's four grotesque wooden faces mimicked living ones until they were the distorted equivalent of twisted souls. They revelled in something crude, primitive and vulgar.

'We have suffered a terrible setback,' said Lady Ann, handing everyone their glasses of sherry. 'Ray Knight has been taken from us, but what better tribute can we pay him than a beautiful garden that will last forever? In his own small way Ray contributed to the creation of a place where people can live out their values in nature. Each new generation will be able to express themselves perfectly in tune with something undefiled, wholesome, heavenly.'

'Barry and I share your vision for Green Way House. We'll make it the best garden ever. For Ray's sake as well as yours.'

'Bless you child. I can't tell you how much that means to me. Let's raise our glasses. May the dearly departed find the peace he deserves.'

'To Ray,' said Laura readily.

'To Ray,' joined Barry, clinking glasses.

Laura was all renewed enthusiasm. 'We should shape the hedges into topiary your ladyship. We should have towering birds, spirals, spheres and pyramids. They can be new features throughout the grounds. Of course we mustn't do anything too drastic. There must be nothing too roughly made or contrived. Nothing too coarse or artless.'

'Naturally we should experiment with new designs here and there, but... how can I say this? Certain things – *ideas* – don't take too readily in this garden, it has to cooperate first.'

'But isn't that what a garden does best?' argued Laura. 'After it dies back in winter it starts afresh in spring? In slightly different form. With pieces of its old self. I think this life-in-death rebirth is the purest form of existence – that's what is so fascinating.'

Lady Ann refilled her glass with sherry. 'I used to think that. I have tried to think like that. Yet there is a greater truth to be told by what we don't alter.'

'A garden doesn't die,' said Barry, 'it only fades and disappears for a while. If we wait long enough something will return to fill its vacant spaces. It might be a nettle or it might be a wild orchid. We can never wholly predict what will happen.'

'Life is nothing without surprises, that's for sure. Take this morning for instance. The police rang me to say that Lolly Hooper is alive and well and living nine miles away in Gloucester.'

'Lolly is alive?' said Laura and dropped her glass.

'Perhaps now she'll finish that painting I paid her for. I'm so glad nothing bad has happened to her. I must confess I was a bit worried.'

Laura trod broken glass. 'That can't be. She's…?'

'Why her long silence I'll never know. It's so rude.'

'It's a miracle.'

'We can only hope that what comes back from the dead is what we want,' said Lady Ann darkly. 'Now if you'll excuse me, I'll go see if Betty has prepared those honey sandwiches I asked for. I'll get her to sweep up your glass.'

'What? Oh I'm so sorry…'

Barry watched her ladyship quit the room in a hurry. 'That was all very odd, I must say.'

'Agreed,' said Laura, nursing a cut on her hand. She had not so much dropped her glass as crushed it.

'I felt for a moment she was about to confide in us.'

'I also felt we were not going to like what we heard.'

'You did?'

'I don't trust her.'

'Is that why you broke your glass?'

'Forget the glass.'

'We mustn't do anything to upset her.'

'We'll see about that.'

'What are you doing?'

'Inform her ladyship I've gone back to my caravan. Tell her I have to bandage my hand. It'll give me time to take a look upstairs.'

'Are you crazy?' said Barry. 'You'll get us both fired.'

'That's why she mustn't suspect I know a thing.'
'What do you know?'
'I've talked to her son.'
'What? How can that be? Where?'
'In the hayloft over the coach house.'
'And you were going to tell me, when?'
'I'm telling you now.'
'But Lady Ann says William is dead.'
'I'm not talking about him. I'm talking about his twin brother Liam.'
'William has a brother?'
'He lives here in the house.'
'So he's your prowler?'
'Admit it, I was right and you were wrong.'
'Why lie to us? Why keep him a secret?'
'I have to go and find out. Lolly Hooper may be alive, but her two fellow gardeners aren't.'
'You'll take that risk?'

Laura was already at the door. 'Lady Ann has tried to stop us talking to her son ever since we arrived. Is it because of what happened here in the summer? I want the truth and only Liam can give it me. It's now or never.'

***

Laura slipped quietly out of the drawing room and started nimbly upstairs.

She was not worried about meeting Betty since she could hear her whiny voice coming from the kitchen. Mr Mortimer was in there too, chatting to Lady Ann.

Mounting worn, wooden treads she arrived at the portrait that hung on the wall on the quarter landing. Stopped dead. William Lawrence's head of dark, curly hair gleamed under the dirty varnish as he rested his hand as usual on the broken heart that lay on the table before him. He sat very upright on his plain wooden chair with a general air of importance. Sad cypresses lined the garden depicted in the vista behind him, via which he could exit at any time.

Still the painting was changed, or she felt differently about it. William Lawrence might be gripped by grief, but his yellow teeth revealed themselves in his slit of a smile.

He turned his head three-quarters towards her in a polite, discreet way that invited her to approach closer. Suddenly his eyes stared straight at her. It felt like a bold challenge, a calling to account.

He was summoning her to a final test or trial.

'How peculiar,' Laura said to herself and braved the portrait's forbidding if exhilarating gaze to touch the canvas. William Lawrence's white lacy shirt showed at his throat and its cuffs protruded from his sleeves. She used her fingernail to trace the gap between his two long and voluminous strands of black hair that hung down the front of his coat.

There could be no doubt about it.

'What painter paints their sitter with a silvery gold button missing from their gold waistcoat?'

She hurried away. She went from door to door. Tried their handles in vain. She had to wonder what was so vital that so many sealed rooms had to be kept from prying eyes.

She was not the only presence who wandered these upper floors that were forever meant to be off limits?

It was when she reached the third floor that she realised she was at the foot of the stairs that led up to the sunlit study.

On her right was the bedroom from which she had once seen Betty leave with a tray of food and pills.

She pressed her ear to the door's wooden panels. For all her tip-toeing about in the house so far she had heard nothing living in its silent corridors.

Then from the room there issued a sudden moan.

'Who's there? Is that you Betty? It's too early for my medicine.'

'It's me, Laura.'

There followed a startled silence. Then a chair fell over. Next minute someone banged both fists on their side of the door. 'Thank God. You've found me. I knew you would. I staked my life on it…'

47

Police Headquarters
Prism House
Gloucester

'It's gone six already,' said DI Prickett, collecting his coat from its peg. 'Don't work too late.'

'Laura Bloom is right about Lady Ann Frost. It turns out she has literally been leading us up the garden path,' said Alison. 'She's the mother of two sons, not one. The survivor is called Liam. He has been staying in Green Way House all this time. If she can lie about that, what else isn't she telling us?'

Prickett wrinkled his nose. 'Did Lolly Hooper confirm anything else of interest?'

'We can be pretty sure that the aconite which killed Lars Visser came from Green Way House's own garden. Also those oleanders that finished off Paul Carter can be found growing in its glasshouse.'

'What's this about Lars's car?'

'Lolly says Paul drove his green Volvo Estate on the day he disappeared. That would suggest Paul left the house of his own free will. Guess what? She says Lady Ann's butler, John Mortimer, went with him.'

'Forget them for a moment. You say Lars thought Liam tried to kill him? What else do we know about this Liam?'

'It seems he has a drug habit. Paul was a user too. Lady Ann caught them smoking cannabis together in the brewhouse. One reason why she keeps her son cooped up at home is to keep him away from bad company. She polices him day and night with a loaded gun to see off the dealers.'

'You think she's crazy?'

'I think she could blow all our heads off.'

'Someone like that shouldn't own a gun.'

'She has a valid licence.'

Prickett threw his hands in the air. '*What?* How is that possible?'

'Lady Ann's firearms certificate was revoked but later returned to her, after she completed an anger management course.'

'What else about Liam?'

'He isn't well. He could be depressed or he could be dangerously schizophrenic. The drugs might be his way of coping or they could be one reason for his strange delusions. He dresses like his dead brother and believes he is dead too.'

'Why does that sound familiar?'

'He has to be the young man I ran down at the crossroads at the top of Greenway Lane?'

'Don't tell Lady Ann that. She'll probably shoot you too.'

Alison took a deep breath. Exhaled slowly. 'It's imperative I pay Green Way House another visit. We need to know where Paul was driving that night.'

'As you say, we've been played.'

'Did he drive the seven miles to Coombe Hill where his body was found in the canal three months later?'

'Go. Go now sergeant. Find out what we're dealing with here.'

'Okey-dokey.'

'You still not convinced about something?'

'What makes you say that?'

'I know what you're like.'

Alison frowned. 'It's the way Lolly said it. She saw Paul drive out of Green Way House as if in a trance. He was as white as a sheet, she said. He turned right out of the gate close by her. Except Lars brought that car with him from the Netherlands. You've seen it: it's left-hand drive. It couldn't have been Paul sitting that close to her because that would put him on the wrong side of the steering wheel.'

'Which means what exactly?'

'Suppose Paul was dead or dying already? He was strapped in the passenger seat beside the driver whose only purpose was to dispose of the body in plain sight. He wanted Paul to be seen departing apparently alive and well from Green Way House by any witnesses? I've checked CCTV footage on all roads out of Cheltenham. One camera records the Volvo Estate on the Tewkesbury Road at 10 p.m. on the night of August 12th. It doesn't show any faces.'

'The road to Tewkesbury goes straight to Coombe Hill.'

'Once at the terminal wharf the driver placed Paul in the refrigerator that Lady Ann had asked him to dump in the disused canal? Could it be John Mortimer wanted to clean up without her knowledge?'

'No, no sergeant, she's in on it, I bet you. She probably planned the whole thing because she wants to hide her son's compulsion to murder innocent people?'

'We don't know that yet.'

'Believe me, she hurts everyone who lets her down.'

'Be prepared to ring Force Response at Bamfurlong Lane. We might need to have armed officers ready to raid Green Way House a.s.a.p.'

'Either way I want results.'

'Her ladyship must find it hard to live with all the lies.'

'She'll find it a lot harder to live without them.'

'Whatever the reason, she's at war with the world,' said Alison.

'Absolutely.'

'Or somebody is at war with her.'

'Say what you have to sergeant.'

'You yourself discovered it on Google Maps: some other person roams Green Way House's garden. We need confirmation from Lady Ann. If it isn't Liam, who is it?'

48

'It's no good, I can't get in,' said Laura, twisting the brass door handle back and forth.

Liam's voice reached her through his room's keyhole. 'Look above you. Betty keeps a key on top of the door frame.'

Laura stood on her toes and felt along the narrow ledge of wood. Her fingers touched something cold and metal.

'Stand back,' she cried as she inserted the key in the lock and gave it a turn. 'I'm coming in.'

The room was sparsely furnished with an old four-poster bed at its centre. Her breath turned white in its frosty air. While a fire had been laid in the grate, no one had lit its wood and coal for ages.

Liam sat up on his bed to protest his lonely existence. All he wore was his usual soiled nightshirt. A large, black fly crawled down his cheek which he failed to notice. Instead his face slowly formed an expression of helpless, tearful hope. His distinctly spidery hair hung long, limp and straight over his thin face. His grey-blue eyes dazzled in his otherwise washed-out, wan features which belonged to someone who was both ill and was being treated very badly. The blankets slipped from his bare torso which looked to be skin and bone.

She had been all set to accuse him of murdering Lolly Hooper, but she had been sadly mistaken. If she had been wrong about Lolly then she might be wrong about Lars and Paul. If Liam was no killer then he lived in fear of who was?

She tried not to scare or embarrass him. 'For heaven's sake, this room is like an ice-box.'

'The dead don't feel a thing.'

'I'm going to help you get out of here.'

'You tried that in the hayloft…'

'Your mother will go too far one of these days. She has to be stopped.'

'I know what I said but it's not so easy.'

'You can walk, can't you?'

'Some days are better than others. Today I have a chest pain and a bit of a fever. My head feels like a lead balloon.'

'It can't do you any good to lie here for hours on end.'

Liam beckoned her closer. His manner was weak but welcoming. 'It's the silence I can't stand...'

'No one should be shut up for so long,' said Laura earnestly and rubbed his cold hand. 'Why *does* your mother do it to you? Is it because of what happened to Lars Visser and Paul Carter?'

'She says she only wants to protect me from myself.'

'Did *she* poison them? She did, didn't she?'

'Believe me, my mother isn't to be trusted.'

'But it's so unfair on you.'

'She has stripped me of my life to keep me alive. She has taken all my power and control and I don't know if I will ever recover.'

'I should take you to a hospital right away.'

'What's the point of that when I don't have a recognised disease?'

'So tell me again. What does 'dead' feel like?'

'The only way I can describe it is like maggots everywhere inside me.'

'I've never spoken to a dead person before.'

'I feel swallowed up by people whenever I meet them. In their company I experience a shortness of breath, a tight chest and my heart races until it is about to burst. Just talking to others is exhausting. It's like an allergic reaction. I suffer from chronic stomach pain, a swollen throat and even stinging in my eyes and tongue…'

'Yes, I understand that,' said Laura eagerly. 'When I was sent down from university I wasn't able to drive, go shopping, or walk my dog Lola for fear of being stalked. It was really upsetting. It still is.'

'My mother is writing a medical paper about me to be published in a psychiatry journal. She lost her job on account of her unorthodox views on how to cure patients. Making sense of my peculiar case is her way of restoring her reputation among her peers. You could say I'm her human Guinea pig. The irony is I'm meant to be her ticket back to the world. Her concern for me is her last throw of the dice, not for my sanity but for her career.'

'What makes her think she has the right?'

A fleeting shadow crossed Liam's face. 'She says I have some sort of brain damage. A history of depression could be the reason or it's on account of my fondness for drugs. She says that's why I've become less social. Some days I don't feel like speaking at all.'

'Or she has invented the whole thing to keep you close?'

'The voice in my head says I'm dead or dying.'

'Anyone will feel like death if they don't eat enough food and get enough exercise.'

'I have no stomach, brain, nerves, soul.'

'Is that what she tells you?'

'She says that only she knows how to save me.'

'How exactly?'

'In summer she takes me into the garden. She points to a flower and asks me to name it.'

'What do you say?'

'I say it's not a flower. I tell her it doesn't exist, no more than I do.'

'Then what happens?'

'She gets very cross. She says only the beauty and tranquillity of the garden can heal my sick soul. She believes its sights, sounds and scents will reset my brain. I'll be like Adam before Eve. Pure. Unblemished. Receptive. All the awful things I have seen and experienced can be wiped clean. No more narcotics for me.'

'Bit of a long shot.'

'She might be right: there are things I would do better to avoid.'

Laura resisted his faux pity. 'Tell me how your brother died. What happened back then to leave you and your mother so traumatised?'

'I know what I said, only…'

'Think about it. You can trust me.'

'William should tell you himself,' said Liam quickly. 'He should sing like a canary.'

'Dead men don't sing.'

'If only.'

'Did Lady Ann shoot him dead the same way she blasts her rabbits and foxes?'

'She might as well have done.'

'I knew it.'

Liam looked spent, empty, drained. If he had given up washing himself it was because survivor's guilt had overcome him? 'My brother and I were helping her tend the garden when it happened. She smashed his head half off with the mini-digger. She rotated its cab and hit him with its steel bucket when she must have known he was standing so close by. What if she was aiming for me? I was drenched in his blood and brains. I've let her get away with it all these years, which is why I helped her stage that crash at the crossroads…'

'*Stage*? Whatever do you mean?'

'Mother and I moved William's body to the top of the hill at the end of Greenway Lane. We made it look as if he had been run over by a large truck. It was meant to be a hit-and-run accident or suicide, or both.'

'She'd do that to save her own skin?'

'You don't know her. She can't risk her professional reputation a second time.'

'And you agreed?'

'She has a way of getting inside your head… Like one of those maggots I mentioned.'

'But all she had to do was tell the police the truth? Who kills their adored son? An accident is an accident.'

'No chance of that.'

'You think the police would have discovered evidence against her?'

'My mother says the digger took on a life of its own. She says she couldn't control the levers as its cab spun round at William. She said it felt as if someone else was driving it. But there wasn't anything wrong with the controls. She made that bit up.'

'So she literally staged her own child's death elsewhere?'

'No one is safe at Green Way House,' said Liam, persisting with the idea of his mother's persecution. 'We're all as good as dead already. You should know that by now. You just said it yourself: Lars and Paul died here. And all because she can't forgive herself for what's she's done.'

'That doesn't explain why you think it's William you see.'

'He won't rest while she hides the truth.'

'No ghost roams the garden.'

'Who else walks around in a seventeenth century coat and wig? Who else carries his hat under his arm?'

'But those are the clothes you wore at the ha-ha.'

'I told you, they belong to my brother. Everything I have of his dates back to the days when he performed plays at college. He particularly loved 17th century comedies by Dryden…'

'That explains a lot.'

'You'll find more under the bed.'

As instructed, Laura bent down and fished out a pair of old-fashioned shoes with red-coloured heels.

Next she drew out a large suitcase by its handle.

'Go ahead, open it,' said Liam.

Inside the case lay a tricorne hat with ostrich trim, an embroidered coat, a white lace shirt, a man's dark stockings and a fancy gold waistcoat. 'So you've managed to keep hold of them ever since the day William died?' she confirmed.

'Not exactly. I found the case dumped in the pit in the ice house.'

'You go to the ice house?'

'It's another place I hide from my mother. Its door is blocked by honeysuckle, but you can wriggle round it if you know how.'

'Who left the suitcase there, do you think?'

'There was a time, years ago, when we used the ice house as a garden shed. My mother must have hidden William's theatre clothes in there after he died. She could neither bear to have them in the house nor destroy them forever, I suppose. I took some of the items but left the rest in case she ever returned and grew suspicious…'

'Those clothes are gone now.'

'Because somebody else has them.'

'Go on.'

'I decided to dress up to feel like William. After a while it became like a drug. At least that way I get to torment my mother.'

'Or someone else is doing the same to you? Somebody very alive is out to frighten you with your own greatest fear?'

'Who?'

'I have my suspicions.'

'Better that than a real ghost.'

'Don't worry, I'll get you out of here. I'll ring the police.'

'No, that won't work. You can't do that. My mother will go berserk.'

'What else do you suggest?'

'The first chance you get, you must steal one of her guns.'

'That won't be easy.'

'I'd do it myself but I've failed every time.'

Laura knit her brows. 'I want to help, I really do.'

'You'll find some shotguns locked in a cabinet in the library.'

'We can make a citizen's arrest.'

'Not before we force her to write a confession absolving me of any guilt.'

'That's a fair point.'

'I'm so lucky to have you.'

'That's a shame,' said Laura suddenly. 'You appear to have lost something.'

'What is it?'

'The waistcoat is missing one of its buttons.'

'Last time I wore it, it was in good shape. You've seen how my mother behaves. She won't let me have normal clothes of my own. She doesn't want me inhabiting the real world which she says is the root cause of all my troubles.'

'All the more reason to get that gun.'

'I have no idea where she keeps the key to the locker.'

'Don't worry, I'm on to it,' said Laura and stole like a thief from the room. She might once have failed to press her complaint at college because everyone in authority had ganged up on her, but this time she wouldn't be such a coward. She still felt ashamed of herself, not because someone had taken advantage of her while she slept but because she had given up on the truth. People in power had bullied her into submission by their inaction. They had even pressed her to sign a Non-disclosure Agreement. Now someone else was having his life ruined because no one would help him. Somebody had to do something fast. She couldn't walk away again like a coward.

Even so, it was hard to believe the all-seeing Lady Ann didn't suspect that he dressed up in his brother's costumes from years ago. It was strange she hadn't yet caught him wearing them in the garden? It was also difficult to believe Betty had kept her mouth shut. Liam had as good as lied to her, Laura suspected, or the alternative truth was too hideous to face. Either way she could be no help to him until she had a lethal weapon. She urgently needed to think of a plan.

***

'Oh there you are,' said Lady Ann, her smile beaming and benevolent. 'Are you feeling better now?'

'I'm all right now I've washed my wound,' said Laura, breezing into the drawing room. It was a risk returning but an even greater one not to.

'Barry said you suddenly came over all faint. I do hope it wasn't the sherry?'

'I don't normally drink alcohol.'

'Goodness. Why didn't you say?'

'I thought one glass wouldn't hurt.'

'That must be it then. I'm so sorry. I'll ask Betty to bring you an orange juice.'

'That would be nice.'

'Meanwhile do help yourself to a honey sandwich. The honey comes from my own bees.'

'No thanks.'

'You should try one,' said Barry, 'they're really good. I've eaten three already.'

'I'm glad someone appreciates my hospitality.'

Lady Ann was being charmingly persuasive, not like a killer at all, thought Laura as she failed to warm herself by the fire. Her trip to the top of the house had left her feeling totally chilled. In her bones. The hideous figures carved above the fireplace eyed her distrustfully. If they could have spoken they would have told her not to start something that could only end very badly.

'So tell me Barry,' Lady Ann was saying. 'What next for my garden? Did Laura tell you? I have drawn up a planting schedule of my own?'

Barry shot Laura a look. He urgently wanted to know what she had just discovered upstairs. 'There's a great deal we can do, your ladyship, now the weather is improving.'

'What do you have planned for tomorrow?'

'In the morning Laura and I will cut back the leaves on the hellebores. That way you'll be able to see their pretty bell-shaped blooms.'

'Can you please take a look at the Viburnum tinus in the upper court. It's a picture of lovely pinkish-white at the moment, but last summer it suffered from a powdery mildew. I really don't want that to happen again this year, I want it to be perfect.'

'I'll keep an eye on it your ladyship. We had a dry summer last year, whereas viburnum likes rain.'

'Good. I don't want to lose it. Did you know people have been growing viburnums here since the 17th century?'

'I'm so sorry,' lied Laura, 'but my head really is killing me. Do you mind if I go back to my caravan?'

'You poor thing,' said Lady Ann. 'Of course you must go and lie down. It's to be expected. These latest events have affected us all.'

Laura smiled sweetly. She backed out of the room with exaggerated apologies. On her way she hissed in Barry's ear: *remember what you told me about bees and rhododendrons. Don't eat any more honey sandwiches.* Then she fled with almost manic haste hellbent on survival.

She was still thinking of the suitcase of clothes that Liam had been so keen to show her. He impersonated his drama-loving brother in some bizarre and sinister re-enactment? Or he played some peculiar game in which his mother had him dress like a doll? Either way, it had everything to do with this world and absolutely nothing to do with the next. That silvery gold button that had appeared in a dead man's hand in the ice house had simply come from someone's theatrical clothes. It was a relief to be given such an innocent explanation for its origins.

Or she should still be very worried.

49

'You in there Barry?' Laura banged her fist on the door of the blue Classic Sprite caravan. It was 8 o'clock in the morning and she needed to share with him her dangerous plan. He might have let her down badly before but this was his chance to make amends.

She used its flat tyre to step up and peep in through its window. Seconds later the caravan's door yielded to her shoulder. A saucepan of porridge boiled black on the stove... She had to switch off the gas before any more damage was done. A full cup of tea was growing cold on the fold-down table. It was imperative Barry keep watch for her while she stole Lady Ann's gun, but something had happened to call him away in a hurry?

'Have you gone to the house,' she wondered, 'or are you somewhere in the grounds? Then again you might be about to return.'

Not for the first time Laura felt the garden observing her, calmly but cruelly.

A half-filled suitcase lay on a bed. Barry had packed most of his clothes but not his mobile phone. Anger gripped her. 'You stupid fool. What makes you think you can leave here on your own terms?'

Laura ran outside. Hurried to the green 1966 Sprite Musketeer. Mr Mortimer had done a good job cleaning it out after Ray's unfortunate demise. It was as if he had never existed.

Every spick and span surface gleamed ready for the next inhabitant.

There was no sign of anyone anywhere. Barry had left of his own accord or he had been taken.

She thought again of Liam shut in his room. Together she and Barry must secure his release without delay. '"Hope for the best, and prepare for the worst... She who hesitates is lost".' She broke into a run, but the ice on the ground meant she had to stop and grope her way forwards on the frozen stones – several times she lost her footing and with it her balance. One careless mistake saw her skate a considerable distance...

Her shouts drowned in the fog. The mist did not just chill her to the bone, it deliberately misled her. Its slimy and elusive motion dragged at her heels. She was in the company of something unreliable, shifting, unscrupulous.

It was necessary to blunder from one part of the garden to another, until she came to the path to the stables.

'Barry? It's me, Laura.'

There was no trace of her co-worker in the stalls or in the coach house. Only the six-in-hand stood with fresh mud on its wheels. Laura's heart hardened as a mocking song recurred in her head:

> My Ladye hath a sable coach...

The world is about to see the truth about Lady Ann Frost despite all her efforts to the contrary, thought Laura and exited the stables to enter Green Way House.

Betty went to block the front door but jumped aside at her approach.

'That's right,' said Laura, 'get out of my way.' Mr Mortimer emerged from the kitchen and he too stopped open-mouthed at her quick advance. The solidly built butler-cum-caretaker was as usual dressed to feel comfortable rather than to impress. That was one way of describing him, she thought – a better one was dirty and dishevelled. Man and wife scowled at her with sullen distrust while she passed boldly by. They exuded an air of decay as strong as the house itself whose power, wealth, energy and beauty had all been allowed to deteriorate so drastically.

'There are going to be some big changes round here,' said Laura, marching into the library, if only because she wanted to sound as bold as she behaved. 'Where does Lady Ann keep the key to the gun cupboard?'

Betty put her hand to her mouth and whimpered. Only then did Laura realise how much she was trembling. 'She keeps it on a chain round her neck. If her son were ever to get hold of it…'

'He's the reason I need it.'

'You're not about to do anything rash, are you?' said Mr Mortimer.

'Not promising anything.'

'Lady Ann won't be happy.'

'No, probably not.'

Laura swept past the many shelves of books that had been acquired over the centuries, until she came to a slender mahogany cabinet. It was about twenty inches wide and eight inches deep and stood five feet high. No present day police force would have approved it. All modern gun cabinets used on her farm in Lincolnshire were made of solid metal. Its top edge was badly scratched where Lady Ann was in the habit of throwing her shooting belt. Two double-barrel shotguns showed through its dusty glass door.

'What are you doing?' asked Betty.

'What does it look like? I'm taking a gun.'

'Say that again.'

'You know what has to be done.'

Laura tried the cabinet's door and confirmed it was locked. What struck her most about the house right now was its sense of excited expectation, like a soft anticipation of applause close by… it might have come from the garden.

Mr Mortimer looked grave. 'I wouldn't do that if I were you.'

'No, I don't suppose you would.'

'At least let me come with you.'

'Not in a hundred years.'

That said, Laura picked up a chair and threw it at the cabinet's door.

She smashed its glass to smithereens. Then she reached in and chose one of the 12-bore weapons.

'Why now?' asked Betty. 'We have a right to know.'

'I'm going to free Liam.'

'But we thought you were such a nice girl.'

'Well, you thought wrong. The present state of affairs has been allowed to go on for too long. Where does Lady Ann keep her cartridges?'

'You'll find those in the drawer below.'

Laura crouched down and pulled hard at the drawer's two brass handles. Slid it open. Legally, shotgun cartridges did not have to be kept under lock and key which was lucky for her.

50

I have come full circle, thought Alison as she neared Green Way House. I first met Liam in a dense fog like this and here it is again, waiting for me at his home.

She crossed Greenway Lane in order to rattle the gate to the garden. To her great surprise it yielded to her touch.

Visibility deteriorated further as she entered somewhere maze-like, confusing, deceptive.

She was invited to lose herself in its wreaths of white vapour.

'Whoever stalks this garden makes the rules,' she murmured, then reproached herself for saying it. To voice it was to accept it as true.

She advanced quietly, since stealth best suited a place so private – she felt it incumbent upon her to walk respectfully along its paths, as in a graveyard.

It was not so bad.

It was not so good.

Twigs and branches littered the ground from storm-tossed trees. She arrived at the entrance to the knot garden and on one side of its stone gateway were the words "media vita", she noted. On the other was the remainder of the motto "in morte sumus". '"In the midst of our lives we die".'

Alison trod grass and weeds grown wild to arrive at another gate ready to exit. More words in Latin were fixed to its metal bars which read "mortui vivos docent", which she translated as "the dead teach the living". She was in some sort of court where rough grass changed to gravel.

She followed the crunch of her boots until she found herself about to climb a flight of stone steps. 'This part I remember,' she thought with relief. 'I'm at the front of the house at the end of its driveway.'

Halfway up the steps her left foot fouled something solid in the fog.

'What the hell!' cried Alison. There was a flash, as when things moved too fast. She lost momentum. Spun sideways. Her breathing couldn't keep up with her brain – she was head over heels and flat on her back. She knew she was down, but felt as though she were floating… Then came the bang. Her right arm struck one of the steps' ornamental pillars as her ankle doubled under her. She went to stand up but could only stay still. Someone yelled out in pain. Then the deafening thump that had been the sound of her hitting the frozen ground ended in silence.

That yell had been hers.

She felt all round. A tree's fallen bough had just felled her?

She went to lift the branch that blocked her way… Twigs were slippery with ice still joined to the bough.

Except this was no branch, it was a human arm stiff with cold. These were not twigs she grasped but someone's fingers.

Next minute she frantically clawed at the bare, white body of a dead man.

She skidded on his frozen vomit…

51

Laura flipped the break-level on her shotgun and hinged its butt from its barrels. With both breeches open she calmly inserted two black 70mm shells side by side in the holes – she had used JK6s before when shooting rooks on the farm. She clicked the gun shut again and checked the safety catch was on. She kept her left hand on its stock and cradled it firmly in the V of her forefinger and thumb. At the same time she used her firing hand to grip her weapon behind its trigger guard... she held it firmly but gently. The 28inch long barrels felt a little top heavy but also very good.

Neither Betty nor Mr Mortimer attempted to stop her. The matter was, they acknowledged, out of their hands.

She mounted the grand staircase at speed to its quarter landing. William Lawrence stared back at her from the wall. His vivacious smile brimmed with satisfaction.

Laura climbed more stairs, then headed in the direction of the study and its lantern on the top floor. A maze of corridors branched out from the original 17th century house via its nineteenth and early twentieth century extensions – she was in the original H-shaped building much altered and expanded. At first the walls were all dark oak panels, but then came a corridor hung with decorative patterns. She knew she was in the oldest part of the house because one narrow, horizontal strip of paper had peeled away from the top of the wall to reveal copper nails. Still it was a shock to realise how far back in time she had gone. Each roll of paper had first been pasted onto canvas then tacked to the wall, well over three hundred years ago.

Suddenly the hairs rose on the back of her neck. She had come to a stop before a very pretty scene depicting a lake set in substantial grounds. A familiar white pavilion stood on an island in the middle of its mirror-like surface. Topping the building's roof was a weathervane in the shape of a freshwater pike. This was Green Way House's garden as it always would be. A man sat fishing at the lakeside with his back to her. The fish wriggled on its hook, the birds flapped their wings, the ducks waddled, the flowers swayed in the invisible breeze. She half expected the angler to turn his head and offer her the same joyous smile that William Lawrence had just given her in his portrait. He, like him, was dressed in a dark coat and black tricorne hat.

Dangling from the angler's line was a fish that he had just hooked from the water.

Elsewhere the block-printed scene displayed ducks, clouds, birds and flowers. Each of its fifteen colours had been applied separately and edged with arabesque red roses. The same scene was repeated all the way to the end of the passage.

'I'm looking at an ideal depiction of someone's perfect garden,' thought Laura, amazed. 'He is sitting in his own little paradise.'

Who are you, she wondered...?

Could anyone achieve such perfection and still be murderously disappointed?

...curator or killer?

It was not until she reached Liam's room that she calmed down. Its door was locked, but its key lay as usual on top of its wooden lintel. She was almost beside herself with joy when she entered. Its semi-naked occupant looked shocked to see her with her gun slung over her shoulder. He fixed her with his wide-open eyes, which was when she noted what strange pupils he had. They were full of surprise, admiration, bewilderment, but also horror.

He couldn't believe she had kept her word since yesterday.

'Quick. Get dressed,' said Laura. 'We're getting out of here.'

'What have you done?'

'I've done what I said I would do, I've broken into your mother's gun cupboard.'

'But I'm dead. I can't go anywhere. I have no muscles, ligaments, veins…'

'I said get dressed. Any minute now Mr and Mrs Mortimer will find your mother and bring her here.'

Still Liam dithered. His face, the colour of parchment, looked blank. Long locks of hair hung down over his thin shoulders and crawled with lice. 'But I've told you I don't have any proper clothes. My mother won't allow it.'

'You have your brother's stage costume, don't you?'

'It's that or nothing.'

She fought back giggles while he donned coat and stockings. He looked very dapper in a dead man's red-heeled shoes. He called to mind the fisherman by the lake. Most of all she thought of William Lawrence in the portrait on the quarter landing. 'Hurry. I think I hear someone coming.'

'Just… give me a moment.'

52

Barry Barnes lay face up on the garden steps. Alison ran her hand over his exposed neck and it was stiff, hard, bleached. No pulse. His skull leaked red, but the intense cold had all but stopped the bleeding. His left leg was badly twisted, obviously broken. 'You slipped on the ice, much as I did. But why were you in such a hurry?'

Prior to his fall something had made him violently sick. He had been sufficiently ill to fear for his life?

He had hoped someone in the house might come to his rescue?

Instead she observed a torn shirt lying on the ground where he had failed to claw his way up the steps in time.

Nearby lay his trousers.

They looked like one of the last bits of clothing he had shed.

'You stopped to vomit. In so doing you stumbled and fell and knocked yourself out. While you were unconscious your body temperature dropped too low,' thought Alison. 'Your hands froze first, even as you shivered violently to generate enough heat to protect your vital organs. By the time you came to, you were totally confused. A lack of oxygen to your brain meant you woke up with visual and auditory hallucinations. You most likely suffered bewilderment and amnesia.'

Her foot came to rest on a patch of ice that had frozen yellow.

'Once your kidneys began to fail you had a real urge to urinate – you weren't even able to control your bladder.'

That was the paradox of freezing to death, it played a final, cruel trick on you. 'Your nakedness explains one thing but not the other,' thought

Alison. 'You were ill but you most likely died from hypothermia. At 85 degrees Fahrenheit your body felt unbearably hot, so you took off all your clothes in the sub-zero temperature. Or someone took them off for you…'

Barry Barnes had expired in less than an hour.

53

'This way,' urged Liam and directed Laura through a shabby, unpainted door at the end of the corridor. 'We can go down these backstairs used by the servants years ago. This is how I escape undetected from the house to the garden.'

The steps were dark, steep and narrow. Laura did not like them. Suddenly it was not only Lady Ann they were defying, it was also the shadows.

The secret stairs spiralled down three floors inside the stone walls. They kept descending until they arrived in the kitchen.

Liam lost his nerve again. The prospect of escape suddenly seemed too daunting. He displayed an abrupt incapacity to step outside his prison! A cruel paralysis possessed him.

She had to seize him by the hand and drag him over the threshold. When he spoke he was barely coherent. 'What next?' he complained.

Laura peered intently at the fog. 'We need go to my caravan to pick up my things. That's when we make a run for it. We'll escape via the gate to Greenway Lane.'

'Mr Mortimer has the key.'

'Then we'll climb over the wall.'

'He will have hidden the ladder.'

'That still leaves the old beech tree.'

'Are you really determined to save me?'

'Do you doubt me?'

'Last time someone tried to help me they nearly ended up dead.'

'Not me. I'm not Lolly Hooper.'

'Good, because there might never be anyone else to ask again.'

A path led via the upper court to the vicinity of Greenway Lane in the direction of the stables. Laura successfully steered by the house. Once past the knot garden it was harder to get her bearings. That's because the mist was an endlessly shifting barrier – whichever way she chose scarcely seemed to be of her own making.

She really should have demanded that Mr Mortimer hand over his skeleton key. Or she should have made him open the garden gate for them at gunpoint. Now it was too late. Liam was no help. He was increasingly like a frightened child.

'Stop right there.' The voice was horribly familiar. The fog warped the sound of the words so that they could have been in front or behind them. 'Liam? Is that you? Come to mummy.'

Laura signalled to him to keep walking…

'I don't know what you hope to achieve,' said Lady Ann, 'but you're making a big mistake.'

…signalled him not to say anything.

Next minute her ladyship emerged from the mist and blocked their way. She gasped to see Liam dressed in his brother's costume. *'William?'* She visibly shook then corrected what her eyes told her. Snapped back into action. 'Lay down your weapon Laura, before one of us gets hurt.'

'Stay back or I shoot. It's not William, it's Liam. And he's coming with me.'

'Don't be stupid. You may think you are helping him, but you're really not. None of this is your fault. You want to do the right thing but that's not enough. It never was.'

'With me,' hissed Laura. She seized Liam's hand whose fingers were already stiff with cold. 'Now!'

'Please Laura, be sensible. Can we at least talk about this? My son isn't safe outside these walls. Not even you can police the whole world.' There was real urgency in Lady Ann's panting voice. Laura saw her hot breath condense in white clouds – she was inhaling and exhaling the spectral garden like someone drowning.

'I already told you, Liam and I are leaving this minute.'

'You know that's not possible.'

'You've a wicked, evil woman. You deserve to rot in hell for what you've done to your own son. You keep him shut up like an animal, but his days of humiliation are finally over.'

'Come back to the house. Let's discuss this amicably.'

'Why should I? For all I know I'm your next victim?'

'What makes you think you'll be anyone's victim?'

'Paul Carter. Lars Visser. Ray Knight. They all worked and died here.'

'You think *I* killed them?'

'Who else? The same way you killed your husband and son.'

'Can anyone vouch for that?'

'Liam can. He has told me everything.'

'Not everything clearly.'

Laura stood her ground. 'What did you and Lars argue about? What did Paul and Ray do wrong in your opinion? Did they threaten to ruin your grand project by not creating your dream garden exactly as you envisaged? Or did they promise to be a bit too successful? They were about to give you what you're too afraid to have? That's the reason why they all had to be punished, isn't it?'

'Who told you that nonsense?'

'Is it really nonsense? I consider you to be a cold-blooded murderer. The more I think about it the more I wonder if you even have a soul?'

'Thanks for asking.' Lady Ann uttered a little laugh. It was an expression of disappointment, pain, hope, scepticism.

She was testing her, thought Laura? If not, she sought to mock her.

'Run Liam, run!'

Laura was first to reach her caravan. She pushed Liam inside and shut the door behind them as she began throwing clothes into a suitcase. 'Stay low. Heaven knows what she'll do next?'

'We should have climbed the tree... jumped over the wall,' said Liam. Pre-occupied and subdued, he did as he was told. At the same time he gave her a look of fury she found incomprehensible. Gone was the hope she had given him. In its place was the discontent of someone who had finished with love and life, who only went through the motions of living because he had no other choice. His momentary flash of vacancy scared her rigid. Was she mistaken about him? She'd been wrong before. 'Now what will happen to us?' he said bitterly.

'I'm just as worried as you.'

They didn't have to wait long. Minutes later Lady Ann marched out of the fog. She had gone back to the house to fetch her other gun. She had found a second store of ammunition for it somewhere. Her ladyship stood with her feet shoulder-width apart. She flexed her knees slightly as she turned her body roughly forty degrees to the side of her target. Then she aligned her eye evenly with the shotgun's sight by keeping her cheek tight to the stock – she let her head rest against it by relaxing her neck ever such a little. 'Come out here Laura while you still can. Don't be afraid to open the door and run. *Run fast* – I'll cover you.'

Instead Laura released her own gun's safety catch. She took aim too, even as her ladyship's weasel words played tricks with her mind...

54

Alison stepped inside Green Way House and it was cold, dark, brooding. A recalcitrant atmosphere hung over its gloomy hallway.

'Hallo. Anyone there?' she shouted and her voice echoed down dusty corridors. Recant, recant they seemed to say. Disavow your fixed opinions... Yet her presence here also felt inevitable, as though she had been summoned back according to someone else's plan.

Mr and Mrs Mortimer came running up to her. 'Thank God you're here detective. Laura Bloom has gone berserk. She has stolen one of Lady Ann's shotguns and will surely kill somebody if she isn't stopped soon.'

Alison looked into Mr Mortimer's one good eye and it burned with virtuous triumph. Had he not known the girl would be trouble from the moment he met her? Now was the time finally to get rid of her. 'Where is she?'

'Laura and Liam ran into the garden. Lady Ann has gone after them.'

'Why Liam?'

Betty screwed up her nose at her. The look on her face was pure hatred. 'Laura wants to seduce the boy and ruin his life. She's a very bad apple.'

'Why threaten her ladyship with a gun?'

'You wouldn't believe me if I told you.'

'Try me.'

'All I'll say is that you can't run away with the dead.'

'Who's dead?'

'Please detective, believe me when I say Liam died years ago and not his brother.'

'Are you saying Liam is really William?'

'I'm certainly not denying it.'

'Please explain how that's even possible.'

'I won't tell you because I can't.'

Alison reached for her phone to call police headquarters in a hurry. 'This is Detective Sergeant Ellis. Request armed back up now. I'm at Green Way House in Shurdington. Suspect has a gun. Send an ambulance.'

Next minute she heard a gunshot.

It came from the garden.

55

After the bang, a deathly silence. The freezing cold air reeked of burnt powder as Laura reloaded her shotgun. She poked it out of the caravan's window. She lowered its barrels in line with her target instead of the sky. 'Get away! Next time I shoot to kill. I'm leaving Green Way House and so is Liam.'

Lady Ann called back from the shifting mist. 'And I thought I could trust you.'

'Why are you such a wicked, wicked person?'

'It's not me to whom you should be directing your question.'

'So much bad stuff has happened since I set foot in this garden.'

'Can't disagree with you there.'

'Liam has told me what you did to his brother. I'm going to see to it that you pay for that.'

'Is that what he says?'

'You staged a road accident to save your own skin after you killed William with the digger.'

'It's not me you should be afraid of.'

But Laura was not taking any chances – she was tracking her opponent's every movement. She might have aimed wide the first time, but she was confident that she could hit what she wanted if she chose to. A shotgun's long barrels allowed more of the powder's pressure to accelerate the shot. The gun's high muzzle velocity meant the pellets would spread out less. 'I'm warning you, Liam and I are ready to fight to the death.'

'How far do you think you'll get?'

'Who cares, so long as it isn't here.'

'Others before you have thought the same and failed.'

'I suppose you have a better idea?'

'Put the gun down and give me my son back.'

'What if I don't?'

'Yes mummy, what if she doesn't?' cried Liam and wrenched the weapon from Laura's hands. 'For the past five years you've told me what to do. It's what medicines to take, where to go and where not to… I can't breathe. You've made me live within these walls as if the real world will always be too big and brash for me…'

'You know I've only ever tried to protect you.'

'The claustrophobic atmosphere of Green Way House, my isolation, my illness – these are the only, bitter fruits that grow here.'

Lady Ann stepped from her protective cloak of mist. Now mother and son stood in a face-off for all to see. 'I didn't kill anyone. You did.'

'You made me take William's body to the crossroads. You made me stage the road accident for your own ends.'

'That was yourself.'

'Damn you, you're my Hell's keeper.'

Laura went to stop him, but Liam was through the caravan's door in a flash with his shotgun aimed low. He targeted his mother with a sharply angled swerve. The incensed young man saw red and with virtually no margin for error, he unleashed a passing shot from one barrel…

Pellets caught Lady Ann in the thigh, but she did not go straight down. Instead she staggered away into the mist with a yell of anguished sorrow. 'You're not him! You're not my sweet Liam!'

56

Alison exited Green Way House in a great hurry, just as a second whip-like bang came at her from the mist.

'What the devil!' The blast shook the garden, which gave an involuntary judder. She felt it recoil, shrink, shrivel for a moment. She did the same, only to feel doubly confused. Because that first bang had only been the muzzle blast. What she experienced now was its ballistic shockwave. A mass of lead shot echoed the burnt propellant already expelled from the gun's barrels. She literally expected some second projectile to hurtle at her from out of nowhere, as the new noise sliced the fog at twice the speed.

The bam-bam took her breath away. The air changed pressure. She felt her head spin and the ground open under her, yet it was a mistake to suppose she had been bloodied.

She straightened up again when someone swept by her in a blur. She glimpsed a figure dressed in a long coat and red-heeled shoes through the fog. With a jerk of her head she was aware of heated voices... all this in a few seconds. Then Lady Ann screamed: 'Leave me alone, damn you! Oh God, oh God, what have I done?'

Her ladyship aimed her gun all round. Her finger was poised on the trigger ready to fire at whoever chased her.

In the air came a song.

'Who's there?' said Alison taking a step back. 'Show yourself, damn you.' The voice was empty, hungry, lacking.

The singer fought to fill their hollow throat with a few words only:

Oh think upon the garden, love,
Where you and I did walk.
The fairest flower that blossomed there,
Is withered on its stalk.

57

It all happened so fast, thought Laura. One minute Liam was crouching and sheltering in the doorway of the caravan, the next he was gone with her shotgun and cartridges... She had tried to wrest the weapon back from him, when a greyness had come over his face like a veil. His dead expression, devoid of feeling, saw his pupils burn without flame. He had ceased to focus on her with living, seeing eyes at all... They'd displayed a detachment which was reckless, mechanical, ruled by purpose.

Now blood streamed from her head where one barrel had blasted her ear in the ensuing struggle.

Her head rang with pain.

He had left her to bleed with no moral or intellectual compunction. His abrupt about-turn had been utterly horrible. She saw his eyelids close like the lids of the dead, as he turned in blind obedience to some unspoken command.

To kill.

She could not be sure if he had already overtaken his mother in the fog. She tried not to wobble as the wet blood down the side of her neck turned sticky. Her burst eardrum hurt so much she had to stop, double up and retch violently... Her head spun. She floated. Rather than walk, she glided... then she exhaled and she was back.

A few steps more and the haze lifted. She again saw her way to Green Way House – icy air chilled her lungs as she breathed less rapidly. Was this what it felt like to be dead and not just deaf, she wondered?

Laura swayed violently left and right, yet somehow managed to advance to the kitchen.

There she selected a sharp knife from a rack on the wall.

She was not about to take any chances.

She saw and heard nothing.

No one was present in the drawing room or anywhere else on the ground floor.

That left her no choice but to keep going. "Forewarned is forearmed… Faint heart never won fair lady".

Liam had said he needed her help, but she was just someone whose trust was to be used and abused. Again! Like everyone else in this vile world he hadn't taken her seriously. It was not her fault if she found people – friends – so hard to fathom. She took them into her life, only they refused to reciprocate. They built walls round themselves so she never got to know their hearts. Instead she was the one to be hurt. Liam was not the victim she had thought to lead to safety. He had gone on the offensive. She didn't recognise him. After what Lady Ann said earlier *she had to doubt if it was him at all…*

For the last few years her ladyship had revived the presence of her dead, beloved William.

Except it took a living, breathing twin to take the dead man's place. Liam was him by nickname only. Like a stage persona! The house was big and dark and terribly heavy. The cold, empty corridors and vacant rooms would have her come right in. It anticipated her complaint before she could utter a groan. It deplored the duplicity.

She arrived on the quarter landing where she stopped at the portrait of the house's original owner.

Light and dark edged the two halves of his face, as his lips mouthed at her in Latin: "*Cura te.*"

'This is all your doing,' said Laura. William Lawrence was telling her to take care of herself. It was not the worst thing she could do – it did not strike her as an act of complicity this time. 'Once seen the truth cannot be unseen. Suddenly I see things through your eyes. This is what you have been attempting to tell me ever since I arrived. How could I have been so blind? *You wanted to warn me that an imposter walks in your shoes.*'

Suddenly she knew what she was charged to do. Her whole life so far had been in preparation for this moment.

No one else had his permission.

Not that she knew of.

Laura gripped her knife firmly in both hands. "Fools rush in where angels fear to tread". Right now she was up against a wicked and cruel masquerade. They might be luckless and wretched, but her enemy was also mischievous, clever and self-willed. Lady Ann had driven Liam to the point where he was jealous of himself – she kept his brother's memory alive to the point where he had to become him just to please her.

Now the dead envied the living.

'Damn it William, you're as hard to kill as the devil himself.'

58

Alison stumbled up to Laura's yellow caravan and its door swung wide open. She climbed inside and her heart sank. It was too much like déja vu. There was blood on the wall in the front apartment – she half expected to find HELP ME written in red on the floor.

She reached for her mobile phone and rang Armed Response. 'It's Detective Sergeant Ellis. I requested backup. Where the hell is it?'

The reply on the line sounded far way in both place and time. She seriously doubted if she was even speaking to anyone living, so distant did the voice speak to her in return: 'ETA is twenty minutes…'

Next moment her phone died.

'Shit, no battery.'

A large black fly buzzed by her face. She saw how it feasted on some gore on the ceiling. Alison used her penknife to prise balls of lead shot from the roof where someone had blasted a hole through two layers of hardboard with their gun. There were other signs of a struggle and more blood on the doorframe.

At her feet lay a spent shotgun cartridge which she left for Forensics.

Whoever had been hurt had headed for Green Way House, she decided. They had just passed her in the fog. She looked up to see a light shine from its glass lantern high on its roof. Its misty halo made for a strange optical illusion. The glow gave her a peculiar feeling: it was not the sun's diffused or reflected rays but something akin to an eye. It was how the house surveyed all it owned.

She was looking at the octagonal 'lighthouse' that William Lawrence had built for his doomed son in the 1690s. It shone white like a beacon with all the brightness of heaven at that moment, its glazed sides emitting such special radiance.

Next minute Alison saw a figure emerge on to the lantern's balcony. It was Lady Ann. Behind her was Liam with his gun pointed at her head.

'Who's there?'

'My name is Detective Sergeant Ellis,' cried Alison as she mounted the steps where Barry Barnes lay frozen.

'I know who you are. I've seen you snooping around.'

Alison kept looking up at the gaps in the swirling mist. 'I need you to calm down Liam. Or should I call you William?'

'He'll never be me. I won't let him.'

'Why are you acting this way?'

'Because I hate him.'

'What does that mean?'

'It means my mother is right. I killed my brother with that digger's shovel. I did it on purpose. Ever since then she's had me pretend to be him in return for her complicity. She's had me act the part of a dead man until I feel dead myself, all because she can't bear to live without him.'

59

Detective Inspector Prickett was in a panic. That telephone call from DS Ellis could not have come at a worse time – the SIO still wanted to know why two men had ended up dead in a canal and a river. Instead he was speeding towards Green Way House with his car's siren at full blast because he feared his best officer was in deep trouble. His life was all about trying to establish what people saw, heard and did as well as when they did it. Now Ellis had called for urgent assistance and he didn't know what to think.

He felt angry as well as sullen – he was always mildly distrustful of "Armed Response" in their big ARVs. Those men and women dressed in black body armour and carrying Heckler and Koch G36 semi-automatic carbines put the fear of God into him.

He listened in to the radio.

K99 control further message over.

K99 go ahead over.

We have our unit at Green Way House. We're going in…

'Damn it,' thought Prickett, 'the AFOs can't be there already?' While his office was situated nine miles from Green Way House, the Armed Response Unit was based near the M5 motorway between Gloucester and Cheltenham – they had a six-mile start on him from Bamfurlong Lane.

He rang Ellis again but she didn't pick up. 'Get the hell out of there right now sergeant. Leave it to the Authorised Firearms Officers. Most of all, don't do anything I wouldn't…'

60

Back at Green Way House Alison retrieved a shotgun from the paved floor of its porch.

Whoever had just dropped it had been forced to flee in a hurry.

Or there had been another fight.

She inspected the weapon and one of its twin, side-by-side barrels was still warm. With no time to lose she flipped its break-level to hinge it apart. Then she snapped the gun shut again. Kept the safety catch on.

That left one live round ready to shoot.

Police sirens sounded close by in Greenway Lane. Alison knew she should wait for backup, except Liam was already set for an armed stand-off on his rooftop balcony?

'If the AFOs can keep him distracted for long enough I can take him from behind,' she told herself hopefully.

That might be wishful thinking.

There was no sign of Laura, only some blood pooling on the hall's paved floor. More red splashes led to the kitchen, then upstairs.

Alison mounted the staircase's bare, wooden steps one by one very cautiously. She hadn't gone far when a shot rang out from a floor high above her. It was quickly followed by another deafening bang as walls and doors shook with a different clatter...

She rushed to the nearest window to peer outside.

A police helicopter had just flown a circle over the house. She saw it orbit at sixty knots to give its occupants an entire 360 degrees view of the scene to film, observe and reconnoitre... the pilot was banking hard so that the officer, who perched in his open door, had an uninterrupted view of events from only a few hundred feet in the air.

Someone had just fired warning shots in its direction to scare its crew away.

The shots were a big distraction which might give her an advantage, thought Alison. Of course it was downright dangerous. She was not even wearing her bullet-proof vest. Nor had she donned a body camera to record everything that might happen.

What had begun as a medium risk had just escalated to something off the scale…

The poised, almost regal figure of William Lawrence eyed her intensely from his portrait as she resumed her climb from the quarter landing. Having only ever seen a reproduction of this former owner of Green Way House in a book before, it was a shock to meet him face to face. The half life-size man in oils was disturbingly enlivened in the flesh, as well as a little ascetic. His stance suggested someone blithely unaware that the artist had captured such a true likeness. For here was a seventeenth century gentleman who was for the most part always discreet, even if he did let slip a wry smile. His right hand held his broken heart on the table before him. Painted on the vital organ was his coat of arms while on the edge of the table she read "et genus et pectus" which translated as "both heart and lineage". If one had shattered then so had the other, which meant there could be no heir to continue his family name. He might be professionally and impeccably correct, yet he could never be entirely happy ever again – that skewed smile of his was disappointment. He behaved as though there were something diseased, injured or rotten in him, body and soul. Most of all he struck her as someone who needed saving from himself.

Dealing with such a person might not be healthy.

William Lawrence was determined that she should not thwart him, or even come close to outwitting him today?

Alison mounted the last stair to arrive in a long, narrow corridor lit by a single window. Woodblock prints on the walls displayed Green Way House's garden with its lake, clouds, birds and flowers. Except this was not so much a representation of an actual place as a state of supreme being. Here was somewhere worthy of Adam and Eve at their creation. The anonymous angler who hooked a fish from the water would catch the emotions of joy and pleasure forever.

The man's bony face was reflected in the lake, Alison noted. With it came a sudden chill. He was looking right at her.

Like a skull.

A brutal laugh crossed his lips in the mirror-like ripples. He stirred, fretted and fussed, already full of cruel remembrance for the coming evil.

He wasn't laughing, he was screaming.

61

Laura arrived in the study that William Lawrence had built for his son. The bitter, acrid smell of gunpowder hung in the air. Its pungent smoke burned blue in the sunlight that penetrated the globe directly above her.

Her grip hardened on the kitchen knife in her right hand, as she passed the desk and approached the open door.

She could see on to the balcony but not beyond.

Liam had the shotgun he had wrested from her hands in her caravan – he was pointing it at the side of his mother's head. Lady Ann, for her part, was now weaponless, Laura noted. He was holding her hostage as he taunted the police in the sky and garden. 'You'll never take me alive.'

Laura advanced another step. If she couldn't observe what was happening in the grounds below then the police must already be in position. They must have Liam in their sights.

A sniper might drop him at any moment, which was why he clung to his mother for dear life? She was his human shield.

Suddenly the downdraught from the helicopter's deafening rotors blasted air into the room. The forced current swept pens and papers off the desk and blew books from the shelves. Laura felt the air compress then rarefy all round her, even as mother and son struggled to stay upright. The machine was above the mist using its searchlight to penetrate the gloom below. It was blowing more holes in the fog with its blades spinning at 400-500 RPM. Whereas a moment ago it had flown in circles to save fuel, now it descended much lower in order to hover. It hung in the air at two hundred feet before the house like a great bird.

She could clearly see the police officer with his loud hailer strapped into the machine's open side, as the pilot sought to fly in line with roof and balcony.

A loud speaker crackled into life. 'Police! Lay down your weapon. You are surrounded.'

She saw her chance: 'Liam? It's me, Laura. Do as they say. Put the gun down. Why are you doing this?'

Lady Ann let out a whimper. She looked frustrated, disappointed, defeated – she was at her son's mercy.

Liam swung round but kept his shotgun trained on his mother. 'Stay out of this Laura. I'm not about to exchange one prison for another. I'll die first.'

'You think acting this way will do any good now?'

'What else am I supposed to do?'

'You said you needed my help.'

'I never set out to lie to you.'

62

DI Prickett had not seen such a strange house before. Its air of dissatisfaction could not be wholly concealed, not even by the mist that clung to its gutters and gables. It was dark, withdrawn, resentful. He had to hang back as the AFOs broke open the main gates to the weed-covered driveway.

'This can only end badly,' he told himself.

He tried phoning Ellis again but there was no reply.

Green Way House wrapped itself in ever thicker bands of fog as if to turn a blind eye to what was happening. He did not trust it. The further he advanced into the grounds, the more he was struck by the recklessness and folly of it. He did not so much resent the silence as dread the consequences. He felt robbed of all judgement both mental and moral. To enter was only to deceive himself? For although he found a path, he had no idea where it led him.

Prickett watched helplessly as the Armed Response Unit took up positions ready to storm the building.

'Surely you can't expect to do anything yet?' he said to the AFO standing closest to him.

'Sorry sir, but I take my orders from my commander.'

'But this is my case.'

'Right now we're in charge.'

'What will you do if the worst happens?'

'We go in with guns blazing.'

'Not the right time.'

'Let's hope he surrenders.'

'Good luck with that.'

No one should get hurt in such a beautiful garden, thought Prickett, admiring winter honeysuckle in full flower.

People were flesh and blood, not mere blooms to be cut or pruned.

The black-clad officer crept forward into the mist when a shot rang out.

Next minute the scream of spinning rotor blades filled the garden.

Prickett's heart missed a beat. 'That doesn't sound good,' he said worriedly, as he raised his eyes high to the sky. 'Not good at all.'

Something wasn't right.

'It's the NPAS helicopter,' he realised, as the distinctive whirr of its turbine turned to a scream.

The pilot desperately accelerated the main rotor system – he was trying to increase his speed to make use of aerodynamics to keep his EC135 flying.

That was another thing "Armed Response" hadn't bothered to tell him, thought Prickett, grimacing. Someone had summoned help from the National Police Air Service. It was nothing to do with him. His police force didn't manage its own helicopters any more, they had to summon them from bases as far away as Birmingham or Bristol.

They had to plead for help sometimes…

63

Laura kept her knife pressed against her thigh… If she was lucky she could strike Liam before he knew what hit him, but first she had to try and talk sense into him. 'Tell me again how your brother died.'

'You ask me this now because?'

'I don't believe you're a killer.'

'No? *I'm* the one who hit William with the mechanical digger. My mother only took the blame to suit her own ends.'

'Why would she do that?'

'Because I loathed him.'

'How exactly did it happen?'

'The controls flew through my hands,' said Liam hopelessly. 'What else?'

'It could have been an accident.'

'But I was *glad* it happened.'

'Doesn't mean you were in the wrong. It doesn't make you a murderer.'

'So it's not my fault suddenly?'

'Not that I can think of, no.'

'How would you know?'

'Because it happened to me when I was driving the same machine to dig out the lake. The handles and foot pedals took on a life of their own. That mini-digger is faulty or it has a mind of its own.'

'I don't believe you.'

'Did you *plan* to kill your brother that day?'

'What if I didn't?'

Laura took another step forward. The knife weighed heavily in her aching fingers. She registered the petrified look on Lady Ann's face as she continued to struggle. Any mother would take the blame for her son's recklessness but this was different – her ladyship had covered for him these past five years because they shared a secret: they were both in thrall to the dead who walked among them in their garden. 'It's time to agree that what happened was most probably a fluke and let William go. You're not the cold-hearted murderer you think you are. You can't be him any longer. *It's time to stop playing the impostor.* He needs to know that, or he'll never let you alone.'

Lady Ann uttered a soft moan. 'Oh God, what should I have done?'

'You should have told the truth from day one.'

Next second Liam aimed his shotgun again at the police below. He pointed it one-handed from his hip over the balcony's rail, while he continued to use his mother as a shield.

He wasn't about to be the opponent who was easily defeated.

He refused to be the gullible person, the easy problem...

So he pulled the trigger.

64

DI Prickett had no choice but to follow the awful noise. The air shook with the screech of the helicopter's labouring engine…

Then he saw it: the civilian pilot – police officers don't fly helicopters – was trying to accelerate to fifty knots ready to climb away into the sky.

Except there wasn't the power to provide the lift. Nor was there time to check for poles, wires or people. Fog obscured trees and buildings so that the pilot could not find a large, flat area to set down.

It was enough to topple the EC135 after its backup engine failed to function.

Prickett waded thick mist to track the sinking machine as the pilot hit the sloping ground at fifteen degrees…

It fell like a stone.

Keeled over.

He raced towards it and there was the unconscious pilot still strapped in his seat on the right-hand side of his machine…

Flames licked what looked like broken hydraulic or fuel lines spewing fluid.

He wrenched the pilot's safety belt loose as he fought to disentangle his legs from the cockpit. Then he pulled him across the burning ground. Seconds later the police cameraman rolled free from under the fuselage – he was bleeding heavily but was otherwise able to help. 'Quick,' he said, 'it's going to blow.'

Together they dragged, then carried the unconscious pilot the rest of the way past the mangled rotor blades.

They ran with him as best they could through the garden as the air erupted at their backs.

The volcanic ball of flame set fire to the fog… turned it black with smoke and the foul smell of ignited jet fuel.

The red-hot wind rolled right over the fleeing men. Blew all three off their feet. Liam must have blasted the EC135's tail rotor with his shotgun, thought Prickett. He had disabled the anti-torque blade designed to stop the machine from spinning in the opposite direction of the main rotors, until the pilot lost control.

Prickett rose unsteadily to his feet again and gazed back at his lucky escape. The helicopter had exploded at one end of a rose walk, demolishing a wall. Flames lit its paths like a funeral pyre.

Silhouetted against the red and black furnace was a man.

Prickett wiped his hot eyes with the back of his hand. Blinked harder. 'What the hell? Who stands that close to an inferno?'

Whoever he could see was no police officer? Deny it if you want to, he told himself, but that figure framed in flame is more like a shadow lit from Hell. His clothes alone suggested someone impervious to the elements: he would rather walk the path than avoid the peril.

'*What* are you?' thought Prickett, since something melancholic, even diabolic, dogged his heels.

65

'Don't do it Liam,' urged Laura and inched closer to the balcony. He couldn't hold on to his mother and watch the police forever? She could not determine exactly where the helicopter had gone down, but she could smell and breathe the ghastly smoke that blew from its wreckage. 'This can only end in disaster. I guess it already has.'

Liam choked on the haze of fire and fumes. This was no game he played, thought Laura. Still he kept Lady Ann in his nerveless grip. He would have her suffer for what he had endured at her hands in Green Way House – she would feel the full weight of his judgement at last. 'You guessed right.'

'You don't have to be your brother any longer.'

'Leave me alone or I'll jump and take my mother with me.'

'No one should have to do the dead's living for them.'

'I've died once so what does it matter?'

'Not true.'

'That's how I see it anyway.'

'Give yourself up to the police and end this nightmare now.'

'The police won't listen.'

Liam's sudden pull turned to shove. He pushed Lady Ann hard against the balcony's rail…

Laura saw her chance. She ran at him with her knife raised. She arced her arm and brought the blade down as hard as she could. Her hand made a sinuous, sweeping motion – it ended in a single blow as she went to stab him in his back. Some power came over her which she couldn't control. Her action was not the great strength she expected, or sense of triumph. Instead she felt childishly self-willed and perverse. *Compelled.* Her strike was capricious, unacceptable, freakish. It was not like the wound she had inflicted on her abuser at college as if she had merely come full circle – she was not back at that moment of blinding rage but somewhere beyond… In the end it was raw courage.

'For heaven's sake Liam,' cried Laura. 'Let her go.'

Liam half spun, then tottered. He took a step sideways… his stricken face seemed to ask if she had any more surprises. He pirouetted and twisted as he tried to finger the blade stuck behind his shoulder.

Then he was gone.

Over the balcony.

With his arm round his mother.

'No!' cried Laura and lunged after them into the void.

Mother and son hit the roof. They took off on its stone tiles next to one of its gables, then shot into space amid the house's great mass of ivy.

Lady Ann clutched its thick woody stems, then flung her hand out to the edge of a gutter as Liam let go.

'Hang on,' Laura shouted. 'I'm coming.' She swung her leg over the balcony's metal rail.

At first she could find little purchase on the rough, lichen-covered roof. But if she were to go very carefully she could work her way down the steep V of the gable. 'Don't worry, I've got you.'

'Hurry, I'm slipping…'

She reached the lead rainwater head to which her ladyship was clinging. She lowered herself via its oak leaf pattern and its four-petal flower motif. 'Grab hold of the drainpipe beside you and step into the ivy.'

'I can try.'

Laura became aware of intense activity below as people rushed to recover Liam's crumpled body. She had no idea if he was alive or dead. Rather she had to concentrate on saving Lady Ann – she stretched out her hand but couldn't quite reach her. The ivy, whose stems appeared so entwined and robust, began to shiver. Leaves and tendrils moved violently up and down. The whole house appeared to tremble, rock and quiver inside its prison. The vibrations became waves, jolts, jars – the ivy moved from side to side in refusal, denial and disapproval. It shook and disturbed the stricken climber to weaken her grip on its stems.

Lady Ann was set to plunge two storeys. 'It's no good, I can't get a footing.'

Laura went to move forwards and nearly fell herself. It was not just that the ivy was apt to shake with her weight. Rather her whole sense of self tottered and wavered as though she were being made to feel unsound inside her own skin. She was being tested and found wanting. Vertigo was like that, she thought – it messed with your head – but never before had she known it turn her soul upside down. 'That's it,' she said as she wriggled head first at the foot of the gable. She anchored the heel of one hand in the gutter and reached out with the other. 'If I can just get a bit closer…'

Lady Ann thrust out her arm.

Laura did the same.

One groped for the other.

Their fingertips touched… when the drainpipe broke. Lady Ann slipped – lost her grip, balance and place all at a stroke. Laura went to grab her but she shot away out of reach. She was on her way down. She crashed at lightning speed through the ivy which seamlessly parted to let her go.

The vines pummelled and belaboured her all the way to the ground, which she hit head first.

'Oh God no,' cried Laura hopelessly. She was staring into space at a drop that looked infinite. For a split second she too was about to plunge after her into the void. Any moment now the upper court would rush up to meet her and in front of her face would be her dashed brains. After her lurch off the roof she heard someone calling. She attempted to fling her arm backwards but could not reach anything solid. Not in time. Tiles cracked beneath her. Ivy ran through her fingers. There was a great whoosh. She saw the sky turn circles and the last breath in her body left her gasping, when a familiar voice sounded calm: 'It's all right. I have you. Grab both barrels…'

***

Laura felt herself hauled back to the balcony by dint of the gun she grasped. She kicked and clawed. There she clung to her saviour with pathetic gratitude.

It was Detective Sergeant Ellis.

66

Police Headquarters
Prism House
Gloucester

'Don't quote me, but you can take it as definite,' said DI Prickett. 'There's no doubt in my mind that Liam lured you up to that balcony to kill you.'

'I knew the risks,' said Alison.

'Next time don't be such a fool. Don't rush in…'

'*Where angels fear to tread*? You sound like Laura.'

'I mean it Ellis. You could have ended up dead.'

'Liam didn't intend to kill me. He just wanted his life back.'

'Don't think so.'

'I mean it.'

Prickett arched his greying eyebrows at her. Feigned outrage. 'Here's what I think. Liam was a true psychopath. That's why he deliberately murdered his brother five years ago. It's why he almost certainly did away with Paul Carter, Lars Visser and Ray Knight, so he could experience the emotions that other people have vicariously. You heard what he said: he felt dead. That's because he had absolutely no feelings of his own. Meanwhile our bird-loving John Mortimer covered for both son and mother – he dumped Lars and Paul in the water at Coombe Hill in a misguided attempt to avoid justice. He admits he is chairman of the Tewkesbury History Re-enactment Club who specialise in recreating battles from the seventeenth century. He even admits to coming home after meetings and roaming Green Way House's grounds in his theatrical clothes and singing old songs. He says he meant no harm, but quite frankly it suited him and Betty to terrify Liam in order to manipulate his mother? By impersonating her ladyship's dead son William he kept her paranoid and dependent on them. Most of all Mr and Mrs Mortimer didn't want any investigation reopened into the suspicious death of her ladyship's husband years ago. Rumour has it he was poisoned.'

'We'll never know. Dead men don't tell.'

'Five deaths and no confession!'

'Our loyal butler is adamant: he insists nobody killed anybody at all. Of course it's a crime not to report a death and a greater one to hide it.'

'You can't possibly believe him?'

'He blames the garden.'

'Nonsense.'

'There's no forensic evidence to prove otherwise. It seems even Barry Barnes poisoned himself with rhododendrons.'

'Ha!'

'The effect of rhododendron poisoning usually only lasts twenty-four hours in humans. However the toxins were enough to induce dizziness, vomiting and frequent defecation. Barry's lungs and heart would have suffered badly and he would have had difficulty breathing, which most likely caused him to lose his balance on the slippery steps – he fell and knocked himself out and the icy weather did the rest.'

'You mean the murderer did,' said Prickett.

'Even William's death five years ago was most likely an accident.'

'Hardly. John and Betty Mortimer have filled in the details. It turns out Liam and William detested each other as children. The siblings fought and did not see eye to eye as adults either, making for an always tense atmosphere in Green Way House. William was first to be born and was his mother's favourite. Liam followed forty minutes later and always walked in his shadow. A further complication was that he envied his brother's artistic abilities and wanted to be a successful actor like him. Liam wanted him gone and slept with a crowbar under his pillow, prompting William to keep a hammer by his bed for his own protection. We may lack proof that Liam *planned* to smash his brother's head open with the mechanical digger's steel bucket, but it all points to the same thing.'

'You're forgetting that it wasn't only William who 'died' back then, it was Liam.'

'Not helpful.'

'Think about it,' said Alison. 'William was Lady Ann's first born. She idolised him to the detriment of his twin. When William was killed she flatly refused to accept he was dead. She kept him 'alive' by insisting Liam be him. In her mind it was he who died that day, not William. The twins already had the same name: Liam was her nickname for William. There was no way Liam could escape his accident of birth except by a fatal accident of his own. The irony is that once he took his brother's place he had what he wanted – he had all his mother's affection. Lady Ann may have called him by her dead son's name but 'Liam' did his best to play along. He dressed up to gain her attention.'

'Until it all went horribly wrong.'

'Liam acted the part of his dead brother quite literally. He became his walking corpse in his own mind. It destroyed him mentally and physically.'

'That doesn't surprise me. In order for Lady Ann to people her perfect garden with her dead son she had to have another, living one to walk its paths. That was Liam's real role in all this, *that* was to become his unbearable burden.'

'I can only say the idea has been tried before.'

'How so?'

'When William Lawrence designed his garden in the 1690s his primary purpose was to bury his beloved child in its grounds. He intended to move Will's bones from the local church in the village of Badgeworth and place them – along with his dead wife Anne – in a new mausoleum on a hill with a fine view of the house and valley. That way mother and son could continue to live with him in their memorial garden. Unfortunately he died before he could complete the task.'

Prickett smiled. 'It's quite a coincidence that Lady Ann and her children have the same names as their seventeenth century predecessors?'

'Or she was really doing William Lawrence's work for him all along.'

'I take it that's a joke.'

It was Alison's turn to smile. 'Let's hope that's the last we ever hear of Green Way House's eccentric owner.'

'All Lady Ann ever did was dream of paradise. She is rather to be pitied, don't you think?'

'Not at all. Her odious butler is right: her perfect garden is the perfect killer.'

67

The Round House
Mercombe Wood

'Coffee's getting cold,' said Ravi. As he spoke, an owl screeched on its way past the window. 'I made it for you half an hour ago. You still haven't touched it.'

'I'll be right there,' said Alison and continued reading. 'I thought I'd take a last look at that book Paul Carter ordered from Bristol.'

'Not the one about Green Way House?'

'Uh-huh.'

'Why, what's wrong?'

'I do wonder why William Lawrence's second wife Dulcibella didn't complete the garden after his demise in 1697.'

'The case is closed. That book should be too.'

'Was it typical of Dulcibella to cheat the dead quite so casually?'

'The estate she inherited most likely ran short of money.'

'But Lawrence's will was quite clear: Dulcibella was specifically instructed to build a mausoleum for his son Will and his first wife Anne. Chapel and tomb were to be the finishing touch to the whole enterprise. His "hortus conclusus" was laid out and planned to house the dead. Without them it was all for nothing.'

Ravi took her cup and set about reheating it on top of the wood stove. 'Why should one wife honour another anyway?'

'What if the garden can never be perfect because it provokes too much jealousy? Old hates new. The dead are liable to resent the living?'

'The other way around, more likely.'

'I meant what I said.'

'I reckon the local vicar objected to the bones being moved, don't you?'

'Or Dulcibella decided the garden was not such a good thing after all, morally, spiritually, physically?'

'She would have been right, as it turns out.'

'Lady Ann Frost tried to do what Dulcibella failed to do over three hundred years ago, only to have it turn against her.'

'You'll be telling me next that the garden has a murderous streak all of its own.'

'"And the LORD God said, 'The man has now become like one of us, knowing good and evil. He must not be allowed to reach out his hand and take also from the tree of life and eat, and live forever.' So the LORD God banished him from the Garden of Eden to work the ground from which he had been taken."'

Ravi stoked the stove with more logs. 'Don't forget all this began when you thought you ran into a ghost at the crossroads at the top of Greenway Lane. That ghost turned out to be a living human being in thrall to his mother and his dead brother. There's nothing remotely biblical about any of it.'

'People can certainly haunt each other, you have to admit.'

'Of course there is one other possible answer.'

'There is?'

'So far two hundred cases have been documented worldwide. It's called "walking corpse syndrome". It was first described by Dr Jules Cotard in 1882, hence it's more scientific name of "Cotard's syndrome".'

Alison set her book aside. 'Go on.'

'The patient comes to believe that they have lost all their internal organs, blood or even limbs. They say they have lost their souls. A typical sufferer might insist they are dead or don't exist anymore.'

'Sounds like Liam all right.'

'The patient refuses to leave their house much or speak to anyone. Voices tell them they are dead or dying. Other sufferers won't eat because it is futile when they are no longer living. Some try to harm themselves.'

'Or other people?'

'That's not typical, but a patient might well demand to be taken to the mortuary where they want to be with other corpses. Sufferers often start with a history of depression, anxiety or substance abuse.'

'One reason Lady Ann shut Liam in the house was to stop him buying any more drugs.'

'Some kind of brain damage is common. It may come from a stroke, tumour, blood clot or injury. The problem is that "walking corpse syndrome" is a symptom of other conditions and not a disease in itself. It's not listed in any medical handbook used to diagnose mental health problems. There are no rules to guide doctors.'

Alison nodded. 'To Lady Ann, Liam's illness was William's way of speaking to her through his living twin. Instead of which one brother stole the other's soul.'

'I think you should drink that cup of coffee now.'

'Yes, I think that's wise.'

***

Before Alison went to bed she did what she always did, she placed a toy police car under her pillow.

'Why that car and no other?' asked Ravi.

'I've told you before.'

'No you haven't. Not really.' He examined the three-inch long, diecast Corgi model and smiled. He ran his finger over its worn blue and silver paint that said Ohio on its side and noted a few dents its metal body. 'It's seen better days.'

'That's because my brother and I played with it in our back garden when we were children. I was nine or ten at the time.'

'So it's a keepsake?'

'I should throw it away but I can't.'

'One axle is bent and its wheels don't turn very well.'

'That's because I was always crashing it.'

'Even at ten you wanted to catch baddies?'

'He played the crook and I was the police officer in high-speed chases. Now I think of those times that we spent together and they seem like paradise.'

'He'll return to you when he chooses.'

'Even in his absence I try to live his life for him.'

'Is that so wrong?'

'Maybe, but I have to keep his memory alive. Love should never be allowed to wither on the vine. It deserves careful tending, don't you think, or it poisons the mind?'

68

A year had passed since she had first set eyes on Green Way House. 'No going back to college for me,' Laura decided. 'No more abusive lovers.'

Back then everyone had told her she had to be some*one* instead of some*where*. All that had changed now she had found the perfect place in her very own walled garden. It was her sister, her spouse, a sanctuary enclosed, her fountain sealed up…

'Who would have thought everything could look so beautiful so soon?' she said aloud as she pushed Lady Ann briskly along in her wheelchair. She bounced and banged her mistress on the cobblestones in the stable yard. 'In twelve months this place has been transformed. You can never tell a garden it's loved too much, can you? Not even you will ever love it the way I do right now.'

Lady Ann made a worm-like motion. The partially paralysed chatelaine went to twist her upper body urgently with many futile turns. At once Laura extended her arm to calm her charge's slippery, practised evasions while they did a quick tour of the paths. 'Don't fidget so much your ladyship, or you'll miss the aconites.'

Next minute Laura braked hard next to a sea of bright yellow flowers. She bent down beside the wheelchair to admire hundreds of blooms shaped like the hoods of medieval monks. 'Is it any wonder some people call them monkshood, friar's cap and auld wife's huid?' she said happily. 'Of course the name I love best is winter wolf's bane.'

Lady Ann flinched. She wriggled again at a creeping sensation – a fat, black fly had just crawled over her face, round her neck and across her knees. At first she tried to protest, but since her brain was damaged beyond all likely repair she could voice no articulate response. She used her good hand to flap her dead one quite uselessly. Like a cat shaking a rat, Laura observed severely. Lady Ann made her chair tremble, rock and finally quiver as she wriggled from side to side in refusal, denial, disapproval – she made a fist to brandish at her keeper.

'Once the aconites fade we can look forward to the Dutch crocuses,' Laura enthused. 'Those varieties of Crocus tommasinianus I planted are popping up quite nicely. You can look forward to seeing Barr's Surprise, Prince Claus and Ruby Giant. By late February the ground will be a sea of different colours. You'll have your garden worthy of the best "hortus conclusus", it will match the legendary Palazzetto del Giardino di San Marco in Venice.'

Lady Ann spat more white phlegm. Her lips were a mass of tiny bubbles in her attempt to deny some undesirable taste. She sought in vain to rouse herself from her dangerous predicament.

'Anyone would think you don't like coming into the garden anymore,' said Laura, resuming their vigorous stroll. 'But you must know, as someone whose job it once was to support people who are experiencing depression, anxiety and low mood, that getting out in the fresh air can work wonders. This garden is ideal, it just needs love and attention. It has been misunderstood, miserably overlooked. You do believe in miracles, don't you? It would be fantastic to believe in something like that for you.'

Although she was now Lady Ann's privately paid career, she had already taken a leaf out of Betty's books. Like any other self-respecting cleaner, housekeeper or nanny, she demanded to work in shifts (two weeks on and two weeks off, or 7a.m. to 3p.m., 3p.m. to 11p.m. daily with breaks), which required backup teams and cover for holidays. No one was going to catch her running this place like Claridge's.

The garden took priority. Even as Lady Ann suffered, the first fruit trees blossomed and flowers bloomed. Only then would they return to paradise. They had to let it grow and grow, largely of its own accord.

Her ladyship threw her arm about in one last forceful effort to get free. She wrestled and jostled as if with an invisible opponent.

'Don't you want to know who you really saw prowling in the garden?' asked Laura irritably.

Lady Ann's panic increased...

'Why would you even think that?' said Laura sadly.

She began to choke...

'Don't do anything stupid your ladyship. This is the best day of your life.'

Her speech was gibberish...

'If you ask my opinion you're only shy. What are you feeling right now? Come on, be honest. *Really*? You don't trust me? I admit I'm a bit scared too.'

Her grey-blue eyes rolled into her head...

'You're about to experience something truly great. I'm very happy for us both,' said Laura.

She couldn't catch her breath.

'You really were afraid of what you wished for, weren't you, when you searched the grounds each night with a loaded shotgun in your hands? *Now it's time to meet in person.* It is, after all, what you've wanted all along. I can't say exactly if it's quite what you expected, but I know it's no bad thing.'

They turned left by the knot garden and passed through the upper court. Then they proceeded via the fruit trees to the rose walk. The burnt-out helicopter had long since been removed and only blackened earth and an embarrassing dip in the ground remained to show where it had fallen. Already the garden was healing itself with fresh red roses just as the blood and brains at the front of the house had washed away in the rain. By great luck Old Father Time had escaped demolition on his plinth. He continued to point with his blunted scythe to the single line of cypress trees, while his wolf and serpent still lazed at his feet.

It made for the perfect rendezvous place.

'You literally not ready for this?' asked Laura snappily. She turned her deaf ear her way. 'You not happy? Sorry to hear that. What can I say? *He* wants to meet *you*, I can assure you of that.' She watched Lady Ann shake her head. 'Did I not explain? Yes, that could very well be.'

Laura parked the wheelchair where all four paths of the rose walk met to form their cross in the middle. She watched squirrels and blackbirds flee along the nearby walls. 'I don't know what lies ahead of us Lady A, but whatever it is this has to be better than everything we've had so far. I'm thrilled for you. It's not every day your greatest desire comes true.'

Lady Ann's eyes widened. Her heart raced. She attempted to raise her good hand as she punctured unintelligible squawks with apt gestures.

Meanwhile Laura was doing her utmost to direct her attention to the figure that walked their way. 'Remember we have to work together for all our sakes. These last few months in the garden, we've both become different people. Away from others I've stopped thinking about my past, because I have a new one. With you.'

Lady Ann went to scream.

'Relax,' said Laura. 'This is someone you won't want to un-see.'

Her ladyship uttered uncontrollable but stifled cries of terror…

'Today is not the day to flunk it.'

She averted her face in horror. Shut her eyes…

Laura smiled. 'You have perfection here. I have created it. For you and him. And *me*.'

…at someone or something about to be named.

'It's time to give him the garden we promised. It's not all bad. This place makes me feel like nothing horrible will ever happen again.'

Lady Ann whimpered…

'It's time to look love in the eye. Find the courage. The biggest monsters are the ones we imagine?'

...shed a tear.

'No more running! For you or me,' said Laura. Then, raising her voice to the approaching figure, she shouted. 'It's okay, we're not going anywhere. We're staying right here. She wants to meet you for real. No more false shit. No more lies. You're all she has left now.'

Their newcomer was dressed in wig and coat and he leaned heavily on his crow-head cane as if fresh from stage. He stood slightly stooped on his blood-red shoes when he turned towards them at some speed. His waistcoat, all buttoned up apart from one silvery gold button, revealed just a trace of his white lace shirt and cravat. The wrinkled shape of his flesh was full of vascular marbling. There was a dark staining of soft tissue whose bloated putrefaction was perpetually decaying. His face had suffered much sloughing of green skin still turning papery, where his skull had been smashed on one side like a pot or vase. His emaciated lips parted to reveal a pink discolouration of teeth and gums, due to lividity in the tissues. His lungless chest puffed breathy gasps. Similar corpse soap saw nose, cheeks and mouth elide into each other, rendering individual features hard to identify.

The same could not be said of his one good eye which shone as clear as glass.

'We did it William,' said Laura, 'we got rid of them all! Now it's just us. We're all the company the garden needs from now on. I only regret that, thanks to that old oil painting, I mistook you for someone else for too long.'

That said, she took tight hold of Lady Ann's arm by her wrist. She held up her floppy, dead limb for him to seize. '"Perfectio vera in coelestibus",' she declared absolutely delighted. '"True perfection is to be found only in heavenly things". Hurry up your ladyship and open your eyes. See what I see. Come meet your child.'

Laura marvelled at the wonder she felt as one hand sought another. She was equally curious to know if he spoke to Lady Ann in her dreams at night as he did hers? It was not as though he had ever really left, not when he lay at the base of the yew tree where he was interred.

Suddenly he took his tricorne hat from under his arm and swept it past his knee to give her a thankful bow.

His waxy lips stuck tenderly to the back of her proffered hand, after which he sang her a few words:

The living to the living hold,
Dead to the dead belong.

It was her good fortune that she had stumbled across someone's tragic story which only she could finish, since no one deserved to be consumed by their own shadow.

She wasn't afraid. With his polite salutation all terrors were gone. Instead she was thrilled by the clasp of his cloying fingers.

'I'm sorry about Liam, I really am, but sometimes we have to let something die to let something live.'

Getting this far hadn't been easy. The dead needed a route back to where they began. He had set out to gain her attention via the garden's memorial pillars, sundials, gates and paths the minute she had arrived. Most of all he had wooed her with his sweet serenades and gifts from the orchard. She had seen something she hadn't understood at first, but now she did: 'Never who but *where*,' she confirmed. 'Let others doubt what they like, but this Eden is real.'

In her hand was an apple.

Printed in Great Britain
by Amazon